HOLIDAY FOREVER

by

Neil Haugerud

TELEMACHUS PRESS

If you purchased this book without a cover you should be aware that this book is stolen property. It was reported as "unsold and destroyed" to the publisher and neither the author nor the publisher has received any payment for this "stripped book."

This book is a work of fiction. Names, characters, places and incidents are either the product of the author's imagination or are used fictitiously. Any resemblance to actual persons, living or dead, or to actual events or locales is entirely coincidental.

Holiday Forever

Copyright © 2011 by Neil Haugerud. All rights reserved, including the right to reproduce this book, or portions thereof, in any form. No part of this text may be reproduced, transmitted, downloaded, decompiled, reverse engineered, or stored in or introduced into any information storage and retrieval system, in any form or by any means, whether electronic or mechanical without the express written permission of the author. The scanning, uploading, and distribution of this book via the Internet or via any other means without the permission of the publisher is illegal and punishable by law. Please purchase only authorized electronic editions and do not participate in or encourage electronic piracy of copyrighted materials.

The publisher does not have any control over and does not assume any responsibility for author or third-party websites or their content.

Cover designed by Telemachus Press, LLC

Cover art
Copyright © Maxxximum Madcap, Funny Bone Productions

Published by Telemachus Press, LLC
http://www.telemachuspress.com

ISBN #978-1-937387-26-6 (paperback)
ISBN #978-1-937387-85-3 (eBook)

Version 2011.11.02

Printed in the United States of America
10 9 8 7 6 5 4 3 2 1

HOLIDAY FOREVER

Chapter 1

JUDGE PLUMB SENSED something unusual—sounds, much like the buzzing of wasps, filtered into his chambers. The next case on his docket had received abundant publicity, even a smattering of national press. He appreciated the attention; an opportunity to put on a little show—say some quotable things for the press; something that would get published in the newspapers.

A feeling of restlessness had engulfed the courtroom. Nervous fidgeting, along with a low din of voices, arose from the spectators. Everyone quieted as the Judge entered the courtroom. From the bench he nodded greetings to the jurors, and shuffled a few papers, calling attention to himself, before calling court to order. Judge Plumb appreciated the packed courtroom. It was good for his ego, even though the attendees were the usual curious and disgruntled town-gossip types.

George, the first witness on the list, sat near the back of the courtroom. He listened attentively when the judge called the court to order. The onlookers discontinued the whispering among themselves, but the feeling of restlessness continued.

The court clerk called the case. "The state versus Nancy Bartel. Conspiracy to conceal and distribute a controlled substance."

The impeccably dressed county attorney, with a white carnation in his lapel, peered over the top of his half-glasses, nodded, and smiled at the jury. He paraded before the jury box twice, looking directly at each juror. With one hand placed on the rail of the jury box, he turned, and faced the judge.

"Your Honor, the state calls George O. Rudnik."

George, acknowledging the call, grasped the back of the bench in front of him and pulled himself upright. His thin gray-white hair was neatly combed. His face was white, like that of a shut-in.

A gasp, as loud as the sucking of a Hoover cleaner, washed through the crowd when George removed his rumpled tan trench coat. George folded his coat, draped it over the bench in front of him, and proceeded toward the witness chair—totally naked except for his black- and-white tennis shoes.

The judge leaped to his feet, and flailed his arms like a bat in a cave.

"Order in the court," he shouted, but couldn't be heard above the new ruckus from the crowd.

From his lofty perch of authority, Judge Plumb rapped his gavel again. "Bailiff! Bailiff!" he shouted. "Remove that man from the courtroom!"

The bailiff, a retired justice of the peace, old and stiff with arthritis, was slow to rise. George seized the opportunity and addressed the court.

"I'll gladly leave, Your Honor." He returned to the bench, picked up his coat, folded it across his arm, and began walking toward the exit.

"Stop that man!" Angry spittle flew from the judge's mouth.

The crowd roared with laughter.

At this point, Sheriff Smith rose from his seat and approached George.

"George." Sheriff Smith was soft-spoken. "What would you think of a conference in judge's chambers? Do you mind putting your coat on till we get there?"

"Okay. I guess I could do that."

Naked George put on his coat, pausing while buttoning each button, as if performing a reverse striptease. At first the crowd applauded, then slowly quieted until only the tick of the courtroom clock could be heard. When he had finished, George and the sheriff approached the bench.

"Your Honor," the sheriff said. "Mr. Rudnik, not being represented by an attorney, has requested a meeting with you in your chambers."

The judge; purple with rage and disgust, thrust his blown up, reddened face in George's direction.

"Who the hell do you think you are? Making a mockery of my court! There will be no conference in chambers. You will do as ordered by the court."

George began unbuttoning his coat.

The judge rapped his gavel with such violence that the head broke from its shaft, flew into the air, and struck the court reporter on the neck. Startled, she jumped backwards and kicked over her steno machine as the gavel's head bounced off her neck and onto the courtroom floor, finally rolling to a stop in front of the jury box.

"Court is recessed for twenty minutes," Judge Plumb announced. He was appalled at the events that had just unfolded in his courtroom, a place of respect and decorum. "Bring that disruptive son of a bitch to my chambers," he whispered to the sheriff.

A clapping began, tentatively at first but with growing enthusiasm, when George and the sheriff neared the entrance to judge's chambers.

"Atta way, George."

"We're with you, George." There were cheers, laughter and by now a prolonged applause.

The judge's chambers were ostentatious, furnished with a large mahogany desk and table, leather chairs and couch, dark walnut-paneled walls, and expensive lace-trimmed draperies. The judge was seated behind his desk in his large, high-backed, leather swivel chair, feeling deserving of every expensive item in the chambers. The county attorney and his assistant had taken seats facing the judge.

"You nitwit fuckers have really got me pissed off, this time," Judge Plumb said. "And I am going to see to …"

And discontinued his speech as George was ushered in by the sheriff.

Judge Plumb contorted his face, winced and shut his eyes when George reclined, nude and seemingly comfortable, on the judges' leather couch.

"Goddamn it, man! Am I going to have to put you in jail for contempt of court? You are required by the law of this state to testify when subpoenaed. I will recess the court while the sheriff takes you back to the home; where you will put on a suit and tie appropriate to these proceedings. Do you understand that, old man?" the judge said.

George had sympathy for the judge.

"I'll make a deal with you, Your Honor," he said. "I know it takes awhile to accustom oneself to my lack of attire, and I know you don't want any disruption in your courtroom. I'll keep my coat on, except when I am giving testimony. You could clear the courtroom of spectators when I testify."

"Since when does a naked derelict from the old people's home tell me what to do in my court?" asked the judge. "Your refusal to give testimony is contempt of court."

"I am not refusing to testify, Your Honor. I will gladly testify—naked. I doubt that contempt is appropriate for my lack of attire."

"I'm the judge and I can cite you for contempt on any dammed ground I choose. You will testify as I instruct you or else …"

Judge Plumb felt his blood pressure rising to a dangerous level. Taking a deep breath, he opted for a different tactic. "Why are you doing this, old man? You appear normal in many aspects."

"I believe my nakedness attests to the rights and freedoms of action and thought that have been preserved and protected by the policies of Miss Bartel; at the home. I am sure, that given the opportunity, the jury would soon become oblivious to my nudity. My nudity, while not a verbal statement, is part of my testimony. It speaks to the peace, comfort and propriety of living conditions at Miss Bartel's care facility."

"I'll make the damn decisions in this court, you crazy bastard!" Judge Plumb shouted. "Get this man out of here, Sheriff. He's in your custody until I contact you. If you don't hear from me in one hour, put him in jail."

"Let's go get a cup of coffee, George," the sheriff said. Every eye in chambers was directed on Naked George as he put his trench coat on and left with the sheriff.

When they were gone, Judge Plumb turned to the county attorney. "What the fuck is going on in this world?" he asked brusquely. "You should have known better than to let this happen in my courtroom. I can't lock that crazy old son of a bitch up at his age and in his condition. After tomorrow's news reports everybody in the fucking country will be watching this trial. I'll not be made a laughingstock. What the hell do you need his testimony for anyway? You saw that jury. They think he's funny as hell."

The county attorney felt boxed in. It was an election year and what he thought was an opportunity for an attention-getting, vote-generating raid was turning into a nightmare.

"We're positive he knows about a large amount of marijuana at the rest home. We didn't find it during the raid. We believe he had it in a shopping bag. We're sure he hid it somewhere. We know the old codger won't lie under oath. He has refused to talk to any of the cops. They can't budge him. Let's clear the courtroom and put him on the stand naked," the county attorney said.

The judge leaned over and slapped at the county attorney's forehead.

"Get your head out of your ass so you can see the light of day. We can't keep the press out. The courtroom will be packed with every newspaper reporter in the country."

"Don't announce it, Judge. Just do it quickly the next time. The sooner, the better. Let's just hope we don't make the national news because of the naked guy. He's drawing the wrong attention to this case. I need a couple of quick convictions. If public sentiment gets turned the wrong way, I could lose the election because of this case."

"Come up with something." the judge said. "I can't let the guy get on the stand naked. We'll be in every tabloid in the country. He's got us in a no-win situation unless you come up with some brilliance. We can't let him thumb his nose at a subpoena. The way it looks, the stubborn bastard won't testify with his clothes on. The public will crucify us if we lock the bastard up for contempt. Think of something, or we're screwed by that wily old son of a bitch."

The county attorney paced a circle around his chair. His palms were wet and sweat literally dripped from his underarms. He pounded his right fist into the palm of his left hand.

"Is there anything we can do with that goddamn smug sheriff?" he asked. "He's been no help at all. He should be thrown out of office. He knew all along about the illegal activity going on at that rest home, and never did a goddamn thing about it. He's romantically involved with one of the defendants, that Adele. She's the one who cold cocked the cop when she found out he'd shot the dog."

"You and the sheriff, you're both up for election, aren't you?" The judge wiped his face with his handkerchief. "Get out of here, now. I gotta think," he said.

Chapter 2
Four Years Earlier

NANCY STOOD HELPLESSLY and watched the three men struggle to haul her car out of the ditch. She had been driving for a couple of days, from California across the Rockies, without any problems, except wondering where Jim had disappeared to and why. She was even doing all right when the snow began to accumulate. By then she was in the middle of nowhere, but she knew Norwood couldn't be far. She had no choice but to continue, or find some farmhouse where the lights were still on, and ask whoever answered her knock for a place to spend the night. Better, she thought, to grip the steering wheel, decrease her speed, and keep going.

The quick left-right-left combination from County road 10 to County 52 and back onto 10 in less than three-quarters of a mile was what did her in. No one could make turns like that in a blizzard without losing control. It wasn't her first blizzard and she knew out on the Minnesota plains, nothing stopped the wind and snow. *I'd have to drive half way back to Cheyenne to find a windbreak,* she thought.

Huge snowflakes hurled by the howling blizzard slapped Nancy's cheeks. A freezing chill crawled through the thin leather soles of her shoes and up her legs. Nancy stomped her feet to keep the circulation going, while the men who had stopped were doing her a big, fat favor working in this cold by the bright white cones created by the truck's headlights. But she wished they would hurry up.

"Come on, girl, sit in here with me." An old man in the passenger seat of the truck's cab had cracked open his window to call down to her. "I promise I ain't gonna hurt you. I'm too damned ancient."

Nancy laughed. "Yeah, you are," she agreed. "In this cold, whatever you tried to attack me with would break clean off your body."

She looked again at her Mazda. "I'll stay put," she said, "and not because you worry me."

"Suit yourself," the man said, and closed the window.

Her Mazda, a two-seater sports car, had sucked up the twists and turns and devoured the hilly terrain of northern California, the place she now called home. If she decided to stay in Minnesota, though, she'd have to go looking for something that rode high off the ground, with four-wheel drive and studs sticking out of the tires.

When she had begun to fishtail in the snowstorm, she downshifted, thinking that would slow her, same as it did on dry roads. Instead the wheels locked, and the car swung around, perpendicular to the road.

Never one to panic, she took a deep breath and made sure her seat belt was fastened. She thought back to the days of Driver's Ed at Norwood High: *Am I supposed to turn the steering wheel into the direction of the skid or the other way to correct my path?* She still hadn't figured it out when the Mazda, now leading with its weightless and almost nonexistent rear end, tipped like a sunken ship and came to rest on its rump in the ditch.

Nancy peered up at the hood. From what she could see, which wasn't much, only the Mazda's sleek silver nose would be visible from the road. She turned off the headlights and ignition, then checked herself for injury; finding none, she then wriggled out of the car and up to the soft shoulder, taking the full force of the wind. She looked in all directions; there were no houses or farmsteads, at least none with lights powerful enough to cut through the dark of the storm. And Nancy wondered if she'd come all this way, just to freeze to death, alone in the middle of nowhere? Other thoughts darted through her mind.

Should I freeze to death in my car or begin walking and die by the roadside? I'd be more comfortable in the car, but it would appear as if I had given up and killed myself, like uncle Al did. That would bother Ruth, probably more than she could bear ...

In mid-thought—headlights materialized out of the storm.

That the two men in the Lexus had noticed her was a miracle. They stopped a few yards down the highway, and then backed up to where she stood.

They immediately asked if she was injured, and what had happened. Both men were well dressed with stylish overcoats and dress suits; but that didn't stop them from trying to push her car free after they found out what had happened.

A semi, traveling from the opposite direction was the second miracle. It arrived just after the men in suits had given up the fight. The tractor trailer's huge wheels sprayed a wake of snow over the threesome before it came to a stop. The trucker's deep horn gave a blast, before backing up.

A big man in denims and a sheepskin vest climbed down from his cab. A length of chain was looped under his arm and over his broad shoulder. He released one end of the chain, as he walked. The chain extended from his semi all the way to the ditch. He was bare-handed and seemingly immune to the effects of the cold.

The trucker took charge.

Nancy took refuge from the wind along-side the tractor trailer, while the men looped the chain around something under her car.

The old man, in the cab, opened his window again.

"Looks like you'll be on your way pretty soon," he said. "You must've done something right, to have the cavalry all show up for you in the middle of nowhere."

"Hey! You girl!" the trucker shouted from the ditch. "Get over to your car. Sit behind the wheel, and when I give you the signal, put her into first and feed her some gas!" He scrambled from the ditch and busied himself with the end of the chain.

Nancy scrambled through the snow. She already felt useless in front of these men. About the only thing that could make her feel any more ridiculous was landing on her butt in front of them. She paused by the edge of the ditch.

A hand in a fine leather glove reached up to her. "Let me help you."

She looked down into smiling eyes—rich brown like cowhide.

"Thank you sir," she said, grasping his hand firmly.

"I'm Andrew Curtis. Andy. My colleague over there is Judge Morris Norton."

His other hand gripped her firmly under her elbow. With knees bent, she allowed him to ease her down the embankment. A very pleasant current traveled up her arms, as he guided her, with his hand around her waist.

"When you're settled in, I'll shut the door, and you roll down your window so you can be heard."

Meanwhile, Judge Norton had climbed out of the ditch and stood by the side of the road.

"You in?" asked Andy.

Nancy nodded and felt a blush in her cheeks. *Oh, for God's sake, Nancy, she thought. Get a grip!*

Andy closed her car door and cupped his hands around his mouth. "Okay, Your Honor!" he shouted.

"We're all set here!" the judge relayed back.

She listened carefully, as Andy gave instructions. *Kind eyes*, she was thinking, when suddenly, the chain was taut, and with a jolt and a lurch the Mazda came back to the roadway.

"Is my car still in one piece?" she asked.

"Looks that way."

Andy disconnected the chain and tossed it onto the roadway. The trucker and the judge reeled in the chain.

Nancy, the Californian, didn't have a purse or billfold; her cash was in a silver money clip in her front pocket. She held out a twenty for Andy.

"Thank you for—"

Andy held up his hand. "There'll be another chance for thanks. Are you here just for the holidays or—?"

"I'm not sure. I don't mean to be vague. I really haven't thought everything out."

"While you're here, let's have dinner—my treat.

Nancy was used to slick California guys, and their fast moves, but this country bumpkin was coming on like gangbusters.

"I'll give it some thought—would you mind a chaperone?

"Chaperone?"

"In California, I always took a chaperone along on the first date."

"Oh, if you're thinking of a full-fledged date … I might go for that."

"Give me a week to settle in, and visit my dad. Okay. And forget the chaperone bit, Californians tend to be a little phony and silly sometimes."

"I'll thank the truck driver—then I'll give you all my contact information."

Nancy slid carefully through the snow, and held out the twenty to the trucker.

"Thanks, you've been a great help," she said.

The trucker nodded, took the money and shoved it into a denim jacket pocket.

"If you're gonna stay around these parts, girl, you're gonna want to think about a dif'rent breed of horse, he said. "That toy car you've got is too wimpy for Minnesota winters. We'd have to get a patrol together, just to follow you around till June and pull your ass out of ditches."

"Thanks soooo much for your advice," Nancy said in a condescending manner. "But I grew up in Norwood, and if I decide to stay here for any length of time, I'll know exactly what sort of car is suited to the climate."

"You grew up here?" The trucker squinted at her. "I thought I knew everybody from 'round here. What's your name, girl?"

She didn't want to continue the conversation, but he had just pulled her car from a ditch, and she maybe owed him some courtesy, beyond the twenty bucks she'd already given him.

"Nancy Bartel." she replied.

"You?" The trucker threw his head back and hooted. "You're Nancy Bartel?" He opened the cab door, stood on the step, and yelled, to his passenger. "Pa! You ain't gonna believe who this is! This here girl is Nancy Bartel! Ol' Billy's daughter! Jesus H. Christ! Imagine that!"

"No shit!" The old man joined in. "Ol' Billy. That son o' bitch couldn't win fer losin'. How about you, girl? Your luck been any better than your daddy's, or does some curse run in the blood?"

Nancy felt a loathing for these men. She understood very little about her father, he had shown little interest in her whereabouts. But, her dad, William F. Bartel was the real reason she had returned to Norwood. At first, Nancy wasn't sure how much she wanted to learn about her father. She'd have to be diligent to find out a lot about him. And if she did, hopefully, she might come to better understand herself.

She wasn't going to leave her father as a shadowy stranger from the past. She knew she had to learn about herself too, and change; or for the rest of her life she would be stuck in a rut, just like her car had been. Maybe not having a father was a key to why Jim had vanished. And to why she wasn't able to connect with him on a deep, intimate level—or to anyone else, for that matter. She was about to tell the trucker to cut the bullshit about her dad—when he shouted to her against the wind.

"Yeah, my granddad Theo bought out the Bartel farm after your granddad got himself killed in an accident with his team. As Grandpa told the story, he bought the farm for his boys, and he got the widow; that would be your grandmother, in the bargain. Ain't that somethin', girl? We're almost kin!"

"If I thought for a minute that I was a kin of yours, I'd have you push me back in the ditch so I could freeze to death."

Nancy took a step back and bumped into the judge.

"Excuse me, Your Honor, but I—"

"May I assist you back to your car, Miss Bartel?" He offered his arm.

"Please." Her throat was so tight with anger and shame, she could hardly speak.

"Hey!" the trucker said. "Wait a minute!" He grabbed the vertical bar beside the driver's door and levered himself up onto the step. "My pa and my uncle used to walk to school with Ol' Billy. Here's the funny part. Billy was always flyin' off into some ditch, just like you did tonight."

Chapter 3

THE SHADED DAYLIGHT in the hospital room seemed hard, like limestone, and looked the washed-out color of a hangover. Flashes of lightning played across the shaded windowpanes and Billy couldn't figure out if he was five or fifty. Often he was dreaming, sometimes hallucinating, and other times consciously living the past. Perhaps he was just coming off a bad drunk. He'd never experienced the DT's before—he'd heard about them though.

When Billy gained consciousness the next day, a plump, black-haired nurse took his pulse, while a frail nurse with thick glasses adjusted the flow of an intravenous tube to a vein on the back of his hand. He was awake, but only occasionally comprehended anything happening in the room.

"Where am I? What's going on?" he asked.

The nurse with the thick glasses looked at Billy and he saw the reflection in the lenses; a haggard man with shaggy eyebrows and sallow, puffy skin, with dark half moon circles under his eyes. The black-haired nurse spoke to her counterpart.

"This guy is acting awfully weird. Better go get Doctor Samuelson," she said, with a wave of the hand.

"Oh, just wait a minute," Billy said. This time he was listening to himself and realized that all he had said was just blah, blah, blahs.

Doctor Samuelson, a tall, slim, middle-aged man with a noticeable limp, came into the room. He took a Kleenex from the dispenser on the nightstand and wiped a gob of spittle from Billy's chin.

"Billy, can you hear me?" he asked loudly. In his mind, Billy said *yes,* and thought *what gives this guy the idea I'm hard of hearing*; but his words still came out as blah, blah, blah. His lips felt like half-inflated inner tubes, and his mind like a worn-out gearbox. Billy attempted to speak again. More blah, blah, blahs.

Doc placed his hands on the back of Billy's hands.

"Move your fingers if you understand what I'm saying," the doctor said. Billy made a valiant effort. His right hand didn't move but the left responded mildly to the doctor's request.

"That's good," Doc said. "You've been drinking way too much and way too long. You came in here with the DTs, and now we expect you've had a stroke. It will be several days before we have completely diagnosed your condition."

Stroke, Billy thought. He knew what that meant, but surprised himself that he didn't much care.

"You rest for now and dry out," the Doctor said. "We'll keep close watch on you."

Billy thought maybe it would be best if he had a bigger stroke while they weren't watching and could be gone for good. Then he drifted off to another time and place.

He heard the doctor ask, "Isn't there a daughter somewhere?"

"Yes," the nurse's answer. "She's a nurse in California."

Billy had been christened William Francis Bartel—born to Lloyd and Theona Bartel in 1917, born in the same farmhouse near Samhill, Minnesota where his Norwegian father had been born. His mother, of Irish and German descent, had lived on a neighboring farm. She married Lloyd three years after graduating from eighth grade. His mother had taught Billy the alphabet and how to count to one hundred; and by the fall of 1913 he was ready for school.

His first day of school began when his father's gruff voice resounded up the stairway of the farmhouse to his room.

"Billy! Get up! Chore time."

Billy kicked his bed-covers away, rolled over, sat on the edge of the bed, and ran his callused hands through his hair. He rubbed his eyes awake, then looked out the window at a long band of tawny clouds—the beginning of morning light. He fumbled through the pile of clothes on the floor looking for a wooden match to light the kerosene lamp out in the dark hallway. The lamp chimney was all sooted up, so most of the lamplight shone to the ceiling. He put on his coarse, blue, cotton shirt and his bib overalls, then pondered the brindle colors on the heels and toes of his socks. A frayed rawhide shoe lacing broke as he cinched it. Hurriedly he tied it in a knot and skipped the top shoe clip, knowing that his father had already gone to the barn and a second call would be trouble. He blew out the lamp and went downstairs. He moved about softly so as not to wake his mother.

His mother, Theona, was a hard woman, periodically out of sorts, but not a chronic complainer like Billy's Aunt May. Theona had been ill for several days now. Billy was puzzled. His mother didn't have a fever or anything; she just wanted to be left alone. His father had said not to worry—it was just 'the woman thing'.

Billy deftly parted the burlap curtains, which served as his parents' bedroom door. From the corner of the room he fetched a slop jar of human waste. Breathing through his mouth to diminish the odor, he carried it to the outhouse. Black flies the size of small bees swarmed from the tepid outhouse hole and circled his head as he emptied the contents of the jar.

After chores, his time was his own. Early fall colors had edged into the leaves of the stately oaks and the elms; whose reaching limbs seemed bent on gathering in every cloud in the sky. Like an elderly congregation, whispering in church pews, the leaves on the trees near the house rustled in the morning breeze. Billy made his way to the ancient, unpainted woodshed next to the house. A layer of wood bark, accumulated over the years, covered the dirt floor of the shed. As Billy gathered the firewood, centipedes scurried from their hiding places, and a black-green salamander ambled from its damp, bark-laden home. Continuing his morning routine, Billy's short arms barely reached the pump handle at the end of the sink in the pantry. He pumped a pail of water to fill the reservoir on the kitchen stove; then he noticed the red worms.

"Darn red worms," he mumbled to himself. Red worms occasionally appeared in the cistern water after a long spell, so to strain them out, he tied a washrag around the waterspout and left it secured so his mother would know about the worms if she came to wash her hands and face.

Then, Billy set about to check his gopher traps. Sunrise was peeking above the horizon and pried itself between heavy clouds, splashing them with colors of ash and gold. First, he stopped at the windmill, removed the wire bail from the bowl on the water pipe, and sucked a long drink from his cupped left hand.

Billy had no ill will towards gophers, but frequently he'd endured his father's temper tantrums and tirades of swearing, when their mounds had plugged the sickle bar on the hay mower:

"God damn it, Billy, you'll have to catch the rest of those sons-a-bitches after we get the hay up. You should have caught more of them this spring."

Earlier, in April, Billy had caught his first gopher. He pulled the gopher from the hole; the jaws on the trap had separated the skin away from the muscle on the front leg. The leg-meat was bruised, bloodied, dirty, and black and blue. The gopher was plump and sleek with tiny, triangle ears and small black eyes. His fur was a leafy brown with a touch of grey on his chest. He hissed defiantly—kishh kishh kishh—through his curving, yellow teeth. With its short tail upright it darted at Billy. "kishh kish kish." Billy, though startled for a moment, thought it would be fun to try to tame a gopher for a pet and regretted the task ahead. He knew he couldn't hesitate forever. He took the oak stake from the ring of the trap, closed his eyes, and whacked the gopher on the head. The blow only grazed the critter, and the wounded gopher let out a sickly squeak. Billy hit it again, harder, looking closely at it this time. The gopher's eyes bulged out and blood came from the gopher's ears and nose. Billy still remembered the feeling of the skull cracking beneath his stick.

But it was fall now and more than forty gophers later, so Billy dispatched this gopher calmly with two swift blows to the head, then cut off the front feet with his jackknife; and put them in the Prince Albert tobacco can he carried in his pocket. He'd salt down the feet, and later take them to the annual township board meeting to collect the bounty.

Then he was on to the barn, where he was greeted by Stacy, the calico cat, and her five half-grown kittens. Stacy purred deep in her throat and rubbed against Billy's leg. Billy reached down and let his hand glide over her back. Two kittens bravely followed Billy as he carried a coffee can of feed to Bess in the second stanchion. All of the cows had names and Billy would have spoken to them on a first name basis had his father not been in the barn milking. Mabel, with a newborn calf, bellowed with anger at the sight of the kittens, who puffed their hair on end, spat defiantly, then scrambled back to the feed room.

"Get those goddamn cats out of here," his father shouted, as the cow he was milking kicked at the milk pail. Billy knew better than to reply, so he locked the cats in the milk-room before continuing with the feeding. His next chore was at the henhouse, where he paused for a moment to enjoy the call of a rooster pheasant from off in the distance. After he gathered the eggs, he waited at the well house for his father to finish milking. His father came from the barn carrying two cans of milk.

His father, Lloyd, usually strode as if he were going uphill and against the wind. There was no fat on Lloyd. He had a rawboned, weathered face; expressionless except when showing anger. His hazel eyes were shaded by the sweat-stained, charcoal felt hat he'd worn all summer. Lloyd put the milk cans in the water tank in the well house, and turned to Billy.

"How many eggs this morning?" he asked.

Billy showed him the egg basket. "Twelve," he said. "Do you think I will ever get as big as you, Dad?"

"I expect so. I'm only five-eleven."

Billy wanted to talk more, so he followed his father to the kitchen. He was surprised to see his mother at the stove.

"Don't set that egg basket there," she said. "Put it in the corner, out of the way."

She scowled, and Billy didn't care for that because he thought his mother was pretty, although today, her normally rosy cheekbones were pale and her full head of auburn hair was uncombed. Even the light in her round blue eyes was dimmed. Billy put the egg basket in the corner as instructed, then sat down at the table with his father.

"Feeling better, Ma? I caught another gopher." She stood with her back to the table and shrugged her shoulders.

"Only one?" she asked, without turning and continued stirring a pan of steaming oatmeal on the cook stove.

"Yeah. The other two holes were plugged," Billy said, disappointed by her indifference. When she said nothing more, Billy looked hopefully toward his father for acknowledgement, but his father, who habitually smoked a pipe after breakfast, was concentrating on scraping the inside of his pipe bowl with the small blade of his jackknife.

"Better hurry and clean up. Your first day of school today, you know," his mother said. She rattled the grate crank on the stove, shaking ashes in to the pit.

Billy's empty stomach growled, and as he waited he fingered the tattered blue and white checked oilcloth which had covered the table for as long as he could remember.

Theona set out homemade bread, chokecherry jelly, fresh cream, and a bowl of sugar. Billy inhaled the scents. With the first taste of chokecherry jelly, he closed his eyes and, in his mind, returned to the trees by the sinkhole where he had gathered the fruit. He remembered the comfort of being alone there, the hot sun, and the buzzing of insects. He felt warm and contented. He came out of his trance when his mother set his oatmeal in front of him.

"Go up and change now," she'd said when he finished. "Put on your flannel shirt and your oxfords." She handed him the butter dish. "Here, take this to the cellar before you go. Hurry on now—the Kasen boys will be by any minute. You can walk to school with them,"

Billy went upstairs, scratching at his cheek with the stump of his right forefinger. A third of the finger had been amputated after an entanglement with a hay pulley a year ago.

He had hoped his folks would be taking him to school on the first day. He didn't know what to expect. Only thing he knew was, he'd overheard the Kasen boys at a basket social in June say their teacher was an old maid—she had black hair on her upper lip and a rat's nest of hair under her arms. *What's an old maid?* Billy thought.

"Hurry up, Billy. The Kasen boys are here," his mother shouted from the base of the unpainted stairway. Billy hurried down and paused at the doorway by his mother, hoping for a touch or a hug.

"You pay attention in school, now" his father said. "And get right back afterwards. I'm goin' to the mill with the corn—don't know when I'll be back. You start chores—get as much done as you can."

Billy saw that the Kasen boys were waiting on the dusty road at the end of the driveway. Leonard, a tall, lean sixth grader with reddish, rough-cut hair was whittling on a stick with his jackknife. And Vance, a round-faced, smiling third grader with a smattering of freckles across the bridge of his nose, was looking up at a circling red-tailed hawk. Billy had met the two boys on a couple of occasions, but had never really talked to them. He'd never had a good talk with anyone.

"You didn't comb your hair, Billy," his mother said as he walked out the door.

"Don't got no comb."

"Turn your cap around on your head a few times. That will make your hair lie down in one direction at least."

"Billy twisted his plaid wool cap around on his head as he ran toward the Kasen boys, who were walking away. When he caught up to them, the boys made room for Billy between them, and they walked silently three abreast. When they were out of view of the house, Vance tripped Billy, and Leonard gave him a hard shove into the ditch. With a hearty laugh, they slapped each other on the back, and continued on their way.

Billy crawled out of the deep ditch and picked sticktights and burrs from his clothing. Continuing on, he stayed well behind, with his jaw set tight and a cold stare for the Kasen boys.

"Come on, Billy. Don't be so serious," Leonard said. "Come on up and walk with us. That was just your initiation. All first graders have to have an initiation. Come on. We won't do it again."

"What's initiation," Billy thought. *"I wonder what other big words I'll hafta learn in school. Will everyone be this mean? But, I guess if this is all there is to 'imitation' it won't be so bad. I'll pretend I'm not scared."* He approached the boys cautiously; searching their eyes for any new signs of trouble. When they offered him a space between them, he held back, but Leonard pulled him forward and gave him an affectionate pat on the back.

Billy relaxed. *"Everything would be ok now."*

"There's that hawk again," Vance said. Billy looked up, and then Vance tripped him and Leonard shoved him rolling into the ditch. All of Billy's breath escaped his lungs when he landed. He wanted to cry, but couldn't even get his breath. He'd had the wind knocked out of him before, but now when he couldn't get any air, he panicked, gasped for breath and thrashed around on the ground.

"He's kind of a dumb shit, too, ain't he?" Leonard guffawed.

When Billy recovered, he licked a trickle of blood from his cheek with his stump forefinger and spat defiantly onto the dusty roadway. His cap was full of the briars. But when he came from the ditch this time he brandished a hardwood stick. It was a good three feet long and there was fire in Billy's eyes.

"That ain't gonna you no good, you little fart." Leonard said, and faked a move toward Billy.

Billy had had enough; his temper took over.

"I'm maybe little. But this stick is hard oak."

Billy would be satisfied even if he got one blow to the side of their head. He didn't catch them, but he chased them all the way to the schoolhouse.

After the Kasen boys entered the faded, one room schoolhouse, Billy hid his stick by a corner post and then paused to catch his breath.

A herd of white-faced cattle grazed in their pasture beyond the schoolyard. The herd bull raised his head and watched as Billy wiped the last trace of blood from his cheek. There were two drab outhouses, a faded red woodshed, and a crude set of swings in the yard.

Billy stepped into the schoolhouse entryway, where caps and thin jackets hung on wall pegs. Firewood was stacked along the east wall near a ten-gallon porcelain crock with a hinged wooden cover.

"Hello. I'm Miss Maybelle Berkin, your teacher. What is your name?" A pleasant voice from behind him asked.

A startled Billy turned toward the voice. The woman standing next to him had warm, smiling eyes; an old woman, maybe thirty; with short dark hair. She had black hair on her upper lip; just as the Kasen boys had said. Billy looked for the rats' nests of hair under her arms, but was prevented from seeing by her cream colored sweater.

Billy, with a faraway look in his eyes, absently finger-combed his unruly head of hair, and stared at a mop pail in the corner.

"William Francis Bartel," he said, more to the mop pail than the teacher. "They call me Billy."

"My, what a nice name. Did you come to school all by yourself?" She put her hand on his shoulder.

"Came with the Kasen boys."

"Well, come right on in. I'll show you to your desk. Put your lunch bucket on the table. What happened to your cheek?" she asked.

"It's all right. Cut myself on a big weed."

"I'll get some gauze to put on it for you."

"It's okay. I've cut myself before."

"Yes, but let me help you."

Help me? thought Billy. *Why would she want to help me?* He liked Miss Berkin's soft reassuring voice. She gently led him to a cupboard, dipped water from the crock, and sponged his face tenderly with a wet washcloth. Billy sneaked a look past the washcloth to see if any of the students were watching. All he saw was their backs, but he figured they were listening.

"I'll tape this gauze on your cut."

"No, it's okay."

Miss Berkin put her arm around him and patted his shoulder. Billy smiled, and then flushed with embarrassment.

"We'll find you a desk," she said. Billy followed her from the entryway to the classroom. There were three rows of desks, five desks in each row. The large, worn teacher's desk was at the front of the room. Miss Berkin ushered Billy past a black potbellied stove to the second desk in the middle row. The two Kasen boys and nine other students, none of whom he knew, turned in their desks and stared.

"Students, this is our new first-grader, Billy Bartel. Would each of you introduce yourselves to Billy, please."

A violent rainstorm followed the lightning. Billy was conscious of the sound of water dripping into a galvanized pail in the corner of his hospital room and aware of the medical staff in his room; they were deep in a discussion about him, much as if he were a dog or cat.

"We'll just have to wait and see. He's either going to come out of it to some degree, or he isn't," Doc Samuelson said, looking at a medical chart. "Time will tell."

Billy became angry, when the doctor decided on continued treatment without consulting him or even speaking directly to him. Doc merely stood at the foot of Billy's bed with two nurse attendants and spoke to them about him.

"I understand you're transferring him to the nursing home," the head nurse said.

"Yes," the doctor said. "He's just as well off there. He doesn't need hospital care now. I can check on him when I make my rounds at the home, and they can make sure he's fed and his ass is wiped."

"You sons-a-bitches," Billy said, but the sounds, that came through his rubber lips, were just more "blah blah blahs." Before drifting off, he made a vow to himself—*he was going to beat this thing and learn to speak again, and when he did he was going to have some choice words for Doc Samuelson and the hospital staff. He'd show them what he was made of.*

Two days later, at the rest home, the intravenous tube had been removed, and Billy was being fed gruel.

"*Just like pablum,*" he thought.

Three times a day they stuffed the gruel in his mouth. They held his head back and then they'd wait till he choked or swallowed.

When Ruth Krankus came to visit him, she spoke to him as though he were a real person. By the time she left, Billy tried to say her name.

"Wooth," he said.

Chapter 4
Ruth

"YOU'D THINK A judge and an attorney would have more sense than to drive around in this weather," Ruth said. She set a round wooden tray on the ottoman in front of Nancy's chair. "Help yourself, dear."

Nancy speared a wedge of cheese from the assortment of Minnesotan farmland delicacies: orange and ivory wedges of cheese, crackers in a bowl lined with a loose-weave napkin, pickled herring with rings of raw onion, and cold cuts rolled up, secured with a toothpick, and slathered with horseradish mustard. Bottles of eggnog and brandy were on the coffee table; within easy reach of both women, but protected from the heat of Ruth's brick fireplace.

Memories whirled through Nancy's mind, triggered by the scent of pine from the Christmas tree, cinnamon and clove from the ham baking in the kitchen, and cedar from the green-cut log near the fireplace.

"Mmm. Cheese and eggnog! Is December Osteoporosis Awareness Month?"

Ruth swiped at her with a napkin.

"Is that what they taught you in nursing school? How to smart-talk to your elders?" Ruth teased.

"No," Nancy said, while making a cracker sandwich. "We were also taught how to keep our calcium intake sufficient to stave off broken bones." She handed the cracker to her aunt. "Judge Norton and Attorney Curtis were traveling home from some labor-union dinner at the Hormel plant. Thank God," she added.

"I was so worried about you. They were real gentlemen, to follow you home."

"Yes." Nancy looked around the living room. "This is a beautiful place. I'm happy for you."

Ruth's previous house, where Nancy had spent much of her childhood, just a few blocks away on Oak Street, had been a holy mess when she and Ruth moved in. Hard work never scared Ruth, though, and the two of them had soon transformed the hovel into a comfy and attractive cottage.

This new home, a rambling brick ranch majestically landscaped, fell into a different classification altogether. The bones of the house were good. Nancy could hear the wind wailing and tree branches clicking against the storm windows, but no drafts invaded the room. The walls, painted warm butterscotch yellow, showed no cracks or seams, and neither did the ceiling. It was square, settled, and solid, just like Ruth. Nancy smiled.

"You've always been here for me. Thank you."

"Well, of course I have," Ruth said matter-of-factly. "And I always will be. I love you, dear. So why don't you tell me what's bothering you?"

Nancy's gaze settled on a photograph of her mother, Clair, prominently displayed to Ruth's left, atop an antique glass-fronted credenza.

Chapter 5

And down went McGinty to the bottom of the wall
Sure his nose, ribs, and back were broke
From getting such a fall
Dressed in his best suit of clothes
From "Down Went McGinty" by Joseph Flynn, 1889

BY THE TIME he was in fifth grade, Billy's legs fit snugly against the underside of the desk. It was a spring day without a breath of breeze; the sun had warmed the room to laziness. Billy leaned absently on an open book with his chin in his hands. Outside in the schoolyard, robins chirped and searched for worms beneath the bare late-budding walnut trees. Miss Berkin, in her usual plain housedress and cream cardigan, came up behind him and leaned over.

"You did well on the spelling test, Billy," Miss Berkin said. "You only misspelled one word, but *separate* is difficult. It's easy to remember if you think of paring apples, separating the skin from the fruit. But you got the bonus word right." She let his test fall softly to his desk, and then smiled. "You look dreamy today. A touch of spring fever, perhaps?"

Billy felt his face blush and turned his head. Miss Berkin was staring at the rough calluses, much like oat hulls, on Billy's hands.

"Oh no, Miss Berkin. I guess I'm just a little tired."

She frowned, and for a moment Billy feared she might reach out and brush the unruly lock of hair from his eyes. He quickly swiped at the hair himself. He knew she was aware of his two hours of chores before school and the two hours of chores after school. She didn't send much homework with him.

"Next year, we will have advanced math. If you want, I can give you the books now so you could look at them throughout the summer. You're somewhat behind in math." She knew he did not have much study time.

"Dad says you don't need to be a genius to clean calf pens or plant oats."

"I won't contradict your dad, but math can exercise your mind, and your mind is just as important as your body. Look at yourself. You see what exercise and hard work can do for your body? Well, your mind needs the same thing." Billy looked toward the window. Behind him, he heard Miss Berkin sigh, and he felt sorry for her. She seemed to take a special interest in him, but he felt she was wasting her time.

Miss Berkin was aware of Billy's appreciation of music. There were even times when he tried to harmonize, adding a querulous higher note on top of the low notes from the other boys. Earlier in the year she had surprised Billy. She gave him a Tonette. He had turned it over in his hands, giving a low whistle of appreciation.

"For me?" he'd asked, looking up at her.

"Yes, Billy. For you."

"Miss Berkin, I ... I ...," he stammered.

"You're welcome, Billy."

By now she had developed a concern for Billy.

"There's more to life than farm work, Billy." She said.

"Dad says I get enough schoolin' at school, and I shouldn't be doing it at home when there's work to be done."

"Billy, schooling is also to teach you to think for yourself, and maybe you would do well to do more of it."

Billy turned away, shuffled his feet, and clenched his jaw.

Miss Berkin sighed. "I'm sorry, Billy. I'm sorry you're upset. It's just that you have such great potential. I wish you would understand."

She asked Billy to remain, while she sent everyone else out for morning recess.

There was a thin silence following the last closing of the schoolhouse door.

"Let's try to work this out. Okay, Billy?"

"Yes, ma'am," Billy said.

"Would you like for me to tutor you in math this summer?"

"No, ma'am."

"Is there something else bothering you, Billy? Something at home?"

"No, ma'am."

Miss Berkin gave up. Billy slid from his desk and ran to the schoolyard.

After recess at a quarter past two, there was a knock on the schoolroom door. When Miss Berkin responded, Billy thought he heard his Uncle Theo's voice.

"I have bad news for Billy," he whispered to Miss Berkin. "There's been an accident. His father was thrown from a wagon. I'm afraid he ... I've come to take Billy home."

"Just a moment," Miss Berkin said, muffling her voice.

"Billy," she called softly. "Your uncle is here. Will you come, please?"

"Yes, ma'am," he answered curtly, continuing to be somewhat miffed at Miss Berkin. Just shy of the entryway he was confronted with the somber looks of Uncle Theo and Miss Berkin.

"Billy," said Uncle Theo. "Your father has been in an accident with the team. Your mother needs you at home." He put his arm around the boy's shoulders and walked with him to the surrey and team tied in the schoolyard. Just before he stepped into the buggy, Miss Berkin, wiped her eyes, and lifted her hand in a feeble wave.

"Is my dad hurt real bad?" Billy asked his uncle.

"It's best if you wait and talk to your mother," Uncle Theo said. Thereafter Billy and his uncle rode silently. The lithe hackneys set a steady pace. Billy, worried and thinking only of his father, found himself absently tapping his foot to the "cling-clang, cling-clang," even chime rings from the harness traces. He stopped and tucked his feet way back under the seat, when his uncle glanced at him.

An agonizing fifteen minutes later Billy reached the farm. He was sickened by the sight of the broken corner post entangled with a crushed and upended wagon box. Many of his neighbors' carriages were parked in the yard. He looked to his uncle for some type of consolation, but Uncle Theo just took him by the hand and walked with him to the house.

Billy's stomach tightened further at the sight of his mother in the kitchen, wearing a washed-out faded flower print dress and clenching the edge of her chair. He'd never seen her like this. Her face was sallow and wet, her eyes were red, and her hair appeared as if glued to her forehead and temples. She seemed unable to move, but when Billy took her hand, she allowed him to pull her up, then she half-led, half-shoved him through the room of whispering men and women. She stretched the purple gunnysack curtain across the bedroom doorway and drew him tightly to her. Billy couldn't relax in her arms and he had to ask. So he pushed himself back.

"He's dead, isn't he?"

His mother nodded and sobbed. She answered a barely audible, "yes." Then she toppled sideways onto the bed and buried her head in the pillow. She cried, "Oh Billy, it was awful—I was looking out the window. Your Dad had the team and the wagon. He unloaded some corn in the hog lot. When he came through the gate and stopped, the team just stood there, gentle as lambs. He shut the gate and climbed into the back of the wagon. When he reached for the lines—they just ... just ... bolted, ran away, wild. He was thrown to the floor. I saw him get up and reach out again, but the horses swerved by the lane, and the front wheels hit the corner post. The wagon tongue broke, and the horses kept going. Your father—he was thrown high in the air and out the front of the wagon. I ran as fast as I could to him, but he was dead. He was dead." She sobbed and buried her face in the pillow again.

Billy's mouth filled with saliva, and a deep chill swept through his body. Resisting the urge to bolt from the room, he swallowed hard and shut his eyes.

Uncle Theo and Aunt May parted the curtain and entered the bedroom. Aunt May stroked Theona's face and hair.

"I better see after the team," Billy said, searching for a way to get off by himself.

"Don't concern yourself about that," said Uncle Theo. "I'll see to it."

His mother lifted her head from the pillow and through a web of snarled hair asked, "What are we to do, Billy?"

"Don't worry, Ma. We'll be all right. I can take care of things."

His mother dropped back to the bed. Her shoulders shook, the pillow muffling her crying. Billy gagged and swallowed as vomit rose in his throat. He wiped his eyes, blew his nose, and coughed. Aunty May gently pulled his grieving mother's unattended hair into a twisted ponytail. After a few moments of unnatural silence, Aunt May smoothed wrinkles from her starched black skirt, and nodded to Billy and his uncle.

"Will you leave us alone for a few moments?" she asked softly, drawing the curtain back from the doorway.

Uncle Theo put an arm around Billy's stooping shoulders, then guided him from the bedroom to a chair in the parlor, where the neighbors ringed the room—all looking at the floor or at each other—anywhere other than at Billy.

Mrs. Simpson murmured something Billy couldn't hear to Uncle Theo; breaking a silence that had persisted ever since Billy entered the room. Theo had taken a chair beside Mrs. Simpson and more than once his hand brushed her thigh or rested on her knee momentarily. Other voices were hushed, like impatient church people before a sermon. And they whispered to each other, as if Billy were not there.

Billy reflected on the disadvantages of being an only child, thinking it would help if he were able to comfort a younger sibling or be comforted by an older one. He understood that for now, he could only comfort himself, and that wouldn't happen in this room of blank darting eyes, where calloused hands twisted kerchiefs or crumpled the caps in their laps. Billy needed solitary time and he felt it would help if he could get to the barn and be alone. He ladled a drink from the water pail in the kitchen, and, when he was sure nobody was looking, he sidled out the back entryway.

"Dad's dead, Dad's dead," kept repeating over and over in his mind. Subdued light and pungent odors of cattle, horses, and ammonia-laced manure occupied the barn. For distraction Billy pulled hay from the alleyway and tossed it to the calves. The cats mewed and clamored about his feet, but he couldn't give them any attention. He wished he had a pet, maybe a dog.

That might take "*Dad's dead,*" from his mind. Then he began talking to the farm animals.

"Hey, you cows, how come you eat so much and shit so much? How come you eat the same hay as the horses and your shit is sloppy and green, while the horses shit firm, brown turds? How come most people call cow and horse shit manure while cat shit is cat shit and dog shit is plain shit –or poop? Who's going to milk all you cows tonight—my dad is dead."

He became quite embarrassed by his method of detaching himself and peered out the barn door to make sure nobody was listening. The restlessness continued as he walked toward the woods, alternately glancing down at his shoes, then up at the sky. Wild raspberry and gooseberry bushes in the woods slowed his travel. He pushed his way forward, listening to each dry crunch beneath his feet as he made his way. He allowed himself to collapse by his favorite tree; a bush chokecherry in a grassy area. "*Dad's dead*" crept into his mind again.

It was late afternoon now, the warmth from the sun had gone, and the ground became damp and cool. The brown-gray buds on the oak trees wiggled in the breeze like squirrel's ears. Billy yanked grass up by the handful and tossed it aimlessly in every direction.

He became conscious of a constant "tick tock, tick tock", and recalled the first birthday present he ever received; a pocket watch. It ticked away, over his heart, in the breast pocket of his overalls. His dad came to him then, dressed in the brown Sunday suit he'd seldom worn—the one he would be buried in. The deep worry lines on his face were gone, and somehow, he conveyed an unspoken message to Billy.

"Be strong and care for your mother and cherish the farm." Then his dad smiled and waved good-bye.

Billy brushed off his overalls, braced his shoulders, and walked toward the house. The dreaded voice in his mind had stilled, but he wished again for the sister and brothers his parents had also longed for. He felt bad for sometimes thinking his parents wanted more children; just for help on the farm. He regretted never having had a real heart to heart talk with his dad. He longed for a real talk with anyone; or to be held in someone's lap, like his mother did once a few years ago.

Billy was hoping the neighbors would have gone. But by chore time, nearly half the carriages were still in the yard. And he was puzzled when Miss Berkin sought him out, when he neared the barn. She held her cardigan sweater together with one hand while shading her eyes with the other.

"Are you all right, Billy?" she asked.

"Yeah, I'm okay now," Billy shoved his hands into his pockets.

"I won't be back in school for maybe a little over a week. I'll have to get the rest of the crop in."

"Oh, Billy, you're just a boy," Miss Berkin said, tilting her head to one side. "Let someone else take care of the farm now."

"Who?" Billy asked.

For the second time that day, Billy had the distinct sense that Miss Berkin was about to touch him, maybe wrap him in a hug. She pulled her sweater tighter around her, as if only to give her arms something to do; but she didn't give him a hug.

Uncle Theo and many of the neighbors came by and began putting up the crop the day after the funeral. Billy appreciated it and worked alongside the adults; keeping up with their pace. For two long days he trudged behind the steel-toothed drag, across plowed fields with a team of horses, from sunrise till sunset.

On his first day back at school, Billy waited. After dismissal, when all of the students were gone, he approached Miss Berkin at her desk.

"Could I sit with you for a moment, Miss Berkin?" he asked.

"Of course, Billy. Come here." She welcomed him to her chair. There wasn't room beside her, so Billy was pleased when she allowed him to sit on her lap. He sat stiffly for a moment, then laid his head against Miss Berkin's shoulder and closed his eyes. His muscles softened and relaxed. She put her arms around him and they sat in silence for nearly twenty minutes, then Billy slid from her lap.

"I'll be going home now," he said. He had reached the door before he turned around, and without meeting Miss Berkin's eyes, he asked. "It was alright for me to do that, wasn't it?"

Miss Berkin's eyes grew misty. "Yes. That was fine, Billy. You go on home now."

Chapter 6
Music

From the hospital Mac went home
Where they'd fixed his broken bones
To find his wife was of a child
And to celebrate his right
All his friends he did invite
And soon began to drink whisky, fast and wild
From "Down Went McGinty" by Joseph Flynn, 1889

SOON AFTER THE funeral, his mother rented the farm to Uncle Theo and sold him all the livestock. Billy protested his mother's actions vehemently, arguing that he was able to take care of the farm, but she wouldn't change her mind. The purchase agreement stated that Billy would continue with chores in exchange for eggs, milk, and meat, enough for him and his mother.

Fall arrived and a crisp November wind chilled Billy into buttoning his jacket as he walked from the barn. It was a Saturday; he'd finished his morning barn chores, and was hungry. After he arrived at the kitchen, his mother, wearing a neatly pressed dress, continued her scurrying around.

Her cheeks were rouged and her hair was twisted neatly into a fluffy upsweep. She hummed continuously. Billy figured Uncle Theo was due to arrive any moment.

His mother was peeling apples when he came in for breakfast that morning. It always astounded him to watch the thin curls spiral from beneath her hand. She could skin an apple from top to bottom without once lifting the knife. And Billy savored how the scent of an apple pie baking in an oven could enliven even the dreariest rooms.

After the noon meal, Billy met Uncle Theo coming up the front walk, and Theo wasn't dressed for work, what with his new striped bib overalls, a white shirt, a brown suit coat, and burnished oxfords. Billy had noticed that Theo never wore socks.

"Hey there, Billy. What do you say? Fine weather we're having." He patted Billy on the head and further messed up his unruly hair.

"It's all right if you like cloudy days." Billy felt safe contradicting his uncle, even though he never would have talked back to his father like that.

"A farmer likes rain on the horizon after the harvest is brought in. Of course I wouldn't be saying this if we had hay down." Theo said.

Billy knew that wasn't exactly true, because over the past few months he had become accustomed to this standard greeting from Theo, no matter what was going on in the sky. In fact, a number of things about Uncle Theo didn't ring true, like his fake smile and how he laughed at most anything.

His mother held the screen door open for Theo, and admonished Billy.

"You haven't put the storm window in this door yet, Billy. You should have done that when you did the others on the house." She removed her apron and hung it on the screen door latch.

"Supper will be late. After you empty the slop pail, get started on cleaning the calf pens," she said.

Billy didn't care for the way Uncle Theo was eyeing his mother.

"Sure smells good ... I mean the baking." Theo laughed and winked at Billy. "Smells like apple pie today."

Billy preferred not to be watching. He couldn't understand why and how Uncle Theo could treat his mother so affectionately, he being married and all. He didn't think about it too much, because the world of adults was too baffling, and whatever Uncle Theo was up to; the visits had softened his mother. She even baked during the week, not just on Sundays.

Miss Berkin became ill and dismissed school early. Billy's mother wasn't home when Billy arrived. He'd just fixed himself a jelly sandwich when his dog, Lucky, began to bark. Glancing out the window, he saw Uncle Theo and his mother in the yard alighting from a new Ford touring car. They laughed and embraced. Theo hurried and held the car door open and then kissed his mother on the lips before she stepped down. He took her in his arms and held her tightly with his hands behind her hips and kissed her again. They held hands and raced for the house. Billy quickly stepped out the back door and waited outside by the corner of the house until they were inside.

"Theo!" he heard his mother say from the bedroom. "It's only two in the afternoon!"

"I know. You're especially good this time of day!"

"Slow down a little, Theo. Be more romantic. Let's get our clothes off first this time!"

Billy sneaked around to the other side of the house and ran to the barn, hushing Lucky, who ran beside him. He laid down in the hay in front of the horse mangers with his hand on his dog's head and shut off his mind. It was near four o'clock when he was awakened from a restless sleep by the sound of the touring car leaving the yard.

Near Christmas time, Billy was finishing chores and talking to Lucky, when he thought he heard music. He hushed his dog and sure enough music was coming from the house. There had never been music in his house and he couldn't help but smile as he rubbed his nose with both hands, which he did whenever he got excited.

Is it a Victrola? he thought. *Did Uncle Theo bring an actual phonograph? Will he take it when he leaves, or will it still be there when I get to the house?* The music was intriguing. It was nothing like the serious hymns that dragged on forever at church. It was like the music he heard coming out of the back of the country store sometimes, with horns and a woman's voice singing sad words.

Lucky whined and howled at the strange sounds. Billy finished his chores with renewed energy.

"Can you believe it, Lucky? Music in our house? Even Dad would have liked that." He leaned on the pitchfork and gazed in the direction of the house.

"I figure nothing is going to be the same around here, old boy; so let's just make the best of it. I gotta see what's making that music." Billy said to Lucky.

And as soon as Uncle Theo's car left the driveway, Billy hurried to the house, bounded up the porch, and raced inside. There, in the parlor, was a brand new Victrola with the metal tulip on top. He ran his fingers across the top of the shiny wooden box, looking closely at the arm.

"Don't you touch that now, you hear? That's a gift from your uncle, and I don't mean to let anything happen to it."

Even though his mother sounded as though she was scolding him, she acted like a young girl about to giggle. The rouge on her cheeks had worn off; her tight bun of hair had loosened. She looked younger, even though she was wearing her apron again.

"Isn't it beautiful? You should hear it! I never knew of such music. Uncle Theo says it's the rage, and everybody dances to it. He tried to show me, but he'd better stick to his farming." She held her apron to her face and stifled her laughter.

"Did he give it to you?" Billy asked. "I mean, it must have cost a lot of money."

"Would you like to listen to it? I only have the two records he brought me today and I want to be careful not to scratch them."

"I heard it from the barn. It's great. Show me how it works?"

She cranked the Victrola tight, put on "Till We Meet Again," and asked Billy to dance. Billy couldn't figure out this change in his mother. Rarely had she said more than two words to him and now here she was, twittering like a sparrow and dancing with him.

"What's Aunt May going to think if she finds out Uncle Theo gave you this Victrola?" Billy asked.

His mother stopped dancing, turned from Billy, and waited until the record had finished. When she turned back and faced Billy, it was as if she were a different person. Her face was stern and drawn, with the hard color of a weathered fence.

"Billy, let me have my life, alright? I don't like lying, but as far as anyone else is concerned, I bought the Victrola, okay? And don't ever express judgment of me again."

"Yes, Mother." Billy said and shrank like washed wool.

While setting gopher traps the next morning, Billy conversed with Lucky.

"I sure liked it when Mom was talking to me and dancing with me. I spoiled things for her when I mentioned Aunt May. If she's happy, I guess I better just be quiet about her and Theo."

Billy patted Lucky on the head, wishing the dog could talk back, but the dog only whined.

"I'm not even going to talk to you about them anymore, okay?"

A few days later, he and Theo were unhitching the team after putting up a load of wood.

"I hear you liked the Victrola," Theo said. "I brought a special record for you. It's in the car. It's kind of a sing-songy, talking record."

"I'll bet I'll like it." Billy was thrilled and thought maybe Theo wasn't such a bad guy after all. Then he put the horses in the barn, tied them to their mangers, and fed them their hay. Theo went to the car and came back with a gift-wrapped package.

"Here it is, boy," Theo said. "I've got to go now. You go up to the house, play the record, see what you think."

"Theo gave me my own record. Can I play it right now?" Billy shouted when he came into the house.

"Of course, Billy. I want to hear it too." Billy pulled a chair up to the Victrola, wound the crank, placed the record on the turntable, and sat back in the chair and listened as a man's deep voice intoned the verses of "Dan McGinty".

Billy played the record over and over until he knew the words and the tune by heart. He recited it so many times that when he began, Lucky would bark and beg to go out.

By mid-November, a year later, Billy continued to ignore Uncle Theo's presence around his mother. Billy was thirteen now and looking forward to graduating from eighth grade in May. He would run the farm by himself then, and that would be the end of renting to Uncle Theo.

That afternoon, he and Theo husked a load of corn and shoveled it into the corncrib. They had stopped for a drink of water and were resting by the windmill. Snow geese cruised overhead, making their noisy way south. The crisp air carried the spicy scent of thawing frost from the afternoon sun. Billy rested on the well platform. He and Uncle Theo were sweaty from shoveling and beginning to chill from inactivity. Theo wiped his hands on his jacket, put on his gloves, and announced to Billy.

"Billy," he said. "I've bought the farm from your mother. She retains a lifetime lease on the homestead." Billy looked at Theo in absolute disbelief.

"I've got five sons who are old enough now so we can do all the work I need done. I'll have work for you until school is out in May. Then you'll be on your own. Maybe I can help get you in at the machine shop over in Norwood. I know the owner, Clarence Thurmond."

Billy stammered with a voice as shattered as broken glass.

"But what will I do? You can't buy the farm. It's not for sale."

Resentment revved up his voice. "I've been working this farm from the time I could walk. It's part of me. I've earned it. I'm going to run the farm by myself after graduation. *I'm* the one who won't need *you*."

"Billy," Theo said. "The sale papers have already been signed. It's done. You're not needed here anymore." Uncle Theo took a big blue handkerchief from his back pocket and wiped his forehead.

Hot blood was boiling in Billy's veins—frustrated for his lack of ability to express the degree of anger he was feeling, he stared blankly toward the starlings gathered in the red oak near the barn. His face was hot and his hands shook with an onrushing anger he had never experienced before. He shoved his uncle backwards and with clenched fists he took a swing at him. Theo stepped back and held his hands up to ward Billy off.

    Billy stumbled back and his mouth filled with sticky saliva. He spit, attempting to keep his anger in check. Never before had he felt such a strong urge to injure someone.

Chapter 7
The Machine Shop

And he waddled down the street
In his Sunday suit so neat
Holdin' up his head, as swell as John the Great
But in the sidewalk was a hole
To receive a ton of coal
That McGinty never saw till just too late
From "Down Went McGinty" by Joseph Flynn, 1889

A PLEASANT GRAY moonlight filtered through the frayed edges of the tattered window shade on the curtainless window and into the musty bedroom. Billy peered out the window. Fireflies flickered in the grass like incandescent dewdrops. Stripped to his under shorts and ready for bed, he sat cold-eyed in a straight-backed brown chair, whose varnished surface was crackled with age like ice crystals in root beer. The room was musty. Faded blue and yellow lined wallpaper had peeled from the wall near the door and the ceiling. A muted yellow light found its way through the oily chimney of a kerosene lamp sitting atop a vintage, four-drawer dresser by the wall. The persistent smell of mouse droppings from the nests

Billy had found in the drawers still lingered in the air. This is home now, he thought.

All of Billy's worldly possessions were in the room: the pocket watch his father had given him, which had long since quit working, his Remington bolt-action rifle leaning in the corner, two sets of work clothes, a jackknife, the Tonette Miss Berkin had given him, the McGinty record, and two Edgar Rice Burroughs Tarzan books. His graduation suit, a white shirt, and a tie hung on a wire hanger on a rusty nail in the west wall. He'd worn the suit twice: last Sunday, at his eighth grade graduation, and Monday, when Uncle Theo had taken him to meet Mr. Thurmond at the foundry to apply for a job.

The year was 1931. Billy wasn't fully aware that Mr. Thurmond was adding a small foundry to his machine shop and he needed additional manpower. Any well-developed male, who had worked hard and reached the age of fourteen without being maimed, was considered manpower in those days.

Uncle Theo informed Billy that he had secured a job at the foundry for him. Theo took Billy to meet Ernie Blair, a sixty-five year old bachelor farmer who lived on a small farm on the outskirts of town. Earlier in March, a cow with a newborn calf had pinned Ernie against the barn wall. By the time he'd gotten free; the cow had busted a few of his ribs and banged his legs up so it was still difficult for him to get around. After making sure it was okay to bring his dog Lucky with him, Billy rented a room in exchange for doing some of the farm chores before and after work at the machine shop.

Billy and his mother had long since talked out their differences. All that was left for Billy was resentment. As much as he loved the farm, he knew he would never be back, even to see his mother, whose last words on the subject on selling the farm had been, "It's finished Billy—done, sold—you don't have a say in it."

"Okay," he'd said to her at last. "I'll go to the Blair place to live, and go to the machine shop to work, and I won't be back here. I've been orphaned now. I've lost my father, and my mother."

Sunday, his last day at the farm, Billy and his mother didn't converse, except to say goodbye. And there was no warmth in their parting hug.

"You needn't be so sullen," his uncle said, on the way to the Blair place. Billy, intentionally tight-lipped, slouched near the right door in the front seat of the Ford touring car. *You'd be sullen too*, he thought. *If your uncle had chiseled you out of your birthright and made an adulteress of your mother.* Billy wondered if all men were like his uncle. And women, what were they like? Could anybody be trusted? He'd keep his distance from the people at the foundry and keep his feelings to himself at work. Billy turned from his uncle and gazed back. Dust trailed from the tires, rising like two dirty brown ribbons, and drifted across the countryside. Green fields stretched between occasional woodlots, cultivated dark earth showed between the rows of six-inch tall cornrows.

"Don't fret so. Everything will work out okay," his uncle said. "You can walk to work from the Blair place. You won't have to pay for a ride or have a car. I think you'll find yourself in very good circumstances working at the foundry."

Billy didn't appreciate being pandered to by his uncle. He was fourteen; he could fend and think for himself.

"Well, you're rid of me now," Billy said with mock cheerfulness. "Aren't you, Uncle?" Theo didn't reply, and nothing more was said until their formal good-bye at the Blair farm.

On Billy's first day at work, Mr. Thurmond gave him a tour of the machine shop. He stood in awe of the noise and sights of all the wide belts and pulleys on the ceiling and along the walls.

"I want you to become familiar with all of these machines," Mr. Thurmond told Billy. "By year's end you should be able to work with any of them. People who work here need to know how to weld, too," he said, pointing out a man wearing a welding helmet, and making a sizzling blue arc—fusing two pieces of metal together.

"Look away, young man. Don't ever look at a welding arc without a helmet on. It doesn't take much of that light to permanently damage your eyes."

Billy noticed the rectangle of nearly black glass in the helmet the welder was wearing.

Mr. Thurmond introduced Billy to the drill presses, lathes, metal saws, forges, grinding machines, and blow torches. Everything produced an assortment of smells and sounds. Billy found nothing appealing about any of it.

Wary of making friends, Billy adapted cautiously to the machine shop culture. Working regular scheduled hours and having free time from work, was a new and welcome experience for him. There was a new challenge nearly every day at work, and soon his bitterness began to fade; and his new education began.

He began going to the Red Bird roadhouse with his co-workers. At first shy and timid, Billy became a determined student, observing and listening; although without much active participation until he was sixteen. At sixteen he joined with the group, drinking liquor, telling dirty jokes, and talking disparagingly about "Catholics, niggers, and Indians." He got drunk with his buddies on Friday and Saturday nights and eventually, with the help of the liquor, approached one of the

Elsville girls. One who the guys said was always game for a romp in the hay.

The Elsville girls were older and more experienced than Billy. It got so he wasn't that particular about which girl he left the dance with. For his purposes, they were interchangeable. Liquored up, and fumbling and groping in the dark, Billy didn't care what the girl looked like or what her name was. The guys had told him, "You don't need a fancy rig to have your ashes hauled."

The Elsville girls never pressured him for anything more than the pleasure of the moment. The Blair place gradually became home to Billy. He genuinely liked Ernie Blair, and tolerated, with interest, his myna bird, Cletus. Cletus was a dirty-talking bird, with dirty personal habits, who would foul his cage while sitting on his perch, then hop down and walk in the droppings until they were caked to his feet. Cletus learned how to mimic Billy's voice. "Here, Lucky," the bird would say. At first Lucky ran all around—confused. Often Lucky couldn't tell the difference between Billy and Cletus' voices.

Mr. Thurmond grew to respect Billy. He complimented his intelligence and industriousness, and began giving him increasingly responsible positions. Billy noticed that Thurmond neglected to attach a title to the new positions or increase the salary to match the increased responsibilities.

Mr. Thurmond's wife, Myrtle, a muscular, raw-boned woman with dark red, wiry hair, and rock-hard, red-painted lips, came to the shop one day, for a private meeting with Clarence.

"I've decided we need to modernize," she said. We'll start with Clair, our hired girl? In three weeks she graduates from eighth grade. I told her she could have a job at the machine shop. She starts the first Monday after graduation."

"But, dear—"

"'But', your ass, stenchweed," Myrtle said.

"But there've never been any women at the shop. She's just a little girl. It's a rough place and our guys are uneducated and crude. Plus, there's the depression going on."

"You depression-proofed yourself when you married me and my money," Myrtle said.

Billy had been summoned to the office, and arrived just as Myrtle was leaving. She stood between him and the door. To Billy, Clarence seemed far more uncomfortable than he. Billy sensed Clarence yielding to a fight with his wife, which he'd already lost, and was simply waiting for the next tirade.

"Besides," Myrtle continued, with a glance at Billy. "You hire little boys just out of school, don't you? You're the boss— go and straighten those men out! Just because they're a bunch of men working together doesn't mean they have to always act crude and vulgar. Frankly, I'm tired of doing your damn bookwork and correspondence. I've other things to do. But I'll help Clair get started. We'll sit down with her at this table next Saturday, and you'll hire her."

Myrtle thought Clarence was quite dejected. She swept from the room as Clarence stared at the floor, while rubbing his left earlobe.

Chapter 8
Clair

And down went McGinty to the bottom of the hole
And the driver of the cart
Gave the load of coal a start
And it took a half hour to dig McGinty from the coal
Dressed in his best suit of clothes
From "Down Went McGinty" by Joseph Flynn, 1889

E.J. MULRONEY, the machine shop foreman, called a meeting of all his men. Billy, along with the crusty-looking, mostly untidy laborers gathered around the welding table at the machine shop.

"A new era starts next week," Mulroney said. "A young girl, Clair Isabelle, will be starting work here," he announced.

A surge of sour voices rumbled through the room. The foreman held his hand up for attention.

"She'll be working for Mr. Thurmond, cleaning, running errands, doing correspondence, and whatever else he sees for her to do. Everybody here has to clean up his foul mouth. Your dirty jokes about women, Indians, Catholics, niggers, and the likes are forbidden. Save 'em for the Red Bird Tavern or the Legion Club."

Billy groaned and grumbled with the rest of the men. He'd come to appreciate the raunchy social atmosphere of the shop and didn't want to change.

With the mention of Clair Isabelle, Billy's thoughts returned to the first Sunday after his dad's funeral. He'd gone to church with his mother and shortly after they returned home, Mr. and Mrs. Isabelle, who owned the Highland General Store, came to the house with a hamburger hot dish and fresh home-baked bread.

Their daughter Clair, a tousle-haired girl in a new print dress, stayed outside on the front steps playing with a puppy. She blushed and put her head down when she saw Billy coming. Billy knew her from school, but he'd hardly talked to her.

"Want to pet my puppy?" Clair asked bravely.

"Sure. What's its name?"

"Haven't named him yet. We got three more at home."

Billy reached down to pet the wriggling canine.

"You can hold him if you want. If you like him and promise to take good care of him, you can buy him."

"I sure would like to, but I don't have any money."

"I saw you playing mumbly peg at school. Want to trade your jackknife for him?"

Billy thought of this dad's old pearl-handle jackknife in the milk room of the barn.

"I got an old pearl-handled one with one side missing. The blades are okay. How about that for a trade?" Billy ran to the barn and came back with the knife.

Clair glanced at the knife, and then looked at Billy.

"Okay. It's a deal. Shake on it. When Billy clasped her hand, her face flushed and she began to chatter.

"I'm sorry your dad died. My mother almost died this winter from the flu. She's still kinda sick. I have to take care of my little sister Ruth, and sometimes my mom too. She can't work in the store yet. Lots of people died from the flu this winter. I didn't get it. Did you get the flu?"

Billy wasn't listening and had eyes and thoughts only for the puppy. When a catbird called from a nearby tree, the puppy responded with a growl, and then licked Billy's face. Clair continued her nervous chatter.

"He's half shepherd and half collie. How can a puppy be half one thing and half another? Ruth didn't have the flu, either. Are we half a thing and half another? Everybody says I look just like my dad, but I was born by my mother."

Billy interrupted. "I'm going to the barn with my puppy. You stay here and don't' tell my mom."

Clair Isabelle looked at her new set of clothes, a gift from Myrtle for her first day of work at the foundry. At 7:00 a.m., she walked from her room to the stairway and hollered down.

"Mother, I'm scared. I don't want to go. It's all men there and that Billy Bartel that bought our puppy and never hardly talked to me again after that—he works there. I think I might still like him and I won't know how to act."

Then she ran downstairs, where her mother, frail and drawn, sat at the kitchen table. Clair put her head down, and began to cry. "I don't like that outfit," she said.

"That's okay, dear, but Mrs. Thurmond bought it for you, special, just for today. It's all right if you're scared, but this is a great opportunity. You'll have to be on your own sometime. If I were feeling better, we could keep the store and you could go on to high school. Mrs. Thurmond thinks the world of you; she'll help you get started. I'm sure."

Clair wiped her eyes.

"I don't have to talk to them men, do I?"

"No. You go on and get ready now and I'll take you to work." Clair shuffled up the stairs. The white blouse was starched so stiff it crunched when she moved her arms. Even with a slip on, she felt the scratchiness of the wool skirt. It embarrassed her to wear the white blouse; she thought someone might see her budding breasts through the thin fabric. She hated her tan cotton stockings and the garter belt.

Clair remained rigid and quiet as her mother drove her to work. The sight of the long, gray metal foundry building gave her a cold chill as she stepped from the car. The only real color to the whole building was the black lettering, OFFICE, above a gray metal front door. In the area between the sidewalk and the building were rusted machine parts, smartweeds, and grass that needed mowing. Clarence Thurmond greeted her when she stepped inside the drab office. An office that smelled of metal grindings and hot oil. Clarence showed her around the office and pointed out where the bathroom was. She had hoped for a tour of the foundry, but he led her to the new oak desk, which Myrtle had directed him to buy. And guided her to the storeroom where the safe and the ledgers were kept.

"Make a list of office supplies you'll need," Clarence said. "I have to go see to a problem in the shop."

After he departed, Clair surveyed her surroundings. Her desk was by a side window, looking out into a meadow, where sheep were grazing with spring lambs. Another massive mahogany desk, black with age, sat near the back wall. Shelves of dusty, soiled books lined another grimy wall, where a Brown and Bigelow calendar with a color illustration of a pretty girl hung. Next to that was a painting of a dairy farm, several black and white photograph portraits of old people in oval frames, and a few advertisements for machine parts.

Clair opened each drawer of her desk and found nothing inside. Convinced no one was watching her she smoothed her skirt, and walked to the storeroom, where she shed a few anxious tears. She heard Clarence in another room talking about her.

When Clarence returned to the office, Clair was crumpling the papers she picked up off the floor and pushing them into an overflowing wastebasket.

"The garbage bins are out back," Clarence said. When she went out back and found the bins, Clair caught glimpses of some of the men and felt their eyes on her. Clarence asked her to go to the drugstore and pick up pencils, paper, and other items he thought she would need.

When she returned, there was a bouquet of daffodils, a typewriter, and an instruction manual on her desk.

"Myrtle was here while you were gone," Clarence said. "She wanted me to tell you congratulations on your new job. She said you wanted to learn how to type. She'll be back to help you get started." Mr. Thurmond said he had to leave for a few hours. Before he left, he told her to clean the room.

Chapter 9
Shop Talk

Now McGinty raved and swore
About his clothes he felt so sore
He took an oath to kill the man or die
So he tightly grabbed a stick and hit the driver a lick
And raised a little shanty on his eye
From "Down Went McGinty" by Joseph Flynn, 1889

THE SHOP WORKERS, men in blue overalls adorned with grease and metal burns, gathered around the long wooden table near the end of a large shop room, cluttered with assorted junk. The shop foreman, E.J. Mulroney, banged his monkey wrench on the battered table and called the meeting to order.

"I think it's time we shape up or ship out around here," E.J. said, wiping his scruffy hands with a rough oily rag. "That little fourteen-year-old girl in the office has been here just a little more than six weeks. She's cleaned up her area and straightened things out. She works her shift without stopping. She and Myrtle have put up curtains, added color to the office with a new paint job, and put a smile on this place. By comparison her office makes our area look like the shit it is. No wonder we have so many accidents and so much downtime. This place is a disaster. I don't think that girl has looked up from the floor once since she's been here, and none of us have spoken a word to her. She's so damn scared she tries to hide when she sees one of us. I've got a daughter about her age, and I wouldn't want her treated this way."

"That's right," said Sam Blake, an unshaven man in his sixties with a full head of black hair. "I've worked here since the place was a blacksmith shop owned by Clarence Thurmond's father. It's been a dingy godforsaken place to work for over forty years. That young girl is like a ray of sunshine to a coal miner digging himself out of a cave-in. A good share of the fault of our working conditions is our own." The men muttered.

E.J. rapped his monkey wrench on the bench. "Okay. How do we tell her we want to get along?" he asked.

"You're the foreman," said Billy.

"Okay, then I'll do it. I'll buy her something from all of us, to cheer up her office some more. I'll tell her then."

A tall one-armed man muscled his way to the front of the room. "This is a bunch of bullshit," he said. "I'm not going along with this. If she wants to work here, she can learn to 'root hog, or die' like the rest of us."

"Now see here, Clyde," E.J. said. "We're all in agreement but you. Is two bits too much for you to chip in? Okay, we'll put on the card with the gift, that it's from everybody except Clyde."

"Two bits is five nickel beers," Clyde said. And flipped a quarter to E.J. "Next Goddamn thing you know, we'll be holding ladies aid meetings here and be wearing a tuxedo to work."

A few days later, E.J. removed his black-and-white striped railroad engineer's cap and patted down his thin, carrot-red hair. He swallowed a couple of times, forging enough courage to face the office girl. Shoulders back and chin up, he opened the door and walked briskly to Clair's desk.

E. J. saw that Clair's downcast eyes could see only up to the clips on his suspenders. Without ceremony he placed a pale pink flowered vase on her desk.

"I'm E.J. Mulroney, shop foreman," he said. His new cap slipped from his hand. When he straightened after retrieving it, Clair raised her eyes and looked at his face.

"E.J.," she said timidly, "that's your first name?"

"Yes, Miss. E.J.," he said, and shuffled his feet. "We ... the men thought you might like the new vase. I ... we ... the men ... ah, ah ... like the way you've changed this place. We were wondering if maybe you could show us or tell us how we could straighten up the shop. You wouldn't have to do anything, just maybe give us some suggestions. I'd like to send Clyde, the parts guy, to you, to see if you could help him get some kind of system to the parts department."

"I don't know Mr. Clyde. Maybe he doesn't want me interfering in his area."

"I'll take care of Clyde. Don't you worry about that."

"I'll try if it's okay with Mr. Thurmond and you are sure Mr. Clyde won't be offended."

"Done," E.J. said. "All the guys chipped in two bits for your vase, and I got a little left over if you want some flowers or something, Miss Clair." She felt like grabbing him and giving him a hug, and the chill that plagued her for six weeks ebbed.

"I don't know what to say, Mr. Mulroney."

"E.J.," he corrected her.

At that time Mr. Thurmond came in the front door and hung his coat and hat on the walnut hall tree in the corner. "Good morning Miss Clair—E.J.," he said, nodding.

"Good day, Mr. Thurmond," said E.J. walking towards the shop door. Clair looked his way with steady eyes.

"Thanks," Clair said.

E.J. paused, and Clair saw an easy smile warming E.J.'s face before he closed the door behind him.

Clyde introduced himself to Clair, the next day, extending his left hand in greeting. She glanced at the empty folded shirtsleeve, safety-pinned near his shoulder. His right arm ended as a stump about six inches above where his elbow would have been.

"Had a little argument with a power shaft in the shop a few years ago—and lost," he said. He moved forward awkwardly and, towering above Clair, he frowned down at her.

"Miss Clair, I'm here because E.J. asked me to see you. They all think you're a nice young person and want to give you a chance; but let's get one thing straight. I know where every machinery part and piece of equipment is in this place, how it works, and how to fix it. When I'm not around, these guys couldn't find an egg in the nest where the hen laid it. Hang around with me for a few days and all you'll here is 'Clyde, where is this? Clyde, we got parts for this and that?' It's them that need the help, not me. I can use this stump of an arm to hold a book, a welding torch, a pipe wrench, or a jar of moonshine when I take off the cap. Sure, I could use some help, but don't get the idea I'm some poor, helpless, one-armed, son-of-a-bi—. Ah ... excuse me, Miss Clair."

Clair felt herself shrinking. She cowered, looking for a place to hide if Clyde should become violent. Clyde softened his expression when Clair slinked back a few steps.

"You'll hafta harden your shell a bit, sister, to work around here. Stick with me. I'll feed your gizzard a little grit and that shell of yours will firm up like a tough little pullet egg. This old rooster will take you under his wing and help you over the rough spots, if you'd like," he said.

Miss Clair knew all about grit and gizzards, and her apprehension of this tall, forthright man faded.

From then on, Clyde and Miss Clair were a team. And soon when the men called for Clyde and Clyde didn't respond, they sought out Miss Clair. Everyone took special care with their language and manners whenever Clair was around. While no one ever spoke of it, everyone knew Clair was out of bounds for a come on of any sorts. Not only did the men hold her in high esteem, it was more like a reverence.

If Clyde or E.J. needed something—like new shelves or a counter—and Mr. Thurmond didn't respond, they'd mention it to Clair. When Clair explained things to Mr. Thurmond, there usually would be action.

Then Chuck Hanson's pants leg caught in a drive belt and his leg was broken. First E.J. and Clyde, then Clair, pleaded with Mr. Thurmond for safety shields on all drive shafts and pulleys. Mr. Thurmond refused. "It was just an accident," he said.

At the close of the day, E.J. and Clyde were putting their tools away in the back of the shop.

"What are we going to do about safety for the men?" E.J. asked.

Clyde looked at the uncovered drive shafts, heard their hum, and once again, in his mind, felt his arm shatter as it twisted around the shaft until the belt slipped on the pulley. The smell of blood and smoke continued—clear in his mind.

"Clarence ain't too bad a guy," Clyde said. "His money has come kind of easy for him, if you call living with Myrtle easy, but old Clarence likes to squeeze his every nickel till the buffalo shits. So let's not give up on this. Clarence ain't around today, so let's go see Clair." When they found Clair, they ushered her into Mr. Thurmond's private office and shut the door.

E.J. and Clyde were Clair's favorites at the foundry. When she looked at them in their worn clothes with their hats in their hands, she was sure they had wet their hair and combed it with their fingers before they came to see her.

"This must be serious. What are you two old roosters up to now?" she asked, and guided them to chairs by the desk.

"How long have you been here now, Miss Clair?" E.J. asked.

"Nearly seven years."

Clair's expression turned somber. She thought these two connivers might be up to something she might not want to be involved with.

"Miss Clair, you know you're just like a sister to us guys here at the plant. We really … well, you know, you're just…"

"I know that. You've all been so wonderful. You're family." Clair smiled at Clyde.

Clyde hitched his short arm up in a nervous twitch. "We need you bad," he said, shifting from one foot to another. "We need you to talk to Myrtle Thurmond about the shields and other safety measures around here. We get no response from Mr. Thurmond. You know about our plan. It's all ready … all we need is the go-ahead. You're family to Myrtle too, and she'll make Clarence do it if you ask."

Clair closed her eyes. "I can't do that. Isn't there another way?"

E.J. stood up. There were deep worry lines about his eyes, and he didn't stand as straight as usual.

"We shouldn't have asked you," he said. "Come on, Clyde, we're pushing too hard on Miss Clair."

"Wouldn't I be disloyal to Mr. Thurmond if I did that?" Clair asked. Loyalty was important to Clair. *But what about her loyalty to E.J. and the rest of the men?* Then a bloody severed arm and a broken leg bone crossed her mind.

"Okay, I'll talk to Myrtle, but you guys keep your mouths shut," she said.

Clarence Thurmond sat comfortably at his supper table and lifted his coffee cup to his lips, as his wife Myrtle scanned the weekly newspaper.

"Says here that young Chuck Hanson whose leg was broken at the foundry was pretty lucky and will be back at work in a few months," she said.

"A huh," Clarence mumbled, and thought Myrtle resented his lack of interest.

"A huh? Is that all you've got to say, you sleazy little bastard? A huh?"

Clarence jerked to attention, spilling coffee from the rim of his cup. "No, I mean that was too bad. I'm sorry," he said. "We'll put him back to work when he's healed up."

"Did he get mixed up with the same shaft as Clyde Erickson did years ago?"

"No. That was a belt and pulley."

"Do you have a trophy room down at the foundry with arms, legs, and severed hands up on the wall like stuffed deer heads?"

Clarence put his coffee cup on the table and looked shifty-eyed at Myrtle. She put the weekly paper in her lap. Myrtle's dark brown eyes dilated and her lips tensed.

"What are you doing about safety measures?" she demanded.

"I've talked to Clyde and Miss Clair about it."

"Enough talking. I want action. I'll be at the foundry tomorrow afternoon. Have Clair, E.J., and Clyde in your office at nine. I'll do the talking, and don't you make any noise louder than a popcorn fart."

Around noon the next day, Myrtle arrived at the foundry. Clarence, E.J., Clyde, and Clair were waiting for her in Clarence's office, just as she'd requested. From a manila envelope she was carrying, Myrtle produced a handwritten safety plan, a plan that included safety shields and much more. She instructed Clair to type it up and make carbon copies, and warned her, "If this plan is not carried out—your job is in jeopardy."

Myrtle's round, marble-hard, brown eyes shifted to Clyde and E.J. "And you two, if you don't do what this says, then the next time you lose a limb, we'll hang it like a trophy on the wall." She gave Clair a fleeting smile, and then stalked off in a huff.

Chapter 10
The Proposal

But two policemen saw the fuss, and soon joined in the muss
And they ran McGinty in for being drunk
And the judge said with a smile, "We'll keep you here awhile
In a cell to sleep upon a prison bunk"
From "Down Went McGinty" by Joseph Flynn, 1889

BY 1945, WHEN Clair was twenty-four, she bore little resemblance to the stringy, undeveloped girl who had first appeared at the foundry ten years earlier. She had a mane of radiant flaxen hair, dancing blue eyes, and a nose that wiggled a bit when she talked. She reveled in the adoration of her adopted family at the foundry. Five feet eleven inches tall and well proportioned, her shapely legs were contoured to a sumptuous body that her modest dressing couldn't hide.

She was now assistant general manager. However, being a woman, she was still paid as a cleaning girl and secretary. She relished doing contract work, taking care of sales, paying bills, settling labor disputes, balancing books, and keeping up with correspondence. She particularly delighted in the good-natured banter between the men and herself. Within the confines of the foundry-protected class system, Billy and Miss Clair had become friends. Although Billy didn't know how to flirt with her openly, the thought of asking her out had crossed his mind a number of times, even though Clair rarely dated. This usually happened when he was in the midst of teasing her. Clair was fun to tease and Billy felt safe with her, since she was quick with her own comeback and never took offense.

On a quiet rainy day in April, Clair was sitting at her desk; she didn't look up when Billy wandered in. He swiped a pencil from her desk, and purposely knocked a stapler to the floor. Clair ignored him and continued writing figures in her ledger.

"Miss Clair," Billy said. "All you do is work. You've been here a long time now and you ain't getting any younger." He slouched into an old leather chair. "You should be thinking of getting married," he teased.

Clair shook out her mane of hair, raised her head, paused and, with her pen poised in the air, gazed at Billy. Her velvety deep ocean eyes ran from the top of Billy's head to his feet, and back to his stubborn face. He was leathery, with full dark hair that was handsomely half combed. His deep blue eyes reminded her of the shadows made in snow. His nose was smooth and round, as if he had borrowed it from someone else's face. Clair pictured him dressed in a fine suit and a tie rather than the five-and-dime outfits she'd seen him wearing about town.

Then, with a calculated move, she locked eyes with Billy and laid the pen on the green felt pad on her desk. Clair took a deep breath, and then smiled. "Yes, Billy. I've thought about getting married. For ten years I've been watching you pass by here day after blessed day, only occasionally stopping for a short visit. And I had about given up. I was beginning to think you would never ask, but now that you have, I accept. Yes, I'll marry you."

Billy turned about fourteen shades of red and began to shake. His voice, from somewhere deep in a queasy stomach, came out in stuttering stammers. "I mean just get married to someone, anyone. I mean just get married, I didn't mean ..."

"You don't want to marry me, Billy?" Clair asked in a plaintive voice.

"Yes, but ..." Billy said it before he realized how it sounded.

Miss Clair rose from her chair, smoothed her hair, and walked from behind the desk.

"Let me get you a cool glass of water," she said. Billy stood up and leaned against the wall for support.

"Sit down. Relax," Clair said. "It's not the end of the world, you know."

Billy didn't dare to look at her. He imagined the faces of other men if and when they heard about this situation, and his gut ached with the thought. They'd think he had broken the unwritten rule, and he would have to pay for it.

Clair held out the glass of water to Billy. "Haven't you ever thought of getting married?" she asked. "You're getting pretty old too, you know." Her statement snapped Billy back into awareness, and the hum of machinery from the shop replaced the ringing in his ears.

"I don't know," he said. His voice shook. It was barely audible.

Clair tilted her face provocatively and turned her profile to Billy. "Then think about it." And then she turned abruptly and walked to the storeroom.

Billy took the rest of the day off and went for a walk in the woods down by the river. He urgently needed to talk to someone, and thought of Miss Berkin. She was the only person he'd ever really talked to. She was still teaching. But he decided he didn't dare talk to her about this. He knew he would have to defend himself, explain that he had never been on a date with Clair, had never even touched her. He felt as if he were in deep trouble.

Chapter 11
Prescription for Billy

So McGinty thin and pale, when he finally got out of jail
To learn with joy, his baby was a boy
So home he quickly ran, to meet his wife Cedella Ann
But she skipped and took along the child
From "Down Went McGinty" by Joseph Flynn, 1889

THE ESSENCE OF iodine, ether, alcohol, and mercurochrome permeating the air became stronger with each step as Billy climbed the long flight of stairs from Main Street to Doc Selkirk's office above the drug store. He took a seat on a bench near the back wall in the waiting room, where he waited nervously scratching at the back of his hands.

"Come on in, Billy," Doc Selkirk's voice intoned from the inner office. Billy pushed open the slightly ajar solid oak door to the doctor's office and shuffled in.

The doctor, a man of medium build, was sitting loosely in a dark mahogany captain's chair, in front of a battered roll-top desk that was barely visible for all the papers, *Saturday Evening Post*, magazines, and Velvet tobacco cans piled about. A white mortar and pestle reserved the only clear space. Doc was low in his chair, leaning forward with his forearms across his knees.

He made a loud wheezing sound through his nose when he exhaled. His abundant head of uncombed bushy gray hair complemented a mustache that needed trimming. And below his protruding lower lip was a stylish goatee, with a color and texture that looked like wild rabbits' fur turning white for the winter. He motioned Billy to a wooden chair with a rump-rubbed seat that shone from years of patient fidgeting. Cradling the bowl of an old-fashioned bent pipe with a white bowl in his hand, he wheezed a puff of dense blue smoke through his nose, a portion of which went down the inside of his rumpled white shirt.

"Haven't seen you since your bout with pneumonia when you were what—twelve? Thirteen?" Doc said. His bushy eyebrows shaded pinpoint hazel eyes that grinned. "You sure look okay. What can I do for you?" Billy scratched at the back of his hands, as he'd been doing for nearly four weeks now.

"I've got this rash on my hands," Billy said. "The skin is cracking and flaking and driving me nuts." Doc put his pipe in a tray on the desk and looked at Billy's hands.

"Hmm," he said, picking up the pipe, drawing a few puffs and blowing more smoke down his chest. Then he took Billy's pulse. "How are you otherwise?" he asked.

"Fine," Billy said, and wished he were out of there. He knew he shouldn't have come.

Doc got up from his chair. "Just relax, now," he said, as he pulled his stethoscope out from underneath the Minneapolis morning paper on the desk. "I'll listen to your chest and heart."

Afterwards he looked in Billy's ears and eyes.

"You're in fine health, Billy," Doc said. There was a sneaky grin on his face. "Except for whatever it is that's really bothering you."

"Bothering me?"

"Like nerves. You got a case of the nerves about anything?"

"Well, not exactly." A cold sweat-ball formed on Billy's upper lip. Doc sat back in his chair, viewed the sweat-ball, and then widened his grin.

"Billy," he said. "I've seen all kinds come in and out of here, and you look to me like you got something bottled up inside you that you can't get out. So it's pushing its way out as a rash. Tell me what's bothering you and I bet we can fix you up."

Billy wiped the sweat from his upper lip. "There's nothing bothering me, Doc," he said. "But I'm getting … ahh … married. See, the wedding is set for June and I don't know anything about getting married. I've never really been out with the girl I'm getting married to, see … it all happened by accident. I wanta get married, but it's like for the first time in my life, I'm scared of something."

Doc spent some time picking in his pipe bowl with a wooden match. Then he tapped out the scrapings into and around the ashtray. Tobacco soot smeared the side of his hands and smudged papers on the desk. A glowing tobacco ember descended towards his suit. Billy restrained his inclination to warn Doc, after noticing numerous brown-edged burn holes in Doc's coat and trousers.

"I heard you and Clair Isabelle were getting married. Fine girl," Doc said.

"I don't know how to act around her anymore … and all the men at the foundry…" Billy shifted his posture, got a handkerchief from his back pocket and wiped a new-forming sweat-ball from his upper lip. "I thought they would kill me when they found out, but they think it's great and they all want to be the best man. I had supper with Clair and her parents the other night, and I sat there like I was stupid. Just answered questions and I didn't have a thing to say. Sometimes I get dizzy, and there's ringing in my ears. It's like I'm being swept down river in floodwater. Sometimes I feel like I'm drowning."

"If you're that worried about it, why don't you call it off?" Doc said.

Before Billy could even think, he said, "I love her, Doc," and his face turned crimson.

Old Doc's wizened eyes beamed. "Good job, Billy," Doc said. "You got that cap off the bottle and poured out some feelings. Pretty good! Now that you know how to uncap those feelings, I'll write out a prescription for you that should fix you up. You just keep on talkin' while I'm writin'"

Billy fidgeted. "I'm all mixed up," he said. "But when Clair looks at me the way she does, I feel like I don't have to worry. Then the men start to tease me, and you know that kind of makes me feel good, too. It's when I go home and I'm alone, that's when the shakes come."

Doc wrote the prescription on a sheet of lined notebook paper. Then he folded it into a square and put it in Billy's shirt pocket.

"You're going to have to get this filled in Minneapolis," he said. "I have an account there, so you can pay me now. That'll be twenty bucks."

Twenty Bucks, Billy thought. *That's almost a full week's wages.*

"Awful expensive medicine, isn't it Doc?" Billy asked.

"Worth every cent of it," said Doc. "And by the way, stop off at the drug store and get a tin of cow's udder balm for those hands of yours. That'll take care of the rash you've got now. The prescription will keep it from flaring up again."

Doc ushered Billy out the door, and to a stout, gray-haired woman with long cotton stockings rolled down to her ankles, wearing a huge straw hat adorned with a multitude of fresh-cut spring flowers. Doc said, "Come in, Mrs. Flarity. Nice of you to bring spring with you."

The long wooden stairs, for years treated with sweeping compound, barely creaked as Billy walked down to his car and on to the street. Before he drove off, he pulled the prescription from his shirt pocket and read the unusually clear and concise handwriting.

RX

Wash your car up real nice, and pick some violets and bluebells from the woods behind your house. Then take yourself and Clair Isabelle out of town where you can talk and won't be gawked at. Drive to Minneapolis. There is a restaurant called Charlie's on Fifth Street. Go in and ask for Ralph or Inez. Tell them Doc Selkirk sent you. They'll give you a very private table and bring you an empty vase. Put the violets and bluebells in it. Order something special. Don't worry about the price. It's on me (the twenty dollars you gave me). Then take the cap off that bottle with all your feelings in it and tell that beautiful Clair all about how you feel. Clean your ears out before you go, so you can record what both of you have to say. Talk softly and <u>look at her</u>. And when you want Clair to really know how you feel about her, reach across the table and take her hands in yours. Ralph will have two glasses of wine for you (no more!). Get Clair home by 1:00 a.m.. Kiss her goodnight and go home. Everything will work out fine after that. This prescription is good for life (refills at your own expense, ha ha). Say hello to Clair for me and be sure to send me an invitation to the wedding—Doc Selkirk

Chapter 12
Springtime

Then he gave up in despair, as he madly tore his hair
And he stood one day upon the river's shore
Knowing well he could not swim, did he foolishly jump in
Though it was water he had never took before
From "Down Went McGinty" by Joseph Flynn, 1889

CLAIR FELT AS frilly as the lace collar and trimming on the sleeves of her new spring dress. She pulled back the curtains on the east window of the office and drenched herself in the morning sun. Bouquets of flowers were on each windowsill. Wildflowers had been placed there fresh every day by the foundry men, ever since they learned of the upcoming wedding.

In the office, many of the precious old pictures still hung on the wall, only in new frames. This year's Brown and Bigelow calendar with the leggy picture of a pretty girl was in color now but hung in its usual place.

Clair called her sister, Ruth. Three other receivers on the party line clicked before Ruth answered.

"Ruth, I got a real surprise for you," Clair said.

"Surprise!" Ruth said. "Surprise! The whole county knows about it, and I've been dying to hear from you. I think I'm the last to know, living out here on this farm."

"I just wanted to be certain about it before I told you."

"Well, tell me all about it."

"I can't tell you with all these people listening on the line." They heard two clicks. Now only one neighbor was listening.

"You come out here right after work on Saturday, said Ruth. "You get off at noon, don't you? I'll be getting an anniversary dinner ready for my hubby's folks on Sunday, but we can talk while you're helping me."

"Thanks. Ruth. You don't think I'm too old, do you?"

"Too inexperienced, maybe, but not too old."

Clair laughed. "Okay. I'll see you Saturday at about two then. Bye."

Clair stayed on the line after Ruth hung up and waited until she heard the last click, from the party line listener, then put the receiver back into its cradle and chuckled.

Chapter 13
Ruth

AFTER EIGHTH GRADE graduation, Ruth, unlike her sister Clair, went on to high school. In her sophomore year, the boys began referring to her as "Boobs Isabelle." Five foot three, with distinctive curly brown hair, Ruth was outgoing, had a comely though seductive face and full friendly lips. Boys soon found out that she wasn't easy. She didn't bring any boys home to meet her parents, except for Al, who had just returned from a stint in the army.

Al joined the army at the insistence of his folks during hard times in '29. It was only after he was gone that they understood how much work he had been doing.

Ruth became infatuated with Al the army man and they married one week after her high school graduation. They moved in with Al's parents. Ruth tried, but she couldn't warm up to his parents, mostly because they were all business—nothing else. She and Al moved to another of the farm homes owned by Al's parents. The house was without electricity or plumbing.

Ruth soon became isolated on the new farm. Her natural bounce waned and she became withdrawn, sharing her life by confiding with Clair on occasions. She attended church services by herself except when Al joined her on Easter Sunday, Christmas, and Good Friday. The year's social highlight was the annual legion membership drive, which included dinner and a dance at the legion hall.

Al's only entertainment consisted of drinking and telling war stories with his buddies. He mostly ignored Ruth, who loved to dance.

At times Ruth's dancing style, might give the impression of suggestiveness. She danced nearly every dance. By the time she and Al returned home, Ruth had returned to her role as a dowdy housewife.

Ruth propped herself on one elbow avoiding contact with her husband lying beside her. She had slept soundly and awakened to a cool, Saturday morning in April. The chill in the house became magnified in her mind; by the steady drip of rainwater leaking from broken plaster in the ceiling into a galvanized calf pail on the floor. Al stirred awake, coughed, and threw back the covers. Ruth made no comment, although she was clearly irritated about his three-day growth of beard and the fact he had slept in his dingy long underwear. Underwear which carried the unwashed odor of himself and the hog barn.

"Clair is coming out this afternoon. She's getting married. You know Billy Bartel, don't you?" Ruth asked.

"Yeah, I've had a drink with him a time or two. Pretty quiet guy, like me."

Ruth blinked a couple of times and thought, *God, not like you I hope.*

"She's all excited; said she's been in love with him ever since grade school. I'll be maid of honor. Will you do a favor, just for me?" Ruth asked.

"What's that?"

"When you come in from chores today, will you clean up, and change your underwear?"

"I've only had this set on a week," he said. "Dad only changes twice a year; once for summer and once for winter. It'll be the first of May soon. I'll change out of these woollies into my cotton long johns then."

Al put on the same shirt and overalls he had worn for several days. He spoke without looking up.

"I'll catch two or three roosters now before daylight and put them in a crate for you. Chicken will be a real treat for the folks tomorrow."

Ruth rolled her eyes. "When do we get our treat?" she asked, and reminded Al that last year, when the folks had talked of wiring the house and bringing in electricity, nothing ever came of it. Al just mumbled to himself and went out for his chores.

While waiting for daylight, Ruth washed and candled the eggs she had gathered the previous evening. With a foreboding frown on her face, she filled the kitchen stove with wood, started the fire, and put two teakettles full of water on for scalding the roosters.

At two o'clock, Clair bounced out of the car and ran on tiptoe through the rain to the porch steps. Ruth hugged her, kissed her cheek, and held her hand as they glided into the kitchen and sat by the table.

"I'm so happy for you," Ruth said. "But I can't figure out why. I mean to tell you—marriage isn't all it's cracked up to be, you know."

"Oh, Ruth, now don't put a damper on my plans. Billy is so shy and gentle. He grew up on a farm, you know, and he actually likes animals. He hasn't said much, but I know he wants children, and so do I."

"You're not pregnant, are you, Clair? Have you two been … doing it?"

Clair's cheeks flushed. "For God's sakes, no, we've hardly kissed. I'm still a virgin."

"Oh my God! Oh my God!" Ruth teased. "I lost my virginity with Al in the back seat of his car when he was home on furlough, and for weeks afterwards I worried about getting pregnant. I needn't have worried. Well, I sure hope you can have kids, but aren't you worried that something might happen, considering your age and everything? At the rate you're going, by the time you get around to doing it and getting pregnant you could be forty."

"I know we won't be doing anything before the wedding, but I'm scared to death about the wedding night," Clair said.

Ruth rolled her eyes. "Don't ask me anything about sex," she said. "Al's the only man I've been with. It was romantic and marvelous before we were married and even for a while afterwards. Now however, it's difficult to find anything romantic about dirty underwear, a stubble beard, and beer breath." She wiped her eyes with her apron. "It must be me. Al just isn't interested in romance anymore."

"Do you think it would be risky for me to have a baby?" Clair asked. She thought about a friend her age, who had died giving birth, and the number of retarded children who were the firstborn of older women.

Suddenly, the clouds cleared and the room was flooded with sunshine. Ruth grabbed Clair's arm and tugged her to the front porch. The rain had stopped.

"It's a sign," Clair said, as a dazzling rainbow arched across the sky.

"It's our sign," Ruth said. "Get married. Have babies. I'll take a niece first. It'll be like she has two moms. Don't worry.

Everything will be like heaven. I get to be the maid of honor … or is it matron of honor? Look at that rainbow." They held each other in a tight embrace, oblivious of the ominous return of black clouds.

Chapter 14
The Wedding

So down went McGinty to the bottom of the sea
And he must be very wet, because they haven't found him yet
Though his ghost comes around the dock, just before the break of day
Dressed in his best suit of clothes.
From "Down Went McGinty" by Joseph Flynn, 1889

"I'LL TELL YOU this only one time, my dear. You are going to have the finest wedding Norwood has ever seen—or ever will see. Never mention cost again. I am footing the bill for this wedding. Period. End of discussion.

Myrtle Thurmond refilled her coffee cup, and turned to Clair.

"Now, about those eleven bridesmaids!"

Clair shook her head mildly and smiled. "I'm not sure who I should ask. My sister Ruth will be matron of honor," Clair said. "Except … what about you, Myrtle?"

Myrtle didn't hesitate. "I'll not be an attendant," she said. "I'll sing a solo before and immediately after the ceremony. With your permission, of course."

"You have full permission for anything you think best." Clair knew Myrtle could be trusted not to do anything foolish.

"All right then," Myrtle smiled. "Let's see. Six of the men are married. Two of the others can ask their girlfriends. And I suppose—that will mean a couple of those awful Elsville girls will be attending. I can just see Clarence, that sneaky little weasel, ogling them from the altar. So, Clair all you have to do is show up, and prop up Billy." Myrtle said.

Every pew in the Church was filled. Myrtle outdid herself with the floral arrangements. On the stairs leading to the main door were enormous baskets of red, white, and pink peonies. Bouquets of red roses were placed about the narthex, and inside the church; white gardenias, baby's breath, and pink roses were attached to the end of each pew. In the front of the church were wild flowers, purple violets, honeysuckle, bluebells and fresh ferns from the woods. Everything was perfect—for today was the foundry's own 'Miss Clair's' wedding.

Billy, even as nervous as he was, chuckled to himself as he watched one of the Elsville girls, wearing a bridesmaid dress trying to draw attention from Clyde and E. J., in their tuxedos. Billy's chuckles died in his throat as the door opened and Clair entered.

Her white lace wedding gown had been Clair's mother's wedding dress, and her grandmother's before that. Clair's eyes were smiling up at Billy; he thought he must be living someone else's life, because this was much too good for Billy Bartel. The minister began speaking, and Billy lost track of everything except his struggle to remember what he was supposed to do next.

In the reception line after the wedding, all the foundry men kissed the bride, and wished her well.

After the reception, Billy couldn't believe what had been done to his car. Banners fluttered from the roof's edge. "Just

Married" was scrawled in white shoe-polish on both sides and on the back of the trunk. Tin cans and old shoes were tied to the rear bumper with baling wire.

It wasn't until he got behind the steering wheel that reality hit Billy: he'd made no reservations and had no idea where to go or what to do. He froze at the wheel and glanced at Clair. Everyone was waiting for the traditional parade of the wedding party, with the cars and the guests following the bride and groom through town, honking horns and shouting. Clair rumpled Billy's hair and kissed his cheek.

"Relax," she said. "Drive slowly through the main street, then take highway seven toward Northfield. I've made reservations at the hotel. It's only an hour's drive. We can talk on the way."

Billy drove slowly, but felt as if a cold, wet sponge covered his body, and was embarrassed by a sour odor from beneath his shirt. An odor he had detected about himself when the rash appeared after Clair's proposal. *Fear*, he thought. Dogs were able to detect fear on people; even wimpy dogs would dart and snap at fearful people. *I'll need a few drinks to get through this night*, he said to himself.

"I love you Billy," Clair said suddenly.

"Can we stop for a beer?" he asked, while holding his attention on the road.

Clair was silent for a few moments.

"The wedding night is special," she said. "I hope we don't have to drink."

Clair began talking nonstop, but Billy seemed unable to understand or to respond to her. Billy's real voice was buried somewhere deep in his stomach, while a strange voice babbled silently in his head. *Oh Jesus. What have I done? My life is gone. Oh god. Look at her. She's nagging, turning demanding and different right here in the car on our wedding day.*

"Thanks for getting hotel reservations," he said in a flat voice he didn't recognize as his own. Suddenly it was as if there was no air in the car, and he thought he was about to suffocate. He rolled his window down and felt refreshed by the scent of new-mown hay and the fresh air of an impending rain.

Clair listened to the whine of the tires and their consistent slap-slap crossing tarred joints in the concrete. She made an image of herself and Billy walking into church on a beautiful Sunday a few years hence, holding hands with their charming little daughter, dressed in a new flowered Easter outfit.

"Okay if we stop for just one beer," Billy asked.

Clair seldom drank beer, and the picture of herself on her wedding night did not include sitting at some dark, wet-streaked bar with her elbows tucked in her lap, watching her husband trying to suck courage out of a bottle. "The wedding night is special," she said. "I hope we don't have to drink. Thank goodness you have had some experience with women. You will be patient with me, won't you Billy?"

Night had settled in across a murky moonless sky. Clair hadn't realized how dark it was until far to the west the sky brightened with intermittent lightning flashes.

Clair's courage faltered as she tried to find words to break the silence. A freight train, with its one searching headlight, roared along on the tracks paralleling the road.

"Turn left at the first stop sign in town," Clair said. "The hotel is two blocks down." Billy parked the car in the elm-lined lot by the hotel. Across the street, blinking neon lights signaled: *Bar- Restaurant- Cocktails Bar- Restaurant- Cocktails.*

"Billy, we're both all up tight." Clair said, "and I'm more nervous and scared than you are. A while ago you asked me to take the lead. Okay, at least for tonight, why not follow my lead?

I don't think either of us wants our marriage consummated by a couple of drunken amateurs."

Billy let her hands go and pushed a stone around on the ground with his foot.

Clair lifted Billy's chin so he could see her face. "Can we go forward tonight without the beer?" she asked gently.

Billy nodded, and clasped her hands briefly before gathering their suitcases from the trunk. A light breeze whispered, as the first drops of rain fell through the elms, fresh and cool on their faces.

"Just sign the guest register, please" the night clerk said. The clerk was an older man in a rumpled, brown suit. "We have your reservation right here."

Billy signed *Mr. and Mrs. William F. Bartel.*

"That will be twelve dollars," said the clerk. Billy produced the money from the wallet in his back pocket and blushed as some wedding party rice fell to the marble floor.

"Follow me. I'll show you to your suite." The clerk reached for their luggage, but Billy grabbed the handles first.

I can't carry her across the threshold with this guy watching. Or maybe it's just when I get home I'm supposed to carry her across the threshold. Oh shit, I wish I knew what I was supposed to do.

Clair put her arm around Billy's waist when they reached the room.

Billy entered uncertainly. There was an enormous canopy bed with fancy lamps on bedside tables and a blanket trunk at its foot. In the adjoining room were a couch, a table and chairs, and a fireplace and a stack of wood. Fresh flowers were in both rooms.

"Is everything satisfactory?" the clerk asked, as he wiped a bony hand on his trousers and extended toward Billy.

Clair rummaged through her purse and put a quarter in the clerk's outstretched hand. He smiled faintly, bowed, and left. Clair put her arms around Billy's neck and gave him a light kiss on his lips.

"We should change into our pajamas," Clair said.

Billy flopped into one of the large stuffed chairs and stared at the floor. "Clair, I forgot. I didn't plan, I didn't think ... I've never worn pajamas, I didn't bring any. I'm sorry."

Clair laughed. "You won't believe this, but I brought a pair of pajamas for you, just in case. I'm sorry, I'm just such a ... planner. They're with my things."

Billy took her offering with him to the bathroom, where he held the pajamas up to the mirror in disbelief—black and white striped pajamas. He felt foolish and thought, Black *and white striped pajamas. What does she want, a zebra?*

Summoning a cover of fake bravado he burst from the bathroom.

"Ready or not, here comes your zebra," he called.

Clair gave him a quick kiss, and dashed into the bathroom.

Billy pulled back the covers on the bed and wondered which side to lie on. He decided to just play it safe and lie close to the center. *What could be so different about this*, he thought, *I'll do the same as I do when I'm with the Elsville girls. It'll just be different without the booze.* The thought of touching Clair in the same manner he'd fondled the Elsville girls began to arouse him.

After some time, Clair came from the bathroom, wearing a white, silky, low-cut nightgown. She turned out the light, pulled back the covers, and got in beside Billy. While not quite touching she pulled the covers up to her neck.

Clair reached for Billy's hand. "Billy, I'm a virgin. This is the first time for me," she whispered.

Billy sat halfway up and placed his hand on Clair's breast. Clair shuddered at his touch. Billy kissed Clair hard on the mouth, rolled over on top of her and began pulling her nightgown up. He thought it strange how still and unmoving Clair was; then she began to shake and cry.

"Oh God, Billy. No, no, no! I'm sorry, please ... no, not this way," Her sobs penetrated the room. Billy rolled away and lay on his back at the far edge of the bed.

"Billy," Clair sobbed, while gathering the covers around her neck. She leaned against the headboard and looked over at Billy. "I don't know what to do, but I know what I don't want to happen. I don't want to be raped. I want to love you, but not this way, not this fast. I mean, is that how it's supposed to be? We have our whole lives ahead of us." She paused, before going on. "Would it bother you too much if we waited until tomorrow? Today's been a strain for both of us. Would you please wait and we'll see how things go tomorrow?"

Billy flung the covers aside, flew out of bed and fled to the bathroom where his thoughts swerved about him. *I suppose she thought I was treating her like a whore, but couldn't she have helped me along a bit?* He shuffled from foot to foot, then kicked the bathtub and jumped around on one foot in pain. *"Jesus Christ— what am I supposed to do?"* he mumbled to himself as Clair's words kept repeating in his mind. *No, Billy, let's not have a drink. No, Billy, let's not have sex. No, Billy, don't touch me.*

Billy opened the bathroom window and sat on the toilet seat with his head in his hands, listening to the outside noises.

"Kiss my ass, you son of a bitch," a girl's voice yelled from the street below.

"Screw you, fuck-face," bellowed a masculine voice in return. Looking out the window Billy saw that they were confronting each other near a Ford roadster by the cocktail lounge. The man held the girl by the wrist of her upraised arm. They appeared to be talking, but softly now, so Billy couldn't hear them. Then they kissed in a long embrace, their pelvises pressed against each other. The girl had her arm around the man and was nearly sitting in his lap as they drove away.

Billy returned to the bedroom and stood by Clair in the darkness. She was sobbing intermittently.

"It's okay, Clair. It's okay. Don't be afraid," he said. "I'll never force myself on you. We're in a strange place—away from home." He kissed her forehead. "Let's try to get some rest. I'll sleep on the couch, okay? We'll go home tomorrow."

Along with her sniffling every few minutes, it bothered Billy that Clair hadn't even wished him good night. He held his breath, waiting for her to say something, anything, but as the sniffling subsided he knew she was finally sleeping. Billy was awakened by a gentle kiss on his lips.
"Good morning, Billy," Clair said, acting as if there had been no last night. She kissed him again. Billy responded guardedly. Clair's breasts were partially exposed in the loose-fitting nightgown as she leaned over him.

"Get your things together and get dressed, we can go get breakfast." she said.

Billy welcomed the chance to get out of the bridal suite from hell.

"Hungry?" Clair asked cheerfully, when they were ready to leave the suite.

Billy looked at Clair, wishing that he dared to say what he was thinking. *I wonder how she'd act if I said I was hungry enough to eat the ass out of a skunk and used more of the crude language from around work*, he thought resentfully. *I bet she wouldn't be so damned cheerful then.* "I noticed a restaurant in the lobby," Billy said.

Billy remained quiet at the breakfast table. Clair was first to speak.

"Tell me about our house. Does it need a lot more fixing? What are the curtains like?"

At her word "our", Billy's insides clenched. He'd brought the Blair place seven years ago. Even though he'd not earned much, he'd not spent much either, and the old style farmhouse and the sixty acres were paid for, free and clear.

"I'm not good at describing things," Billy said. "But I've always taken real good care of the place" Clair had her shoes off and brushed Billy's calf with her foot.

"Don't look so frightened," she said when she saw him flinch. I just felt like doing that. Don't you like it?"

Billy didn't know what to think. The chicken he had choked last night was showing signs of life, and he knew it could only lead to disaster. It was only seven thirty in the morning. Billy couldn't figure Clair out. *Is she just a tease?* Clair reached for Billy's hand.

"I want to make up to you for last night," she said. "I'm not afraid now. Everything just went so—fast, and I panicked." Her voice had a purr to it and Billy thought of the calico cat back on the farm.

"What is it, Billy?" Clair asked.

"I was just thinking about the house," he lied.

"I'll carry you across the threshold when we get home," he said. "It's a tradition or something I'm supposed to do, isn't it?"

"I can't wait." Clair said.

Billy's uncertainty took over again—*better yet let's call this whole thing off right now. We didn't make love last night. We can get an annulment. Everything is going all wrong anyway. I could go back to living like a man, the way I was before.*

Clair wanted to stroll beneath the elms on the way to the car. Billy, still angry insisted on a straight line from the hotel. Billy suddenly realized that they hadn't paid their breakfast bill, checked out of their room, or brought their luggage to the car. They looked into each others' eyes, slowly began to smile, then laughed in unison gave each other their first spontaneous kiss.

"You'd better pay for breakfast, before they send the cops after us," Clair said.

On the outskirts of Northfield, Clair slid over in the seat beside Billy. Her right hand was on his thigh, her left arm around his shoulders and neck. The fullness of her breasts was pressed gently on his arm as he drove.

Twenty minutes from Northfield, at 8:42 a. m., on Sunday morning, June 10, l950, on a deserted township road, the marriage of William Francis and Clair Bartel was consummated in the back seat of Billy's l947 Chevrolet four-door.

At the homestead, Clair kicked off her shoes and sprinted barefoot toward the house.

"Wait, Clair!" Billy shouted. "The threshold!"

"Yoo hoo, Clair, Billy—are you home?" Ruth and Al, laden with wedding gifts from the church, came up the path to the door. Clair greeted her sister with a hug and a kiss. Al stood stiffly by the steps. Ruth looked at the newlyweds.

"You two look like you're getting along fine, I mean, for such an old couple," she said. "We brought all your gifts. It's traditional that the family is invited in while you're opening them."

"Come right in," Billy said. He made coffee and put cinnamon rolls from the pantry on the table. Al put the gifts on an end table in the living room, returned to the kitchen and helped himself to the coffee.

"My," said Ruth to her sister. "You got a real winner here, bakes and everything. What are you going to do, Clair, just sit around and look pretty?"

"Sure. Why not?"

Chapter 15

ON SEPTEMBER, 9TH, 1957, Dianne Russy parked her car by the woodshed at the Lavill School. The woodshed's red paint was faded and blistered. While nearby, the one room schoolhouse had a fresh coat of white paint. This was her first day of teaching. While printing MISS RUSSY on the blackboard, Dianne heard a loud noise. Looking out the window she saw a rusty blue pickup, apparently without a muffler, trailed by a cloud of dust, coming down the road by the school. After parking, a thirtyish, worried- looking woman, and a sandy haired little girl, approached the schoolhouse. An unshaven man waited in the truck. Dianne greeted the woman and little girl at the door.

"Good morning, I'm Miss Russy," she said.

The worried-looking woman took a faded scarf from her head and entered the room.

"I'm Ruth Krankus, and this is Nancy Bartel," the woman said.

Dianne took note of Nancy—a stringy six-year-old with an air of independence, plain except for a certain luminescence that seemed to come from her high cheekbones and her dark blue penetrating eyes, deep set and shaded by heavy upper lids.

Ruth nervously twisted the scarf in her hand until it almost looked like a rope.

"Her mother died when she was born," Ruth said. "Nancy is my niece. She has lived with my husband Al and me ever since."

"You can go now, Ruth," Nancy said, "Al is waiting."

Dianne put her hand out to Nancy. "Come, I'll show you to your desk. Did you bring pencil and paper?"

Ruth turned back. "Oh I'm sorry—I didn't know."

"That's okay." said Dianne, "I'll send a list of things back with you. Perhaps you could bring them tomorrow."

The horn honked from the idling pickup.

"I'd better be going," Ruth said. "Are you okay Nancy? We'll pick you up after school."

It took several weeks for Nancy to realize that the other kids viewed her differently; they all had real mothers and fathers and most had sisters and brothers. And one day at recess, some of the kids began a chant.

"Ha, ha, sis boom ba. She ain't got no ma. She ain't got no pa. Ha ha ha." Nancy cried and ran to the schoolhouse.

"Don't let that bother you Nancy. I'll make them stop," Dianne said.

"I do so have a real dad. He comes to see me all the time," Nancy said, "And Ruth is just like a real mom, and Uncle Al he is kind of like a dad, so there, I got two Dads and a Mom, I'm better than they are."

"Be patient. In a short while, when children begin to understand, they'll be your friends."

Nancy's sniffles subsided; she wiped her eyes and nose then lifted her eyes. "Do you really believe so?"

"Let's see what takes place after recess, okay?"

"Okay, but next time I'm not gonna cry, I'm gonna hit 'em."

Chapter 16

DIANNE FOUND HER calling as a schoolteacher, but hardly a week went by when she didn't relive much of the last two years, and wonder when she'd be found out, and if the board would let her continue teaching.

On the first day of teacher training, Dianne eased her slim, straight, five-foot-nine frame into the classroom desk. She smoothed her full, shoulder-length auburn hair. Everything about her was straight and orderly, except for a wisp of unruly hair that occasionally fell across her brow. At twenty-eight, Dianne was the oldest in the class of twelve women attending Normal teacher training. She also had worked at the Norwood Silver Grill, ever since her sophomore year in high school. It had taken twelve years, difficult years, while she fully supported herself and helped support her parents, who were usually unemployed or underemployed. For the past four years her social life centered more or less on Merford Thrane: a beer-guzzling, snoose-chewing, redneck boyfriend.

Dianne had little difficulty getting acquainted at Normal. All her classmates seemed nice; especially Lilla Mae Higgins. Lilla Mae had short brown hair, long, shapely legs crafted and tailored to her body, and soft brown eyes on a face with as many expressions as the cast of a Shakespearian play. Lilla Mae was a person who made a point of saying hello to everyone. Dianne overheard her say she was from a farm near Henrytown, which consisted of a country store and a gas station.

One day during her second week, Dianne sat alone and lonely while lunching in the school cafeteria. Lilla Mae approached with a tray of food.

"Join you?" Lilla Mae asked. Not waiting for an answer, she cleared the dishes from her tray and sat down.

"Sure," Dianne said. "I was hoping for some company."

"Look at this." Lilla Mae motioned towards her food. "I keep on eating like a goddamn farmer. I'll soon weigh two hundred pounds."

Dianne was taken aback by the language. "So ... you live on a farm?"

"Yeah. I got four younger brothers, my old man's a souse, and my mother's a saint. That's my whole friggin' history. How about you?"

"I'm an only child," Dianne said. "I've been working in a restaurant full time since high school. Twelve years."

"How you like that?"

"It's hard work. Long hours. I like the people, though."

"Jesus! I'm going to need some exercise after all this food or it's lard ass city for me," Lilla Mae said. "How about after school we walk down to the train depot? The President is going to be there on a whistle stop."

Dianne welcomed the opportunity to socialize, but thought Lilla Mae's language would take some getting used to.

"That sounds okay to me, but I think I'm a Republican."

"Why, that little wiry-haired, big business, Republican lawyer son of a bitch who's running—he'd be another goddamned Hoover."

"Oh my, Lilla Mae," Dianne said. "Where did you learn to talk like that?"

"Four uncles, four brothers, and a souse father. In Henrytown it's called Higginese. I'm trying to clean it up in class. It bothers you?"

"I'm not used to it. Oh, I kind of am, my boyfriend … he …"

"Don't worry; a year away from home and my language should be all right. I'm going to be a teacher, you know."

"I'm not really political," Dianne said, "I've never seen a president."

"Okay, how about we meet by the water fountain in front of the Admin building at five?"

On the way to the depot with Dianne, Lilla Mae stopped at her rooming house to get a sweater. "I have a room here with a friend of my mother's until I get something permanent," she said.

"I've just got a room at my third cousin's for now, too," Dianne said.

They passed an older woman trudging along wearing a plaid scarf and a man's cap pulled around her ears. The woman stopped, turned and watched them. She shook her head in disgust. "Gooses," she said loudly. "Town's just full of silly girls these days."

Two weeks later Lilla Mae located a two-bedroom apartment for rent. "I'm not sure I could room with a Republican," she told Dianne, "but why don't you take a look at it with me?"

Dianne liked the apartment and said that since she was broadminded enough to make do with a Democrat, she was sure Lilla Mae could manage living with a Republican. They agreed to share the rent and together, two weeks later, they moved in.

At four in the afternoon, Merford Thrane, Dianne's boyfriend, came into the Grill. He ordered green apple pie with cheese and a cup of coffee. When Dianne looked at Merford, it seemed to her she had new receptors on her retinas. Her picture of Merford was much different than before she started school.

There's got to be more to life than Merford Thrane, Dianne thought. She shivered. She knew she wanted to be through with him. Merford finished his pie, pushed back from the counter, and stood.

"I'm a little short of cash," he said to Dianne. "Pay for my lunch and I'll pick you up after work about nine." Dianne didn't comment. As he neared the door, Merford turned. "Leave a good tip for the waitress."

Why am I doing this? Dianne questioned herself as she paid the bill. *I've been going out with him just because he says so. I'll tell him we're through tonight, face to face. Ugh, I can't stand the thought of his grubby face anymore.*

Dianne had reluctantly, and without passion, submitted to Merford's sexual desires. It wasn't really love making; everything was rough, always the same short, animalistic rituals. That would be all through now. At nine p.m. she left the Silver Grill. Merford was parked out on the street waiting for her.

"Merford, I've been thinking," she said. "Our relationship isn't working out. It's nothing in particular; I just want to be free to think and concentrate on school. I'll just walk home."

A greasy grin appeared on Merford's face. "What's up?" he said "Someone at school? I thought it was all girls there. Not the damn professor, is it?" He reached across the seat and opened the right door. His voice was pleasant. "Get in. I'll at least give you a ride home."

Dianne, feeling maybe she'd been a little abrupt, got in and slouched in the seat. "Thanks for understanding," she said.

Merford chuckled, gunned the engine, and drove out of town to a dark, secluded, tree-lined lane in the country. They had been there before. Dianne got out of the car as soon as he stopped.

"Merford, don't you understand? I'm just not going to do this anymore," she said and began walking towards town.

Merford caught her by the arm, pushed her against the trunk of the car, grabbed her skirt with both hands, and ripped it off. Panic-stricken, Dianne pushed at his shoulders and clawed at his face. He slammed her against the car, bending her backwards over the trunk. She braced herself with her hands, thinking her back might break. Merford backhanded her across the face. Then he fumbled his trousers open, forced her legs apart and thrust himself into her again and again.

"This is kind of like school. Us men just have to teach you women to behave, when you tend to get a little uppity. That damn schoolin' you're gettin' over there in Austin must be gettin' you confused. Mixing up your loyalties. A nice, quiet string bean of a girl like you, with nothing bigger than nipples for tits, better keep in mind that you won't ever get aholt of a real man again. You better damned well appreciate it, while you can." He punched her in the mouth, splitting her lip. Merford flipped her over, like he would a beef carcass, and assaulted her again. When he was finished, he gently kissed her on the back of the neck and then on her bloody lips. He even opened the car door for her before taking her home.

"Now get yourself straightened out this week at Normal," he yanked her by the arm and led her to the house. "If your attitude's better, I'll take you to a movie over in Springdale next weekend, but don't try that 'I'm not going to see you anymore' shit again. We're a couple, you and me, until I say we ain't. Nobody walks out on Merford Thrane." He swaggered back towards the car, his upper torso moving from side to side like a walking metronome.

Dianne slunk into her Austin apartment the following evening. She covered her face with a scarf, brushed quickly past Lilla Mae, went to her room and shut the door.

Dianne could hear Lilla Mae putter about the kitchen. Twice she heard Lilla Mae's footsteps near the door. The third time, Lilla Mae didn't walk away.

"Enough of this bullshit," she called through the doorway and flipped on the light. Dianne was sitting up in bed. The sight of Dianne took Lilla Mae's breath away.

"Oh my God, what happened? Were you in an accident?" Lilla Mae asked. Dianne's cheekbones were swollen and there were sickening shades of yellow surrounding the bruises. "No. I just broke up with my boyfriend." Dianne feigned a smile. She tasted blood on her split lip. She squinted at Lilla Mae through her swollen eyes. "As you can see, he didn't take it too well. After all, imagine losing a prize like me."

Lilla Mae stood as if frozen, tears slid down her face. Suddenly she rushed to Dianne, kissed her tears away, hugged her tightly and stroked her hair. "You are a prize, a wonderful, intelligent prize. Be thankful you're through with that roughhouse puke," she said between kisses on Dianne's cheeks, forehead, and lips.

Dianne first felt warm and comfortable, then chilled. She realized she enjoyed being held and kissed by Lilla Mae. The thought of Merford's coarse tongue and the foul taste the flecks of chewing tobacco left in her mouth crossed her mind. With her swollen eyes shut, she felt Lilla Mae's soft clean face, her gentle hands, and the soft sweetness of her kiss. She knew girls shouldn't kiss other girls. It was wrong, sinful. *It's a strange world*, she thought, *where it is sinful to be loved and comforted by a girl, but okay to be raped and beaten by a man. Why do I feel as though I had it coming?*

"Rest now," Lilla Mae said, tucking Dianne in bed and covering her. Dianne reached up and softly kissed Lilla Mae.

The next day while Lilla Mae was at school, Dianne called the Grill and asked to be excused for the weekend. When Lilla Mae came home Dianne told her what had happened with Merford. Lila Mae felt as if steam was about to shoot from her mouth and ears. For the first time, her expressions were inadequate for her feelings..

"Dianne!" Lilla Mae shouted. "You can't let this happen to you. You can't believe all this happy horseshit. You quit your job, didn't you?"

"Yes. I don't dare go back."

You can't let that creep shit-for-brains keep you from your job and home."

"I'm afraid of him." Dianne wrung her hands, her face a mask of fear.

"Report him to the cops."

"I can't. In Norwood, everyone knows everyone else. They'd just get a big laugh out of it and tell it all over town. I'm ashamed."

"Ashamed!"

"I had let him do it to me before, without fighting him."

"You fought him the last time."

"It's not like I'm an innocent young girl any more, you know. I let Merford do it to me before; the police will never do anything about him. He's one of the guys. I'll just have to stay away. I can't lie about what we've done."

"What if he comes over here and catches you on the way to or from school?"

"I didn't think about that," Dianne shuddered. "Maybe if I was real nice to him, apologized, and made up with him, he wouldn't hurt me anymore."

"Oh for God's sake, are you out of your sad-assed mind? Is that what you want to do?"

"No, but—"

"We've got a big problem here. If he's not abusing you he'll probably be abusing some other poor, dumb girl." Then, Lilla Mae said quickly, "I'm sorry, I didn't mean that the way it sounded. A mean son of a bitch like that doesn't even deserve to live. He's a goddamn pig. Somebody has to take care of him. If nobody else will do it, we can."

"What do you mean?"

"We can fix old Merford so he'll never hurt you or anyone else like you again," Lilla Mae said.

Dianne got goose bumps when Lilla Mae's hand stroked her hair and rubbed at the base of her neck. When Lilla Mae kissed her gently on the lips, she kissed back. And she slid her hand just above Lilla Mae's knee. Dianne's nipples tingled, warm and erect, a sensation she had never experienced with Merford's lovemaking.

At sunrise they were cuddled in bed, one of Lilla Mae's breasts cupped tenderly in Dianne's hand. Lilla Mae's sweater and bra were on the floor by the couch, Dianne's skirt in the middle of the room, her bra and panties just inside the bedroom door and two silky slips hung on the bedpost.

With some dread and trepidation Dianne finally agreed to Lilla Mae's plan. First, she called Merford and apologized. She said it was her fault, told him she had learned something new at school and wanted to surprise him. She asked if he could meet her Saturday evening about six o'clock on the abandoned Township Road just beyond Masonic Park. "You know, where we parked a few times," she said.

"Glad to see you've come to your senses, but come on, tell me what the surprise is."

"Oh, you can wait till Saturday. Bring a couple of beers with you."

"You hardly ever drink beer!"

"Part of the surprise, Merford."

The township road, beyond Masonic Park, was Merford's special place for screwing and beer drinking. It was an abandoned road, overgrown with quack grass and secluded; more than a mile from any traffic or people.

Merford arrived, as scheduled, in a brand new red pickup outfitted with a gun rack in the cab, and a spot light for shining deer. Lilla Mae, being from a farm, thought he had a scruffy look, like a hog with mange. He parked across from Lilla Mae's Chevy, and sauntered to the driver's side of her car. Strutting like a peacock, Merford glanced at the driver. Dianne was in the passenger seat.

"Hi, who's your friend here? Dianne," he said. "She's sure a good looker—well-built."

"Oh, she's my friend from school. I told her about the lessons you were teaching me. We thought maybe you might like to learn something too. Lilla Mae, this is Merford Thrane."

" Lilla Mae," repeated Merford. "That sounds like a nice, sweet, southern name. Are you one of those southern belles I hear about, that know how to treat their men and know their place?"

"Well," Lilla Mae drawled her voice low and sexy. "I think I know how to treat a real he-man, like you. I was kind of wondering if you ever thought any daring thoughts, like two girls at once. Ever thought of that, Merford?"

"God, no, never thought of that. What the hell are they teaching over at that school anyway? That can't be Normal," he laughed.

"Would you be interested?"

"You mean do it with both of you?" Merford said, a puzzled look on his face.

"Not exactly, but if you're interested in something a little different, with two girls, go over to the other side of the car and we'll show you what we mean."

Merford sauntered to the other side of the car.

Dianne whispered to Lilla Mae. "I can't go through with it."

"Be quiet. It's too late now; we have to go through with it."

Lilla Mae got out of the car and reached into the back seat. From under a blanket on the floor she pulled out the first surprise for Merford, circled to where he stood and pointed a twelve gauge semi-automatic shotgun at his crotch.

"What the hell you doing with that!" Merford yelled. "Put that thing away. That could be dangerous. Like my Dad always said, never fool around with a gun if you don't intend to use it."

"Oh, don't be concerned about that, Merford," Lilla Mae said. "We're going to use it." Then she swung the gun, and shot from the hip, her arms recoiling as the automatic reloaded. The explosion thundered through the valley, echoing off the limestone bluffs by the river. Air from the shredded left front tire of Merford's pickup whipped through the tall grass like an angry snake. The pickup lurched like a lame bull, and settled in the grass.

Merford charged towards Lilla Mae. She re-directed the shotgun to his crotch.

"I really wouldn't come any further if you ever want to piss again," she said.

Merford stopped, his teeth clenched and his face distorted. He tore the cap from his head and, threw it on the ground.

"Are you bitches crazy?" he shouted.

Lilla Mae's forcefulness had convinced Dianne she could get her revenge and be rid of this menace forever. She moved toward Merford, showing no fear.

"No, we're not crazy. We're just going to show you how being abused and humiliated feels. Sit down." She motioned him to the grass by the side of the road. "Put your hands behind your back. Lilla Mae will be behind you with the shotgun." Dianne went to the car and came back with a peanut butter jar and a Popsicle stick.

Lilla Mae put the muzzle of the gun against Merford's ear. You're a pig, Merford," Dianne said." Lilla Mae lives on a farm, she says pigs eat shit. You're going to eat shit, Merford."

Lilla Mae nudged Merford's ear with the gun barrel again. "That's right Merford. Eat shit. Then we'll decide if we might leave you alone until the next time you try to harass anyone."

"Go to hell, you assholes," Merford shouted. A shotgun blast roared through the valley again. The right front tire of the pickup deflated. The hot shell ejected from the automatic and hit Merford in the face.

"Stay down in the grass there, Merford." Lilla Mae pointed the shotgun. Merford sat down quickly, the smirk long gone from his face.

"Get your jackknife out of your pocket and throw it over to me," Dianne said.

Merford began to cry. "Here," he whimpered, and tossed the jackknife at Dianne's feet. Lilla Mae motioned with the gun.

"Tie his hands behind his back with the twine, Dianne," she said. Merford tipped over sideways in the grass.

"You're going to kill me, aren't you?" he cried.

"Only way we kill you is if you don't eat shit. You do plan on doing it, don't you?"

"You guys are just kidding," Merford said.

Lilla Mae pulled Merford by the hair, up to a sitting position. "Sure, you weasel-faced, moth-eaten, Ethiopian warthog bastard," she said, and rapped Merford on the back of the head with the butt of the gun.

Dianne and Lilla Mae had stopped at a beef farm along the way and put manure from a corn-fed steer, a pig's delicacy, in the peanut butter jar. Dianne placed a gob of manure from the jar on the Popsicle stick and presented it to Merford.

"Eat it, and we're through with you," Lilla Mae said sweetly.

When Merford hesitated; Lilla Mae gave him another rap on the back of the head with the shotgun, grabbed his hair, and pulled his head up again. Merford sobbed uncontrollably. Dianne pushed the gob of manure to his lips and smeared it across his face. A kernel of half-digested corn stuck on his open mouth, as if it were a gold tooth. A wet spot appeared on Medford's crotch. Then he swallowed the gob of manure. Lilla Mae took a Kodak from her jacket pocket and snapped a picture. Dianne spread the rest of the manure across Merford's lips.

"We'll send you a copy of the pictures, Merford," Lilla Mae said. "If you ever bother anyone again, the negatives will be available for public distribution. Imagine how much fun your redneck friends will make of you if anyone finds out. Think about it. We won't tell if you don't tell. Okay, Merford? Now, just stay there in the grass till we get out of here, unless you or your pickup want more of this shotgun." Lilla Mae cut the twine on his wrists. "By the way, here's your jackknife," she said, before burying the blade to the hilt in the spare tire on the side of the pickup.

Dianne, making sure Merford was looking her way, stopped and kissed Lilla Mae on the lips before they drove away.

Chapter 17

AL KRANKUS WATCHED through the barn doorway. At the end of the driveway, Nancy alighted from the school bus, turned and waved to a blond, curly-haired girl with her head out the bus window.

Something tugged at Al's heart when Ruth appeared on the porch. He saw her smile, gather Nancy in, and hug her. He got a cold beer from the water tank and tried to shrug off his feelings. He couldn't remember getting that much attention from Ruth since Nancy had arrived at their home. He grudgingly admitted to himself that he had never given any more attention than he had received. He wondered if he'd ever get the courage to break from his parents yoke. At forty-three, he still was under their domination. He was 'their man' over on the other farm. Every day, with near blood-boiling resentment, he acquiesced to instructions from Dad and Ma.

Al's workday usually began at five a.m. or before, and many times final chores weren't finished until nine at night. Work left little time for Ruth and Nancy.

He didn't receive regular pay from his folks and had to come to them, like a child, for an allowance. He had to ask them if he wanted a new suit, a new pair of overalls, or even overshoes. Once in a while, if he had worked real hard, Dad gave him a hundred dollars, saying, "Here, buy what you need and don't come around begging so often." His father's deep bass voice was always echoing in his ears:

Ma was just as bad. "I have some errands for you," she had groused the last time he had talked to her. "I need the chicken house cleaned out and the nests need repair. You come over after supper tonight and fix them up."

His mother's voice was as coarse as a rasp working on an oak knot. He wondered how and when that dark mole, with the lone black hair, appeared on her chin. That hair was as thick and harsh as the hair in a Belgian mare's tail, and as black as the ace of spades. To Al, it seemed as if that hair was always pointing at him in mockery. When Ma napped in the parlor, that hair curled up like a little black kitten, and went to sleep as soon as she shut her eyes. And when she awakened, that piss ant hair uncurled, arched its back and looked for Al. Al bristled on the inside as he thought of the lecture he had received a couple of months ago.

"What the hell do you think you need a car for?" Dad had said. "We've got a car; and a pickup for the farm. You can use them when you want, just ask. Christ! You young kids think money grows on trees and whisky comes from the well. Shit, nobody wears out shoe leather anymore. I remember when I was a kid; we used to have to get our shoes half-soled every few months. We didn't have to ride everywhere. We used the God-given gifts of our legs. We walked. A car? Shit, you don't need your own car."

And Ma interrupted. And that goddamn black hair agreed with her.

"Wait till Pa and I are dead and you'll have plenty of cars, and plenty of time to use them," she proclaimed. She shut her eyes, and Al saw that hair, the little black son-of-a-bitch, curl up on her chin, smug as hell.

A couple of weeks later, he got up his nerve and asked to buy the farm where he lived from them. "How the hell are you going to buy a farm?" his dad had bellowed. "You don't have any money, it takes money to buy a farm. I got that farm from my dad. You can get it from your dad. But you can't buy it with money or credit. Stay here and farm and one day it will be yours, but until then it's mine."

"I'd just like to have something of my own, a place of my own."

"If you want to buy a farm, save the money you drink up," said Dad Krankus. "Go buy somebody else's farm. I'll bet you don't have a damn thing to buy a farm with except credit. Who would give you credit, Al? The Legion Club or the Red Bird Tavern, I expect, because they know how much money they're making off you, and if you don't pay your bill, I suppose they think I'm good for it. Now get to work and be satisfied. Don't even think of quitting. You've got too much invested. We'd cut you off from any inheritance quicker than scat." Ma nodded approval.

Al looked down, pushed his hands deep in his pockets, and felt his jackknife there.

"You'll have this place someday and the other farm, too," Ma said.

Al suppressed the urge to bring out his jackknife and cut that miserable black hair off her chin. For a moment he saw himself with the severed hair between his thumb and forefinger. In his mind he'd lit a match, all ready to burn the little bastard. *Or maybe I should cut my wrists right here. I bet they'd come a running and "save" me*, he thought.

Then the chalk in Al's backbone turned to mush and he slunk away like a whipped pup and crawled into the cab of the old pickup and he began making plans to break out or break up.

He bought a case of beer, a jug of brandy, and a bottle of peppermint Schnapps. When he opened his billfold he found he didn't have enough money.

"Charge it," he said, and felt he stood a foot taller. "Charge it, and send the bill to my old man." Al had begun having his first beer or drink around eleven, and another nearly every hour until supper time.

Ruth began to dread Al's appearance. Many times he came in the house and immediately crumpled into bed without cleaning up, except to wash his hands.

Ruth kept a neat house, did her assigned chores, made appetizing meals, and was a faithful wife. When Nancy arrived, it brought an additional spark of hope to Ruth, of a better reason for living.

On the Fourth of July, Al's dad surprised him: He told him to take the rest of the day off and he'd do night chores. Al cleaned up and put on his only suit, a white shirt, and a tie. Ruth thought he looked handsome, as lanky and slim as the day they were married. She even phoned Billy and talked him into babysitting with Nancy, like he used to on Sundays.

Ruth wore her best housedress, a print dress with a lot of lavender in it. She never drank at home and only had a few beers when they went out to celebrations. She knew the effect alcohol had on her. Her apprehension and anxiety left her after her first beer. Then that warm feeling took over and all her feet wanted to do was dance.

After dinner, Ruth nudged Al with her elbow. "Come on Al, won't you try just one dance? I can teach you a few steps. You'll just love it," she said.

"Nah, I'd just as soon drink beer and shoot the shit with the boys. You go ahead."

"Circle two-step," Liz the dance caller cried out.

"Come on let's all join in," Linda said as she pulled the men from their chairs. Nearly everyone joined in except Al and the boys.

Ruth received plenty of attention, and she never lacked for a dancing partner all evening. She basked in the attention she didn't get at home, and liked the way the men held her while she danced. After every dance she asked Al to dance, but he refused. "I sat with you all during dinner didn't I?" he said. After that he sat at the table and drank beer with the boys until the dance was over.

Ruth began the last dance of the evening with a young fellow, who was rather drunk and tried to kiss her. Ruth was only interested in dancing so she stalked off the floor.

Ruth and Al conversed more on the way home than they had in a long time. This made Ruth feel romantic; and Al was all cleaned up and even smelled nice.

Billy, half asleep on the front porch looked up when he heard the car door close, and in his half-asleep state he imagined Clair coming towards him in the moonlight. Billy wept silently in the darkness when he realized it was Al and Ruth.

Chapter 18
The Woodshed

AL FINISHED SUNDAY morning chores by ten-thirty. *What's it all for?* He thought. *Old dad thinks he did a great thing by volunteering to do afternoon and evening chores every fourth Sunday, so I can have a full day off every month.* "A full day off every month and work my ass off and beg the rest of the time," he said aloud.

Ruth, also felt trapped, and thought that going to church would do her some good. She fixed her hair in a bun and put a blue and white ribbon in it. She put on her beige dress with a sweetheart neckline, nylons, brown heels, and a gold sand-dollar necklace. Al had even promised to go with her, but their plans were for naught because Nancy felt nauseous shortly before church time, and then went back to bed.

Nancy had been acting troubled lately. Ruth thought it was partly because Billy seldom visited and hadn't even acknowledged her ninth birthday last month. Ruth, feeling rather giddy about being dressed up, decided to leave her nice outfit on for the day. By noon Al, had drifted off to sleep in his easy chair.

"Dinner's ready," Ruth called from the kitchen. Al had been especially bitter and sullen lately, and his frown dampened Ruth's spirits when he sat down at the table.

"What a thrill," he said in a grumpy voice. "To sit at Ma and Dad's table; in Ma and Dad's other house; on Ma and Dad's other farm, and eat Ma and Dad's roast beef with Ma and Dad's silverware and dishes served by Ma and Dad's daughter-in-law."

Ruth patted Al on the shoulder, and gave him a hug.

"Things will get better, Al," she said. "If you'd buck up and help more with Nancy's upbringing, I think you'd feel a lot better about yourself. It would get your mind off the bitterness about your folks. You know they finally did get the house wired for electricity this year."

"Big deal, we're nearly the last ones in the county to get electricity and they skimped on everything. They didn't even wire the chicken house." Al leaned forward, "Beer and booze, that's the only thing that gets my mind off my folks and this goddamn situation we're in. There was a time, seeing you all dressed up like that, would take my mind off my troubles, and I'd feel good, but not lately. Maybe, I've become one of those eunuchs 'cause my folks treat me like one."

"Isn't there something I can do to help?" Ruth really wanted to help, but she felt helpless too.

"You can get drunk with me and go over to the folks and tell them off."

"Be serious, Al."

Al pushed his chair back from the table and speared the last of the roast beef from his plate with his fork.

"Aren't you going to eat your pie?" Ruth said. She'd made Al sour cream-raisin pie, his favorite.

"I'm going to head for the Shell station, and have a few beers with the boys," he said. "Pie and beer ain't the best of combinations."

"Couldn't you find something better to do, maybe something with me?" It's Sunday. I'm all dressed up, how about the matinee at the movies?"

Al didn't pay any attention. Ruth's voice turned sour. "What do you do at that place every Sunday, anyway?"

"No taverns open on Sunday, so a few of us old boys get together. We just drink beer, shoot the shit, and listen to each other tell tall tales." Ruth gave up her quest and cleared dishes from the table.

A draft of cold blustery air whisked through the kitchen as Al walked out the door without speaking another word. Ruth, watched Al from the window, and wiped the tears from her eyes with the dishtowel.

Al's pickup slid halfway across the road at the end of the driveway and fish-tailed as he accelerated. A short time later, his car squealed to a stop in the parking lot at the Shell station.

"What the hell!" the owner, Dewey, exclaimed as the pickup door slammed. Merford Thrane, sitting near a stack of oil cans, shifted his weight in his metal folding chair and leaned back against the wall.

"Hey asshole, whata'ya know," he said. Al smirked and straightened his shoulders.

"Takes a big dog to weigh a ton," he said.

"You better watch your god-damn fast drivin'; a dog that shits fast don't shit long," Merford replied. He then slow-smiled and took a drink from his beer bottle.

And all the good old boys laughed. Three more fellows were hanging out: Bert Hitchcock, Soak Larson and Birdie Johnson. Bert, a huge black-bearded man had watery, almond-shaped eyes, with a wide focus when he looked at you. His beard, which blended in with his dark hair, was so full you didn't see lips, only teeth, when he smiled or opened his mouth.

"How 'bout a game of draw poker?" Bert asked.

"Sure." Dewey cleared his tools from the table near the grease rack. From the storage room he brought an old, brown and white cowhide, and threw it across the table top. "Better than felt to play on," he said.

Al took off his mackinaw, and hung it on a broom handle. Dewey opened a beer and tossed it to Al. "Here ya go, Al," he said. Al caught the beer, walked to the door leading to the grease racks, and sat down on a five-gallon oil pail with a gray canvas boat cushion for a seat.

"Aw hell," Soak Larson said, "let's us just drink a few beers and shoot the breeze. Playing poker with you guys is just like sexing a goose. You know you'll get shit on."

Birdie Johnson, a red haired man, with a long pointed nose and hardly any chin, gave Soak a shove toward the table.

"Play a few hands, Soak," he implored. "We need the money."

"You guys go ahead," Al said. "All I got is enough for three hands of quarter rap. I'll just drink beer with Soak."

Al had three quarters in his pocket, and only two bucks in his billfold.

A car drove across and rang the bell-tape in the drive and stopped by the gas pumps. Dewey looked out the window. "Oh my! Full service here!" he said.

Merford leaned forward for a look. "Fucky Fulton," he said and slunk back out of sight. "Don't let her see me here."

"She too much for you, Merford?" Bert asked. Dewey put on his cap, coat and gloves, looked over his shoulder and turned his collar up for protection against the wind.

"Old Merford, he don't like to share the wealth," Dewey said, as he ambled towards the door. "When Merford's poking it, he thinks he owns it. And Fucky—to her it's just funnin'. If ol' Fucky was to sell it, she'd own half the county."

"Lighten up, Merford," Birdie said, "You look like you're pissed off in a spring-loaded position."

Dewey came back in, looking like the cat that had swallowed the canary.

"Birdie, you sly old fox," he said. "She only bought a dollars' worth of gas. That red dress of hers reaches just below her ass, and she's got 'that night crawler' look about her. It's you she's after, Birdie."

Birdie smoothed his red hair, picked his coat off the desk and looked around the room in slow motion.

"Everybody's gotta be someplace," he said and walked out the doorway.

Soak fetched a half-pint from his coat pocket. "Time for a booster shot, a little bracer," he said.

At approximately the same time as Al pulled into the Shell station, Billy was driving on his way to visit Nancy. Dust, from the county road, seeped through the undercarriage. A steady cold November wind had denuded even the sturdy white oaks of their last, dry, clinging leaves. Only a few, peapod-like leaves of the sumac held tightly to their woody stems against the blustery tug of impending winter. Billy didn't notice. He hardly noticed whether it was spring, summer or fall anymore. He didn't care and didn't want to notice. He tried not to notice the three ring-necked pheasants, hunkered down beneath a discarded rusty cultivator, along the roadway. Billy thought of the first fall he and Clair were married. He'd shot two rooster pheasants; and Clair fixed them in a special recipe with cream sauce and mushrooms. When other memories began flooding his head, he concocted a black cloud inside his skull, which extinguished every spark of thought containing memories of Clair. Billy cleared his throat of dust, and glanced at the package on the seat beside him. He had missed Nancy's ninth birthday last month. He'd missed most of her birthdays since the very first one, when he'd left in tears after fifteen minutes. While it was Nancy's birthday, it was the fact that it was Clair's deathday that cast a shadow over all the birthdays.

This time though, he'd bought Nancy a blouse. The clerk at the store had wrapped it in Christmas paper. Billy knew he should have brought her a card, too. Too late, he thought, as he turned into Ruth and Al's driveway.

Ruth heard the car and met Billy at the front door of the farmhouse.

"Come on in. Nancy's not feeling well today," Ruth said. "I think it's the one-day flu. She's sleeping upstairs right now. Have some coffee—you can go up a little later." Ruth took off her apron.

Billy noticed how lovely she looked, although her eyes were streaked red. Ruth reminded him so much of Clair that at times he had to block her image from his mind.

Ruth plugged in the coffee pot. "Sure is different with electricity in the house, "Ruth said. She glanced to the wood burner by the north wall. "I couldn't give up my Franklin stove, though; there's just something about radiant heat and the aroma from a wood stove in the kitchen."

Billy took his coat off and hung it on the back of a kitchen chair.

"Al's off to his Sunday retreat at the Shell station," Ruth said. She waited through a time of difficult silence. Ruth wanted Billy to say something—contribute to the conversation.

Billy, looking for a way out of the awkwardness, noticed that Ruth had put the last of the wood from the wood box in the stove.

"I'll get some wood from the shed," he said.

"Thanks, but don't be in such a hurry, let's have a beer," Ruth said uncharacteristically.

"I've been drinking too much beer lately. I suppose I could have one, though," Billy said.

This surprised Ruth. She'd never had a beer with Billy.

"I hardly ever drink, and never at home," Ruth said. She opened two bottles of beer, poured two glasses full, handed one to Billy, and took a long drink from her glass.

"First time for everything," she said. "Things aren't going well for Al and I'm sick of it."

Billy shrugged and sipped his beer. "I thought as much," he said.

"Al just doesn't pay any attention to me anymore. Not at all. I'm sure glad we have Nancy; but I still get awfully lonely." Ruth's glass was nearly empty, as was Billy's. Ruth refilled her glass.

"Do you want me to make other arrangements for Nancy?" Billy asked.

"Oh God, no. Don't ever think that, I'd be lost without her. She's like my own daughter. It's just that I think there should be more to life. Al's a lot like you; alive, but there just doesn't seem to be any spirit there. Both of you act like you're half-dead. I could just scream for some damn spirit around here." She felt that warm feeling coming over her; like it did at the dances when she drank. And she'd surprised herself again, she hardly ever said damn. "If Al would just stand up to me, or stand up to his dad or mom, fight, or stand up for himself, or anyone else." Ruth had brought herself into a very angry state.

She was standing with her hands on her hips; her lips pressed together. She looked through narrowed eyes down at Billy.
"I think you're both dead men," She said in disgust. Then she took another long swig of beer while continuing to stare at Billy.
Billy avoided her angry eyes as she paced back and forth in front of him.
"You're both revolting, *I'm* revolting, the *whole fucking world* is revolting!" She was shouting now, her face crimson; this was the first time the obscene word had ever crossed her lips and she was afraid Nancy might have heard even though the stairway door was shut. "Oh Jesus, forgive me," she said. "I didn't mean to say that. Drink some of your beer, Billy. I didn't mean to say that about you. I'm just having a bad day." Ruth opened another beer, filled Billy's glass, added to her own and sat down. Billy hunched forward, his head nearly resting on the table and finished off a glass of beer. He hadn't looked up or spoken since he'd averted Ruth's angry eyes.
"I'll get the wood." he said and went out to the woodshed. He gathered an armful of wood and brought it to the wood box. "I might as well fill it up," he said. Ruth walked with him to the woodshed.
"I'm sorry Billy," she said, tugging at his sleeve as he bent to gather more wood.
Billy turned and could tell that she was no longer angry. She had that look he'd seen at the legion club dances when she'd had a couple of beers. And the beer had affected him too. He'd had a couple of drinks before he came too. Ruth looked so beautiful, and he wanted Clair so badly.
Ruth put her hands on Billy's shoulders. "Forgive me Billy," she said sliding her hands behind his neck. "It's just that I'm feeling so bad. It's not about you, forgive me." Ruth hugged

him and impulsively kissed him lightly on the lips. Billy felt the warm softness of her body against him and it was if an explosion went off in his mind—his eyes glossed over, all he could see or think of was Clair.

"Clair, Clair, Clair." he said. And it was Clair he held in his arms. It was Clair he kissed passionately, oblivious of her struggle, oblivious of terror in her voice.

"Please, Billy, no, no," Ruth cried. She didn't know why she kissed Billy; but she knew it wasn't for this. She struggled to get free, but Billy was too strong for her.

"Clair, Clair," he whispered.

"Please. Please Billy, don't do this; please don't," Ruth cried. "Open your eyes Billy, please, I'm not Clair … I'm not Clair …"

Ruth didn't dare to scream. *Nancy must never know*, she kept thinking.

When Billy's dream came to an end, Ruth was pounding on his chest with her fists and crying hysterically. Billy wanted to wake up from this nightmare. But this was reality and there was no escape.

Billy relived the event thousands of times during the following weeks, and no amount of drinking at the Legion Club bar could prevent it. It had happened as if his mind had left his body. When Ruth kissed him, it was if he were standing off to the side watching, while this other person made love to Clair. It happened, something he couldn't have prevented any more than he could have prevented the sun from rising. Billy couldn't shake the shame. And his mind, full of remorse, kept tormenting him. He recalled his wedding night. He'd controlled his desire with Clair; when she said no. Why not with Ruth? Why?

Thoughts of having a fatal accident crossed his mind. That way Nancy would never have to know.

Chapter 19
The Rabbit Died

"CONGRATULATIONS, YOUR BABY is due the first part of August," the doctor said.

Along with pregnancy came morning sickness, loneliness, depression and crying spells on a daily basis. Al, as yet, had no idea. And Ruth had a dilemma. She longed for someone to talk to. Her mother was a near invalid; the minister would condemn her to hell and Nancy couldn't know. Al would know he wasn't the father; they hadn't made love since the fourth of July. What will he do? She'd also have to tell Billy—he was the father.

Ruth knew that Al had always wanted children, but not this way. Of course, she was going to have the baby. Nancy had been asking her if something was wrong, and why her dad never came by to visit anymore.

"What's wrong, Ruth?" Nancy asked. "He's only seen me that one day after Sunday school during the past two months, just to give me a ride home, and he wouldn't come in even for a minute."

Ruth got all her inner strength together and resolved to make something good of the situation, no matter what it took.

"I'm going to start now," she said silently. Then picked up the phone and called Billy.

"Billy this is Ruth. I need to talk to you, and in private."

Billy was stunned to hear from her. They hadn't talked or seen each other since the incident.

"Ruth, I'm sorry," he said, in a near whisper. "I don't know what to say. I don't know what came over me."

"Billy, be quiet. I need to talk to you. It's urgent. Al's not coming home for dinner this noon and Nancy's in school. I want you to come out to the farm at noon. Ruth heard Billy crying, and his voice was shaking.

"Ruth, I can't ever face you again, Can't we just talk on the phone?"

"No, I want to see you. This is important. I forgive you, Billy. Don't worry about that, but I need to see you when we talk,"

Billy responded weakly. "I'll try, if I can get up enough courage to come out."

Later, it took all of Billy's courage to get out of the car and go to Ruth's house.

Ruth opened the door before he could knock. Billy shuffled into the house. He couldn't look at Ruth and wouldn't look up or speak. Ruth took him by the arm and sat him in a chair by the table.

"Billy, be strong; be a man, and snap out of it," she said. "We've got another problem that's going to take all of our understanding, cooperation, and a lot of deep-thinking. I'm pregnant. I'm going to have your baby, Billy."

Billy's mind landed a hard right to his stomach and a left to the chin. He thought he was going to vomit. All of his muscles tightened, and his hands, though ice cold, became wet with cold sweat.

Ruth went on. "I'm going to tell Al. I don't know what he'll do or say. Whatever it is, I'll need your help and support; not so much for me but for this baby I am carrying. He might throw me out. I don't know. He may accept it or ignore it. It would be my guess he'll just go on like he has in the past. Nothing seems important to him anymore. Anyway … maybe this won't be important either. But I'm going to be strong, and by God, you have some responsibility for what took place and the situation we're in. I expect you to help me through this, no matter what happens. I've decided I can take all of the consequences of our actions. If I can handle it, I can't think of a reason in the world why you and Al can't face up to reality and we can work this out together."

There was a long pause before Billy looked up at Ruth. His voice wouldn't work; sound wouldn't come from his mouth. He looked back at the floor and his feet twisted back and forth before a low murmur came from his lips.

"Ruth, I just can't go through this, I can't be of any help. I don't know what to do. I can't even think. All I can do is get out of here."

Without saying any more Billy hurried out the door. Calling on his past experiences of how he'd dealt with Clair's death, Billy drove back to the foundry and busied himself with work, where his mind had developed the ability to go blank and shut out punishing thoughts. The only problem was after work, but then the tavern would take over.

After Billy had gone, Ruth reflected for a moment, before throwing a cup, full of coffee, at the Franklin stove. The cup shattered. A brown steam rose, leaving a murky stain on the stove.

For the love of God, Ruth thought, *where is there any strength I can draw on?* She drew herself upright, took a deep breath and said loudly. "The strength is within me. I am going to get through this without shame. This is something that has happened to me in life, and it's not going to get me down. I won't let it."

Chapter 20

THE NEXT MORNING, sitting across from Al at the breakfast table, Ruth straightened her hunched shoulders and lifted her head. Al hadn't washed or shaved.

"Probably gonna rain before noon," Al said. "Don't know if I'll be back for dinner or not."

"Al" … Ruth's voice quivered; there was a lump in her throat and a knot in her stomach, but she forced herself to speak. "Listen seriously to me. We don't have many good times together. You've never hurt me or emotionally mistreated me—at least, not intentionally—but … we've been existing rather than living. I've something alarming to tell you. Something distressing for you and me—something we'll need to think about and make some difficult decisions. Whatever you decide is best— I'll respect it. All I ask is that we act rationally and not just think of ourselves."

Al squirmed and rubbed a grubby hand on his chin stubble. "Hey, what are you talking about? You want a divorce or something? If you want to get divorced I don't have much of anything to give you. I don't own the farm, you know, and the livestock …"

"Wait, wait," Ruth interrupted. "I'm not asking for a divorce, but when you hear what I have to say, you'll probably ask for one." She told him about the Sunday Billy came by and glossed over any mention of force regarding the incident in the woodshed. "And now I'm pregnant." she said.

Al hung his head, stirred his coffee and added a spoon of sugar.

"Oh," is all he said, and peering at the coffee, he continued stirring for some time without comment.

"It must've been my fault all along why you didn't get pregnant before. I always thought it was your fault. I always wanted to have kids. I just thought you were one of them women that couldn't have kids. A freemartin. It was me, huh? Never thought of that."

"Oh Jesus, look at me Al. Can't you understand what I said? I'm going to have a baby. Billy Bartel is the father. What are we going to do? I can't believe your reaction. Do you want me to leave? Get out? Al, will you do something normal? Be mad at me. Hit me. Throw something. Say something relevant! Please?"

"Yeah, we'll have to work something out, Al said." His expression hardly changed as he rose from his chair. "I've got a lot of things to do over at the folks today. I'll be back for supper. We can talk tonight at supper."

Ruth swallowed hard but couldn't choke back her tears.

"Can we decide what to do then?" she sobbed.

"Yup", he said. "Don't worry, gotta go now, got sows farrowing."

Ruth sat at the table after Al had gone. Her head and hands were in a cold sweat. Then she went to the bathroom and closed the door. She pulled at her hair with both hands, and screamed: "God, did you make any men that are men or are they all little boys? Is it just women that are able to face this crazy world?"

At six P.M., Ruth, with trembling hands, placed the supper meal before her husband. She'd made Salisbury steak mashed potatoes and gravy, and homemade applesauce. Al sat quietly and ate hurriedly.

"Didn't rain after all. Where's Nancy?" he asked.

"She's staying overnight with the neighbors, so we can talk."

"Have to clean out the hog pen tomorrow. Sows farrowed today. I need to finish chores now."

"Wait. You said we could talk. We can't pretend nothing has happened, can we?"

"We can talk when I come in from chores." He turned his back to Ruth, went to the porch, put on his overshoes and walked to the barn. Some after nine he returned to the house. He smelled of alcohol and hog manure and went directly to bed. On his way to the bedroom he looked back at Ruth.

"We can talk in the morning at breakfast. Better we just sleep on this for the night," he said, dismissing her.

Al was up by five. After morning chores he shaved, washed up and combed his hair before breakfast. Ruth was astonished. He looked handsome and content. She thought, just maybe, Al was going to make something good of this after all.

"Ruth, I know we can work this out," he said. "I don't blame you and I'm not upset with you. I don't think there's anything you could have done to change what happened. Don't ever blame yourself for anything that happens beyond your control, now or ever. That's about all I want to say on the subject, for now." He stood up, turned abruptly, and began walking away.

"Oh thank you so much Al," Ruth said. "With your help and understanding I'm sure this will turn out all right."

Ruth watched Al through the kitchen window as he walked to the hog barn. *"It's a start; he's talking now,"* she thought. *"We'll talk more at noon."* Ruth was feeling much better.

Al cleaned and added golden straw to the hog pens, where he paused, viewed his work silently, and nodded approval. He walked straight, erect and confident; his actions deliberate and precise, while stacking the forks, shovels and other tools neatly in their places. His tight, down-turned mouth had softened, and the tense lines in his face smoothed. The near permanent frown, he'd acquired of late, appeared to be gone.

Al retrieved a few bottles of beer from the feed room, and then climbed the ladder to the haymow, where he opened a beer and sat cross-legged in the musty hay. Absently, he gazed at his surroundings, while savoring the beer. A single white pigeon strutted along the hayfork track near the ridgepole at the top of the barn. A trip rope attached to the hayfork extended to the lower level, where it was neatly coiled and hung on a wooden peg in a structural beam.

Al finished his beer, and put a full bottle in each front pocket before moving up to the trip rope. With the jackknife from his pocket he cut a twenty-foot length of trip line, tied a knot in the fresh-cut end then fashioned a slipknot in the other. In long, slow drinks he drained another beer. Then with rope in hand, he climbed the ladder at the end of the barn and worked his way laboriously along the side near the rafters. When he came to the 8 x 8 beam spanning the middle of the barn, he brushed his hands clear of chaff and pigeon droppings. A white pigeon strutted nervously along the track and perched by the open haymow door. She canted her head and nodded her neck as she strutted, following Al's path with her eyes as he straddled the beam and scooted himself near the center, where he paused and finished another beer. Then he threw his leg over the beam and sat comfortably, tying one end of the rope securely around the beam.

For several years Al had been planning. Little things had been nagging at him. Nothing singularly had been eventful enough to trigger his action. He had needed an excuse. Now, knowing he wasn't even man enough to father a child, his decision was made. His tormented mind was in slow motion, ready for rest.

As he placed the slipknot loop around his neck, he blanked his conscious thoughts and went to a quiet place in his mind. Pensively, he pushed the empty beer bottle sitting on the beam into space. His fixed mind slowed its fall and he watched it tumble in slow motion and bounce in the hay twenty-five feet below.

Al allowed himself to slip from the beam. The barn shuddered, and the startled white pigeon flew skyward.

At one-thirty, when Al hadn't come in for dinner, Ruth called out several times for him from the kitchen doorway. No answer. Krankuses were always prompt about mealtime, dinner at twelve, and supper at six. You could almost set your clock by them. Ruth was sure he was around the farm somewhere. The pickup was still in the yard. She called Mother Krankus and asked if Al was there.

"Not here, we haven't seen him all day," Bess said. "Do you want Russell to come over and look around for him?"

"No, I'm sure everything is all right. If he doesn't come in soon, I'll call you back." She hung up the phone; immediately picked it back up and called the neighbor from across the road.

"Byron," she said, "I'm concerned about Al. He hasn't come in for dinner and it's nearly two o'clock. Would you come over and see if you can find him for me?" Byron thought it strange she hadn't been out to check for herself.

"Sure, I can come right over," he said, and arrived at the farm shortly afterward. He looked around the farmstead and called out for Al several times. Entering the barn, he noticed fresh manure on the ladder steps to the haymow. Byron's climb stopped quickly when he reached the top rung of the ladder. Al was still at the end of the rope and Byron could tell there was nothing he could do for him. He backed down the ladder and paused, thinking about how Al's parents had dominated him. And Byron struggled with the idea of breaking the news to Ruth.

Ruth was quite puzzled when she saw Byron drive off without contacting her. She put on her jacket and scarf for protection from the cold wind. She'd reached the end of the sidewalk when Byron and his wife Layne drove into the yard. Layne came from the car crying. She put her arm around Ruth and told her about Al. Ruth staggered to the house with Layne's help and collapsed into a chair.

Byron used Ruth's phone and called Sheriff Smith. The sheriff said he'd contact the coroner and be right out.

Late that afternoon, the sheriff and Doc Selkirk, helped Hale T., the undertaker place Al Krankus on the white marble slab in the back room of the funeral home in Norwood. The funeral parlor and mortuary were located at the back of a furniture store. The walls, ceiling, and the boarded-over windows of the embalming room were all painted bed sheet white. A large porcelain sink, centered in a gray cement counter, was fastened to the west wall. Below the counter, moist- looking unpainted wood shelving contained an assortment of bottles; some of which held as much as five gallons of urine-colored liquid. Hale took a look at Al on the slab and shook his head.

"Poor bastard's still got his five-buckle overshoes on. Keep the door closed there, boys, until we get these overshoes out of here and the place cleaned up a bit. If we're not careful, that pig-shit smell will permeate every couch and stuffed chair we've got in the place. I hope we don't get an ambulance call before we get the hearse cleaned and fumigated."

Sheriff Smith wondered how Hale T. could smell anything. The sheriff felt that every one of the few times he had personally been exposed to the searing, cauterizing, effect of embalming fluid, his sense of smell had been diminished.

All the next day Ruth's friends and neighbors came by and offered their condolences. Dianne and Lilla Mae had stayed on after everyone else had left and did all the dishes and tidied up the house. And Dianne had put Nancy to bed and stayed with her until she went to sleep.

Chapter 21

BILLY SAT STIFFLY on the red vinyl seat of the chrome-based barstool. The dark lines around his eyes and stubble of rough beard on his stoic face, just shadows, in the dim yellow light at the short end of the L-shaped, mahogany bar in the Red Bird tavern. Funzie, the owner and chief barman, placed a bottle of Hamm's beer in front of Billy; took the five-dollar bill from the counter, made change and put it on the bar in front of Billy. Neither spoke. Funzie just kept setting up more beer when the bottle went dry, and left Billy alone.

Billy drank and pushed life away from himself like he pushed the empty brown beer bottle back on the scarred bar. There was an awful sickness in his stomach. It had been there ever since the unfortunate incident with Ruth in the woodshed. He hardly felt like eating, anymore. Beer mellowed things out a bit. The mornings were the worst. After Ruth told him she was pregnant, often there were times when he couldn't hold the sickness down. The alcohol was just beginning to make Billy feel better when Merford Thrane, sauntered in through the door, and took a seat at the long end of the bar. Funzie, wiped his hands on a dingy, white cotton dishtowel and hung it on the chrome door-handle of the oven.

"What'll it be, Merford," Funzie said. Merford snapped the lid of his Copenhagen box with his right, middle index finger.

"Gimme a Pabst, Funzie," he said. "I just lost one of my Sunday, beer-drinking buddies," Merford said.

"That so? I hadn't heard anything."

"Yeah, Al Krankus cashed in his chips. Turned up his hole card. Hale T's got him over at the funeral parlor, deader'n a doornail. The poor shit hung himself in the barn."

Billy's sickness wouldn't stay down. He ran to the men's room, and when the last of the green bile, in the very bottom of his liver, was gone, the knots in his stomach were so tight they' wrung all the moisture from his system and there was nothing more to give to the toilet stool. A numbness settled in over Billy that was to stay with him for most of the rest of his life. He ran from the restroom and out the back door of the tavern.

"What got into him?" Merford said. "He looked as green as a corpse."

Funzie picked up Billy's half-full beer and walked over to Merford.

"His daughter lives with the Krankuses," Funzie explained. "I don't see that he pays much attention to her the way he has been hanging around here so much lately. It must be nearly nine years since his wife died giving birth to the girl. He's withdrawn from all his friends and everybody has kind of withdrawn from him; and he's been walking around like a zombie ever since. I didn't know him before, but people tell me he was quite a fellow. Went to church and was becoming kind of a community leader. He sure took it hard about Al though, didn't he?"

Chapter 22
The Settlement

A WEEK AFTER Al's funeral, Russell Krankus sat at the dinner table discussing business matters with Bess.

"What now?" Bess said. The black hair, protruding from her mole, had a slight curl to it. Even with the dinner aroma, the house smelled musty, and the stale air slowed the conversation. "Should we sell the farm where Al lived, and just stay farming here?"

"That's a good-producing farm," Russell responded. "It's got a good house on it." Russell sliced a thin, hard-cooked, pork chop on his plate with a long skinning-knife. Bess had said she had to cook pork real hard to prevent trichinosis. "No use us workin' ourselves to death. We could use a farm-hand around. The other place is all set up for a married couple to live, anyhow."

"A man'l work a lot cheaper if you got a good house for him and his Missus," Bess said. "Can get a lot of free work out of a woman too."

Russell scraped the last morsel of charred meat. Bess wiped brown gravy from her mouth with the back of her gnarled hand and added it to the grease stains on her apron.

"Ruth doesn't have anything coming," Bess said. "But I guess if we look at it in a businesslike manner, we should have been paying Al something on a regular basis. If we'd paid him two thousand dollars a year since they got married, that would be twenty thousand dollars. Ruth has done a lot of work around the farm, too, and we never paid her neither," she said. By rights, I suppose that whole farm should have been in Al's name. If we'd of done that; the whole place and a lot of the machinery would have been Ruth's now."

Russell put an elbow on each knee and cupped his hands on his chin. "We both agree it's just good business to get her off the farm though," he said.

Bess nodded agreement. "There's, that pretty nice house in town where old Greasy Lock used to live. It's kind of dirty looking and not well kept up, but Ruth is quite industrious. I'll bet she could make something of it," Russell said. "I hear they're asking ten thousand for it. I'll bet we could get it for six thousand if we paid cash. We could give her the house and offer her ten thousand more in cash as full settlement of our obligation to her. I think that would be fair."

Bess, needing time to think, swept the crumbs from around the table with a straw broom and placed the pork bones in the dog's dish.

"I think that's a good idea," she said. "If she objects, we could give her twenty-thousand outright, to get her to leave the farm and clear everything up."

"Whatever, lets hurry up and get it done. Call Loophole this afternoon and see what he says."

Don Fernt, attorney, took the call. He was aware that many of the townspeople referred to him as Loophole and thought of him as a smooth shyster. He was short, stocky, slightly overweight and expensively dressed with a rumpled appearance. He liked clients who showed a degree of covetousness or selfishness, so he could plant a seed of greed, to spoil their vision. And when the seed matured, they were ripe to be taken by good old Don Fernt.

"Ahem- Ahem-, come right in." Fernt said as the Krankuses entered his office. "What is it I can help you with? He looked down at his hands and unconsciously rubbed them together.

"Our son died several weeks ago and we want to make a settlement of his affairs with his widow," Russell said.

"We've discussed it all and know what we want to do," Bess said. She had a midnight blue hat on, with a wicker weave to it. "We would like you to review our proposal to make sure it is all right in the eyes of the law."

"Uhmm- Uhmm," Fernt said, using his most somber and profound mood inflection. "Let's get to work, then." It was important for Loophole to begin immediately, before any of his clients mentioned fees. Fert figured the Krankuses were unsophisticated and very tight with their money. *These two are about as tight as a bull's ass in fly time*, he thought. And he began calculating the best procedure for fee-generating.

Through probate, he could charge his full fee up front; then put the file aside and work on it at his leisure. His secretary could do most of the real work. She knew more about probate than he did. He paid her minimum wage and charged the client his hourly attorney rate for her work. *I could drag this case out over a couple of years*, thought Fernt. He could help his banker friend out by putting estate money in a checking account drawing no interest. There were many ways the banker would return the favor.

"Ahem—," he said. "It appears that all of this should go through probate to make sure of the proper title to the real estate and make sure nothing backfires on you. Insurance against trouble later. This is a rather complicated legal procedure, but I am sure we can work it out to your advantage. I think the farm you refer to as the 'other farm', where your son lived, will have to be probated. You didn't mention any insurance. Was there any insurance on your son?

Russell and Bess looked at each other. Bess was first to speak.

"We didn't think this had anything to do with the estate. We had a ten thousand dollar policy on Al. Russell and I were named the beneficiaries. We didn't think it was any of Ruth's business. She doesn't know about it." With candid high-tonality, Loophole responded. "Ahem-Ahem-there will be no problem here." Loophole saw his opening. "In a very strict interpretation of the law, it probably should be listed as a non-probate asset. Ahem-Ahem-, but in this case, we'll forget that I asked the question and everything will be all right. Let's see now, Ahem-Ahem-, the court may determine much of the machinery and some of the other assets are rightfully or partially Ruth's because of the contribution of your son and Ruth. I think it best not to mention your tacit agreement that Al inherit all of the farms and property upon your death. You never know what the court might do," he said.

The trap was set; Loophole was ready to proceed with the inexperienced Krankuses. In a deep and resonant voice he continued.

"Ahem-, I appreciate very much your desire to be decent with Ruth. The settlement you have suggested seems ultimately equitable and I'm sure will be looked upon favorably by the court should this become necessary. However if we could handle all of this with Ruth in a negotiated settlement and keep it out of probate it would save a lot of delay and unnecessary court expense. Then you would avoid all of the risk of losing more of the estate. I know you will be more than fair with Ruth; many would not be as generous as you are. I will gladly bargain with her for you. My fee will be twenty-five percent of whatever I save from your initial proposal."

From the look on their faces Loophole knew he had just stepped over the line with the Krankuses.

"Mr. Fernt," Bess responded indignantly, "Definitely not, no we are not interested in that at all. We have in good conscience thought this all through, and we presented to you what we think is right. We only want you to help us with legal matters." Loophole knew he had probed a mite too far.

"Ahem, I think you have misunderstood my concern, Ahem-Ahem-." He told them, how as a lawyer, his code of ethics required him to do the very best for his clients and he only wanted to know for sure about their desired outcome in this proceeding. Certainly he was not suggesting anything other than what was in their best interest. He must always represent clients to the best of his ability. "Ahem-, now let's get on here," he said. "The best way of handling this would be to try to settle with Ruth on the terms you have suggested and keep everything out of probate. I think we can do that. I will charge you the minimum fee set by the bar."

That was okay with the Krankuses. Attorney Fernt knew they had no idea that the minimum fee was in fact a fee set by the local bar association at a social gathering of all the lawyers practicing in the county. A gathering, where the lawyers invited the Probate Judge, who until recently was one of them, and discussed what percentage of the estate a lawyer could bill for without review or criticism of the judge. After discussion, the judge and lawyers would agree on the maximum percentage they thought they could get by with. This became the minimum fee prescribed by the bar. Each individual lawyer could then inform their clients they would give them a special rate and charge the minimum fee.

"About the house you want to buy for Ruth," Fernt continued. "I'll take care of that. With your authorization, I'll make the offer for you and make any down payment from my trust account, holding the property for you, until it's transferred to Ruth."

Unseasoned in matters of law and being quite intimidated by Loophole, Bess nodded to Russell and said meekly, "I guess that is all right if you think it best."

"Yes," Russell said. "Start your offer on the house at six thousand."

"Yes-Ahem. I'll have things in order for a meeting with you folks and your daughter-in-law, by two-fifteen next Wednesday."

After the Krankuses left, Loophole sat at his desk and hummed a few refrains of, *'I Love Those Dear Hearts and Gentle People'*. He felt he had distinguished himself in the art of the practice of law and client bilking. "*Who live and love in my home town*," he sang, as he dialed the phone.

"Mrs. Afton, this is Attorney Don Fernt, speaking. I think I know of someone interested in buying your house. They have been looking around quite a while and have several places in mind. Being an attorney I am also privileged to act as a realtor. I'm sure I can get you a good offer on your house. You know, of course, according to the rules of the bar, I must charge you the minimum realtor's fee or risk my right to practice law. I am sure my party will offer a cash price in full. Does this interest you, Mrs. Afton?"

Mrs. Afton, knew something of the reputation of attorney Fernt, but was also interested in selling the house.

"Well, yes, she said. "I'm asking ten thousand dollars for the place."

"I know," said Loophole, "I'm prepared to offer you seven thousand in cash right now. What do you think of that?"

"Oh my, no, I couldn't possibly accept that. I might consider eight thousand if things were done in cash and finished quickly."

"These buyers are pretty tough customers, but I'm supposed to earn my fee. If I get this much from them I'll sure earn it. Let me work on them and I'll get back to you. I'll get the very best offer and get back to you."

After he hung up the phone, Loophole sang another refrain: *"Because those dear hearts and gentle people will never, ever let you down."* Then he began to appraise his options.

If I were just representing Mrs. Afton, I know I could get the ten thousand for her, but the Krankuses wouldn't think I had done anything for them, he thought. *What I probably should do is sew up a deal on the house with Mrs. Afton for eight thousand. I'll charge her ten-percent. That's $800. I'll convince the Krankuses I got them a real bargain and include in their fee a realtor or finder's fee of $800 after everything is settled. I think they'll just pay it and not ask any questions. I'll charge the Krankuses what would be the minimum fee on all their property, as if it went through probate, even though it doesn't have to.* Everything seemed fair and equitable to Attorney Fernt. He didn't go to law school for nothing.

I should be able to get a fee out of Ruth, too, he thought. *I'll call her in early, before the meeting, and tell her I'll represent her interests, too.* He set about to make it work.

I'll have to spread some of these fees around on Judge Murket and county attorney Lester, he thought. *Just in case they question the fairness of my ways. I can buy them a couple of drinks; treat them to a game of golf or two. The Judge and Lester both like golf and enjoy the country club set. A few drinks and a bite to eat, my treat. That goes on my expense account, too. The most I'll ever get from them is a word of caution if they receive complaints.*

And the attorney sang the last refrain. *'They read the good book, from Fri' till Monday. That's how the weekend goes."*

Ruth arrived at Attorney Fernt's office promptly at one-thirty.

"Uhmm-Uhmm—," Loophole said, greeting her at the door. "Ruth, you have my sympathy. I'm so sorry about your loss." He ushered her into his private office. "Ruth, I'm here to see that you are treated fairly by the law and to help you and the Krankuses come to a legal and fair settlement of the affairs of your husband. I've talked to the Krankuses and don't foresee many problems in my being able to get a fair settlement for you. I'll be representing you in the negotiation. Because of your limited resources and the tragedy you have experienced, I'll charge you only half of the minimum fee; but no one must know of our arrangement. I could risk my law practice, if the bar found out I was charging less than the minimum."

"I don't have any money," Ruth said naively. "Do you think I have some settlement coming from the Krankuses?"

"Well, it's questionable," Loophole said. "But I have talked to Bess and Russell on your behalf. I think I have them convinced to offer you something that will be fair. I can continue to do this, if you agree."

"I don't know anything about legal proceedings." Ruth said.

"*How easy can it get?*" Loophole thought. "Uhumm-Uhmmm-, I'll get you the very most I can. I'll work hard for your interests. If I am not able to get you a fair settlement I won't charge you a thing. The local bar association doesn't need to know."

Ruth didn't have a clue. "I don't know; I'm not familiar with any of this. I don't want to do anything wrong," she said.

"Well, just let me handle it. I've been in these situations before and helped a number of people out when they were short of money. It makes me feel good to help people." He unconsciously licked his lips. "I've looked the whole situation over. Al didn't own anything outright. Everything is in Russell and Bess's name. I have talked to them about what is right and fair play in life. I'm confident they'll see the wisdom of what I say and we'll get you a fair settlement. You just rely on my experience and the great American legal system. Okay?"

"Okay, but I don't know anything about this. I've heard some things about probate. Do we have to go through probate?"

"No, ahem—, ahem—, I think it best that we don't. If we get into strict legal procedures the Krankuses may be able to put you out on the street without anything. Right now I don't think they want to do that. When they come today, let me talk to them alone for a little while. Give me a chance, Ruth." The bell on the cash register of Loophole's mind rang and put a light in his eyes. "I have looked things over with them. What would you think if I got them to give you a settlement of about eighteen thousand dollars? My normal fee would be $2,000 for a settlement of this nature, but in your case I'll do it for $1,000. I won't charge you a thing if I don't get at least eighteen thousand. I see the Krankuses are coming now. We will proceed in that manner, then," Loophole said as he rose to greet the Krankuses.

Loophole convinced everyone involved he was acting in their best interest. Mrs. Afton sold the house for eight thousand dollars, paying Loophole eight hundred dollars for his fee. Ruth got the Afton house and ten thousand dollars from Russell and Bess, of which she paid Loophole one thousand dollars. The Krankuses paid Loophole a full five percent of the estimated value of the farm and all of the machinery; something in excess of three thousand five hundred dollars, in lieu of the probate fee, and were billed eight hundred dollars for a realtor's fee, which they questioned, but paid anyway. Loophole understood only too well all of this realistically could have been done for a total of two hundred dollars in legal fees had any of the parties been experienced in legal matters and not intimidated by Loophole and the legal profession.

Chapter 23

RUTH GAVE A sigh of relief and unpacked the final cardboard box at her new location. When she put the faded towels in the bathroom closet, she caught the faint, acrid smell they carried from the farm; that inescapable scent that never left a hog farm. She thought it might go away with the next washing. She wanted a new scent for this house. Every house has its own individual, unique smell; and she wanted hers to smell like fresh morning air washed by a spring rain. *I could start with cedar*, she thought. She remembered being with Al when they cut cedar for posts, and how wonderful the fragrance was when green cedar sticks made it to the wood box. "Yes, cedar," she said aloud.

Ruth met her image, in the bathroom mirror. Her hair, that once had sheen and bounce, was stringy and matted. But it was her face and skin that had undergone the most dramatic change. Her once-clear, blue eyes looked almost gray, like oysters; loose and liquid. Her skin was dry, taut and colorless. Her lips were tight and pinched together as if locked in sorrow. Her pregnancy, pushed at the seams of her faded print dress; the cloth had yellowed and the true colors were all washed out. She'd gotten the fabric at Caw's feed mill, on a day when Al had taken her and Nancy to town, when Nancy was three years old. Old Mr. Caw's eyebrows and the hairs of his hawk-like nose were coated with white flour. He had shown them samples of the bright-colored, print, flour sacks. Three sacks were free with the purchase of a full sack of flour.

"I remember you, Ruth," Mr. Caw had said. "You were one of my wife's favorite students. She still speaks of you; said you had great talent for the piano. You still play?"

"Hardly ever."

Ruth had taken piano lessons from Mr. Caw's wife Nona. Ruth thought of Nona as a great pianist, with long graceful fingers that floated across the piano keys and searched out notes, like silence searches a room.

A few weeks later, Ruth made the dress she had on now, and one for Nancy. When the dresses were finished they ran outside to see themselves twirling and frolicking in the sunshine.

That was six years ago. Now, Ruth put her red-chapped hands to her brittle hair, and paused before going to the kitchen. She looked at the dull, white wainscoting on the walls. Painting would have to wait. Doc Selkirk had warned her about fresh paint fumes.

Ruth glanced out the kitchen window and saw Nancy talking with one of her newfound friends.

Nancy didn't care much about the move to town. She missed the country and the wildlife. She had wide mood swings, from sad and quiet to covering her insecurity with incessant chatter. Her little girl emotions were on a roller coaster since the death of Uncle Al. She cried and complained to Ruth about being like an orphan, never seeing her father anymore.

Ruth knew she should spend a lot of serious time with Nancy, but she was barely surviving herself, after being pummeled repeatedly with emotional blows. She felt much like a punch-drunk fighter; reeling and searching endlessly for the strength to fight back; all the while thinking it easier to give up like Al and Billy had. But she couldn't take a dive. There was a new life, a second little heart beating inside her. Somehow, she was going to give it a fighting chance.

She spoke aloud, to an imaginary counselor.

"Things are manageable," she said. *"If I try real hard and look at it positively, I'm actually pretty well off."*

Even without conscious thought, Ruth wrote "skip" on the paper before her. *Skip-what's that all about?* She thought. Thinking back—some of her happiest moments were associated with skipping; when little girls, even little boys skipped.

I can't skip if I'm not happy. Or could I? In her mind's eye, the word **SKIP**, appeared in bold black letters and she remembered her mother saying—"Ruth, don't you ever walk? Do you skip everywhere?" Determined to skip, her feet only shuffled and made a scuffing sound.

"Keep trying you old coot," she said. *"Hold your head up, be forceful."* She made a feeble hop, then tried again, with a bounce in her step. *Almost,* she thought, as one foot lifted off the floor. Amused, she spoke aloud to herself again. *"It says skip damn it, and I'm going to skip."* Then a warm shiver went through her body and a smile so radiant it lit up the room changed into laughter. The word **SKIP,** in the front of her mind, gleamed like a diamond, then settled and shone in her eyes as she skipped around the table. Unabashed laughter, burst from her mouth when the seams of her old dress gave way. And she was more alive than she had been in many years. She skipped and laughed, skipped and laughed, until her pregnant, exhilarated body was exhausted. *What if someone were to see me?* she thought. Then the newfound gaze of white light in her eyes, settled on the old upright piano in the living room; its brown-finished surface cracked and split from the dry air from the farmhouse.

"Be spontaneous," she said out loud.

Smiling both inwardly and outwardly, she skipped to the piano bench and sat down. She ran her chapped red fingers over the keys, and then haltingly attempted playing her favorite piece, "*Clair de Lune*". She started, stopped and practiced, over and over. She remembered how Mrs. Caw had taught her music. She played for a while, gradually becoming surer of her touch, until the excitement of the rhythm and the words washed over her, and she felt renewed. Finally she rose from the bench and went to the kitchen. Nancy would have a very special supper. She spread her ivory, Quaker Lace tablecloth over the living room table, and set places for two, with candles, napkins, Sunday dishes and real silver.

She had washed her hair, changed her dress and was back at the piano, when Nancy came in the house.

"What's for supper, Ruth? I'm hungry." Nancy said.

The well-played, melodic sound of "*Clair de Lune*" wafted through the air.

"What's for supper," Nancy repeated loudly. Then she babbled on, in the childlike way that had become a habit for her ever since they moved to town.

"What's going on? I didn't know you could play like that. That's really good. You look so different. Your eyes are all shiny-like. You fixed your hair. Neat. Whoee!! Look at that table. Wowee, company coming for supper? You only have two places set. I suppose I have to eat in my room when you have company. Not fair!"

"Slow down, Nancy," Ruth said, swinging around on the piano bench. "You're the company. Come over here. I want to take a good look at you." Nancy's long, inquisitive face was streaked with dirt; her knees were skinned and scraped and her scruffy old saddle shoes were nearly falling apart. Dust and dirt was riddled through her disorderly, reddish-brown hair.

Nevertheless a twinkle was in her eyes, a wrinkle in her nose and a permanent, impish grin on her face.

Ruth gathered Nancy's scrawny little body in her arms, softly and lovingly, held her close, and kissed her cheeks. Tears of joy welled in Ruth's eyes and the wet tears put dirty streaks on Nancy's face. She looked up at Aunt Ruth and slapped her hand to her forehead.

"Gone bananas, out of your bird, Ruth?" Nancy asked.

"I don't know maybe," said Ruth. "Just bear with me a little bit. If I'm out of my bird, it's a good bird to be out of. Ready to eat? I fixed supper just for you; hamburgers, pickles, French fries, everything, just the way my honored guest for life would like it."

Nancy hardly knew how to respond to this renewed attention. It made her feel special, cared for, and important. *Honored guest, me, Nancy Bartel,* she thought. *Nine years old, an honored supper guest, with candle light, the best linens and dishes. This must be a joke or a prank, but Ruth had hardly ever joked of late.*

Nancy began to wonder why Ruth was doing all this. A worried look came across Nancy's face.

"Hey, hey" Ruth said. "Everything's going to be all right. I love you, Nancy".

Nancy began to cry.

"Don't cry, now," Ruth said. "We're going to be okay."

"Don't ever leave me, Ruth. I don't want to be alone."

"No, no, Nancy, you're not going to lose me. Maybe you're going to lose some of me; the old, cold, part of me; but it won't be a loss. Let's eat. I've a lot I want to talk to you about. I need your help."

"You need me!" Nancy said. "What can I do? I'm just a little kid, I can't do nuthin'."

"You can let me love you, and if you find it possible to love me back we'll both be blessed. But let's not be so serious right now. I want to show you something. Go wash your hands for supper, and do me a favor, don't wash your face, comb your hair, or change your clothes. I think you're beautiful just the way you are. I want to look at you, as you are, across the table from me. After your hands are washed, wait for me by the bathroom door. I have a surprise for you, something fun."

Nancy was totally baffled. What had happened to Ruth? Her sad and distant look was gone. There was a new light in her eyes that brightened and softened her whole face. Nancy washed her hands, looked in the bathroom mirror and began laughing at herself. *What a mess I am. Ruth likes me this way? I guess she really is out of her bird.*

"Take my hand," Ruth said. When Nancy same from the bathroom, she was nearly jerked off her feet, with Ruth's running and pulling her towards the kitchen. Ruth was skipping and laughing. *Laughing? Ruth doesn't laugh*, thought Nancy. *She doesn't skip either*, she concluded.

"Come on Nancy, skip with me." Ruth said. "You can skip. I've seen you skip." Then they skipped around the table; skipping, laughing, being silly and almost crying, until they were both out of breath. Ruth led Nancy to her chair, bowed, swept her hand in front of her in an arc and announced, "Your dinner seat, Madame." Ruth took a seat across from Nancy. They looked at each other in one of those embarrassing silences, and then they broke out in laughter again, until Ruth got up from the table and departed to the kitchen.

"I'll get the hamburgers," she said, beaming. "There's a book of matches by your plate. Light the candles, Nancy."

They ate by candlelight. Nancy was excited by the attention. Ruth told her how life was going to be different; better, she needn't be frightened by the past.

"Can I invite my friends into the house once in awhile, now too?" Nancy asked. "And can we skip again, soon? But let's not skip when my friends are here, they'll think we're weird." Then Nancy said something she had never said before.

"I love you, Ruth."

At the first clap of thunder, that night, Nancy stood by Ruth's bed. Ruth turned back the covers. Nancy hopped in close to Ruth and pulled the covers up around her neck.

The next day Nancy daydreamed at school. *I wonder what's really wrong with my dad,* she thought. *There's no reason he couldn't be like Ruth and change. How come he don't want me around? I suppose it's because I look so much like mom did. If he doesn't want to come and see me—maybe I'll go and see him. The school bus goes by his place.*

One time when they didn't know she was in the stairway listening, Nancy had heard Dianne Russy and Ruth talk about Billy drinking so much beer and shuffling when he walked. *Maybe I could teach him to skip,* Nancy thought. *I could take the bus to his place after school, but Dianne said he drinks and doesn't come home till after the bars close.*

For two weeks now Billy's only job at work had been drilling one-inch holes in iron plating. It was okay with Billy—that way he didn't have to think. It alarmed him when Red told him he had a phone call; he hardly ever got calls at work.

"Daddy, this is Nancy." Billy wasn't sure he heard right because of the background noise. Clyde was sharpening a plow lathe on the grinder.

"Who?" Billy asked. "I can't hear you." Billy motioned for Clyde to stop the grinding.

"Nancy —- Daddy, this is Nancy. Your daughter."

Billy thought there must be another emergency. She had never called him before.

"What's wrong Nancy," he said.

"Nothing Daddy," she said. "I took the bus from school to your place. And I would like it if you would come right home after work."

Billy hadn't shaved or changed clothes for nearly a week. "I can't today," he said.

"Okay then I'll just stay here till you get home, no matter what the time."

"I don't want for you to see me like this Nancy."

"Tomorrow then?"

Billy didn't have the courage to tell her no.

"Okay tomorrow."

"Good," Nancy said. "It doesn't look like you got much for groceries around here. Bring some hamburger and some buns when you come back tonight. I'll make hamburgers for supper tomorrow."

"Ah, okay Nancy."

"And could you take me home after supper?"

"Yes, I guess so."

"Okay, bye Daddy."

Nancy was shaking like she had the chills. She'd picked up the phone a dozen times before she made the call to Billy. And now she had to deal with Ruth. She hadn't told her she was taking the bus to Billy's. "And if that ain't enough," she said. "She'll blow her top when I ask her to come and get me. Maybe not, this is the new Ruth", she thought. "I can just tell her to '**SKIP**' it." And Nancy laughed.

Ruth felt good about what Nancy had done. In fact she thought it was wonderful, and admired Nancy for her gumption. "You could have told me ahead of time though," she said. The first thing Nancy noticed when she arrived at Billy's place the next day was that the house had been tidied up. The dirty dishes were gone from the sink. The piles of old newspapers and magazines had disappeared and the screen door was patched up and back on its hinges. The windows were open, the stale July air and the smells from dirty clothes and rancid fry cooking from the previous day had been carried away on the breeze. The yard was still a mess, grass and weeds three feet high in places. There was hamburger in the refrigerator—one of the few things that didn't have mold on it, other than the root beer that hadn't been there yesterday.

Nancy got goose bumps when she saw the car come up the drive and her dad park by the house. He didn't look like a bum, that's what she'd heard Dianne say. He was clean-shaven, his hair was combed and his clothes were clean. In fact his clothes were new.

Billy thought Nancy's first visit went well. They were both quite hesitant at first, but he started a fire outside with some oak wood between two cement blocks.

"What's that for," Nancy said.

"You can cook the hamburgers out here." Billy took the oven grille from the kitchen stove and placed it across the cement blocks.

"Clever," Nancy said. She was glad they had something to do. Getting reacquainted wasn't easy.

"What else do you need?" Billy asked. He was glad Nancy wasn't jabbering like Clair used to when she was little. He had to look away from her eyes because every time he looked at them all he saw was Clair and had to turn away to keep from crying. It had been nearly a day and a half now since he'd had a beer and his nerves were not that steady yet.

"I'll need a spatula and butter for the buns," Nancy said.

"Oh, I forgot the butter," Billy said.

"I saw a quart of cream in the fridge; we can make butter while the fire is burning down. You can shake when I'm making the hamburger patties."

Billy knew all about making butter, shaking cream in a quart jar, he'd done it a hundred times when he was a kid. Ruth must be quite the mom, Billy thought. Here's this kid not quite ten years old with as much initiative as a young adult.

"How'd it go? Ruth asked.

"Swell, I think," Nancy said. "Dad's awful quiet, so I didn't say a lot either—you know like we do, but he was all cleaned up and didn't shuffle. And he said I can come back next week if I want. That's okay isn't it?"

"That's wonderful," Ruth said.

Chapter 24

THE FIRST CRAMP came suddenly, pushing the air out of her lungs. "Oooff," Ruth said. She heard the lead typeset fall into place as Buster readied the paper. She took a white-knuckled grip on the sides of her chair and waited for the next cramp.

Anguish had eventually turned to anger; cold, hard anger about the manner in which her child was conceived. Eventually her anger gave way to excitement, then acceptance. She eased her cumbersome body out of the golden oak chair's generous seat and came face to face with Buster's anxious scrutiny.

"What's up, the baby coming?" he asked.

"Nature is sending a signal. We'll have to get hold of Nancy."

"I'll drive you," Buster said.

"No, it's only a few blocks."

"Now, you sit down," Nancy admonished Ruth."I knew this would happen," Nancy continued. "You aren't taking this serious enough. I put some clothes aside a week ago for you."

Ruth clucked like a chicken. "Little mother hen," she said.

"I'm going to call my dad, he'll take you to the hospital," Nancy said.

There was reluctance in Billy's voice when Nancy reached him, but he agreed to come right away.

Billy met them on the porch; Nancy took charge.

"Now you take Ruth's arm and help her down the steps. I'll put the bags in the car," she declared.

"Once, quite a long time ago, I learned to say I love you, and never had the chance to say it." Billy spoke directly to Nancy. "The only person I wanted to say it to was your mother." Billy's voice quivered. "I love you Nancy," he said. Nancy let his hand go when she felt it tug as he took a step.

In the waiting room, Billy shuffled his feet and paced. He knew he couldn't go through with it. It was the same waiting room, the same picture on the wall, and the same cracks in the ceiling.

Nancy noticed that Billy kept shutting his eyes and clenching his jaw, before he told her he was going back to work.

"Can't you stay?" she asked.

"It could be a long time, yet," Billy said, and walked toward the exit.

Then a nurse came by. "Ruth is resting in her room, now," she said. "Come, I'll take you to her. You can wait with her until she goes to delivery." "Where's Billy?" Ruth asked.

"Some job at the foundry that needs to be done today."

"I like the pink nightgown you picked out and sent along for me," Ruth said.

"You should look nice when you have a baby."

"Do I look nice?" Ruth asked

"Yes. Your cheeks are nice and rosy, but your lips don't have any color."

Nancy found the compact and lipstick she had packed for Ruth. "I think you should have bright red lipstick on when you have a baby. I brought the real red kind." she said. Ruth applied the lipstick generously to her lips, and then powdered her face.

"I think a sister should have bright red lipstick on when she first sees her brother or sister," Ruth said.

Nancy's eyes popped open wide. Ruth handed her the lipstick. Nancy hesitated.

"Are you sure?" she said.

"Sure as rain."

Nancy rolled her eyes and posed for Ruth with her lipstick on and they laughed.

"My, aren't we all pretty," the nurse said. "Which lady is the mother?" Nodding to Ruth she said, "We will be going to delivery in about fifteen minutes," she said.

Back at work Billy was thinking, maybe everything is going to work out for the best. *"Maybe,"* he was thinking when the phone rang. It was Nancy. She said they had taken Ruth to the delivery room and she pleaded with him to come back to the hospital.

On the way to the hospital, Billy stopped at the drugstore and bought a pink, fabric rabbit for the baby. It had a white face, a pink tip on its nose, and a rattle embodied in its midsection. He bought a book of paper dolls for Nancy. He thought she might especially like the perforated cut-outs of Martha and George Washington in the front of the book. The clerk gift-wrapped the presents. He thought of buying something for Ruth, perfume maybe, but his courage wasn't strong enough yet.

When Billy came to the waiting room, Nancy, thought the gift-wrapped packages were all for Ruth and the baby.

"For me?" she questioned when Billy handed her a gift.

Nancy quickly untied the bow and carefully folded the gilt paper back. She looked up at Billy with a wide grin, then back down at present again. A lank of hair fell forward and covered her cheek as she traced the outline of one of the gowns with her finger.

"Thank you, Daddy; I really like it," she said softly. Could I stay out at your place with you tonight?" Nancy asked.

"I don't have a spare bedroom fixed up yet," he said

"Maybe, next week, I could help you and we could fix one up," Nancy said.

"Maybe."

The door opened and the dark-haired nurse came into the room. "Ruth has a baby boy." The nurse was curt and dour, not at all like she was before. Nancy leaped from the chair, the book of paper dolls falling from her lap. "I knew it. I knew it. I knew it would be a boy," she cried.

Billy didn't like the dour look on the dark-haired nurse's face. He had seen the look before.

"Is Ruth all right?" he asked urgently.

"Ruth is fine," the nurse said. But the nurse's dour look persisted as she motioned to Billy.

"The doctor would like to talk to you privately, now," she said.

The doctor told Billy the birth had been moderately difficult but Ruth was fine. The baby, however, was hydrocephalic, an intense case, indicative of severe mental retardation. He would require special, lifetime care in a unit at the State Hospital.

"I'm sorry," Billy searched for words and mumbled. "I'm not aware of what hydrocephalic is."

"It's a condition where there is an abnormal increase of fluid in the cranium. In this case, it is possible the fluid pressure has pushed the brain flat against the skull. It has also expanded and distorted the shape of the head," the doctor said. Before Billy even adjusted to the shock, the nurse brought the baby to the room. When Billy saw the baby's misshapen head, disproportionately large for its body, he stood motionless until he tasted the salt from the soundless tears that had streaked his face and reached his lips.

Billy had thought the reunion with Nancy had lit a candle of hope. But now it was if his past had put out the flame again. Nancy saw him, running past the waiting room and watched as he reached the exit and fled.

"Give me a beer, Billy said. He had driven aimlessly for an hour before stopping at the roadside tavern. Glenn Miller's 'In the Mood' was playing on the jukebox. Two aged men, with weathered faces sat at the far end of the bar. Two couples in their late twenties were drinking beer in a booth near the Wurlitzer.

"My name's Cliff," the bartender said. "You look somewhat familiar, but I can't place you."

"Gimme another beer." Billy said. From the tone in Billy's voice Cliff knew it was time to move along so hustled over to the table where the two couples sat.

"Flip you a quarter for the jukebox, Art," Cliff said.

Art was a big man. His upper arms were as large as an average man's thighs, and covered with thick black hair.

"Sure." The huge man's voice was as high-pitched as if it had come from one of the girls. He took a quarter from the loose change on the table and flipped it in the air.

"Call it," he said to Cliff.

"Tails."

"Heads, you lose."

"Okay. Pick your tunes, six for a quarter. Play Tuxedo Junction, Sentimental Journey and any other four you want."

Art's girl said she'd play them. She snapped her fingers to the music, and swung her hips about, shaking her wide black velveteen skirt.

The second girl, dressed in a little black slinky dress with a tight skirt, reached down and straightened the seams of her nylons, then adjusted her tiny black hat with the veil in front and joined Art's girl swaying to the music.

"Now I remember," Cliff said to Billy. "It must have been nine or ten years ago. I was just a kid. You came here one morning way before eight o'clock. You had really hung one on. You could hardly wait … needed a little of the hair of the dog that bit you. Parked your car over by the tool shed, puked all over it. Haven't seen you since. That was you, wasn't it?"

Billy took the full bottle of beer and walked out.

"That's a queer duck," Cliff said to the patrons. "Comes in twice in nine or ten years and acts about the same both times. Funny he is still alive drinking like that."

Nancy telephoned Buster. "Can you please come and wait with me? I'm here all alone and no one is talking to me," she said.

Buster first stopped and talked to the doctor. Now it was his job to inform Nancy.

First she screamed, and then shouted.

"You mean he'll never get better. Never! And he'll never get to come home!" Her fists were clenched, her face was flushed and veins on her neck stood out like drop chords. She didn't cry … yet. She ran to the ladies room, locked the door and kicked the wastebasket, sending it skidding across the floor. Nancy ripped a paper towel from the dispenser, looked defiantly into the mirror and rubbed at her lipstick until her lips were raw, and traces of blood appeared on the towel. When the last trace of lipstick was gone she marched back to Buster in the waiting room. The dark-haired nurse was there.

"I want to see Ruth, now!" she demanded.

"She's still in the recovery room," the nurse said. "It will be some time before the anesthetic wears off. I think it might be best now for the two of you to go home and come back tomorrow."

Nancy's muscles knotted with the fear and the anger of a cornered animal. Her voice was detached and indifferent as though from a far off place. "Okay," she said.

Ruth named her baby Burton. Life had made Ruth strong and she was back at work within two weeks. She needed all her strength, for life continued to be cruel. Four months later Buster's son Phil died. And three days later, Ruth's baby, Burton passed away.

For the first time ever, the weekly issue of the *Norwood Journal* was not published. In the following issue there were two obituaries; each with their own full page.

CHAPTER 25

AFTER BREAKFAST ON his third day at the nursing home, Billy was trying to hum a tune, one he used to like to whistle—when two nurses brought Martin Bently, an old farmer into his room. By then Billy had diagnosed himself—he'd had the DT's. However, he couldn't remember any of his delusions. And, yes, he'd had a mild stroke, but not the kind where you just lie there and with unfocused eyes. His stroke had clogged up the wiring from his brain to a few body parts, but not the wiring to the rest of his being. Time hadn't stopped for him—he could think and dream and remember—that was the worst. He didn't think he'd ever drink again, but already he was getting thirsty.

Billy remembered Martin. After they got married, Clair had Billy going to church every Sunday and even attending Bible study class. Martin had been the lay leader of the study group. And Billy already had had his fill of Martin and his pious visitors.

Billy could sit up now and feed himself, though his left arm and the left side of his face and mouth wouldn't respond to the instructions from his brain. He could say yes and no and a few other short words by twisting them out of the right side of his mouth.

"I'm eighty-eight," Martin said. His pious visitors had left, but Martin wasn't talked out yet.

"Uh-huh," Billy said.

"I've got diabetes and can't always remember to take my medications. My mind's good, and I can remember way back. I remember you too, Billy. You were in my bible class for a while. You quit after that unfortunate situation with your wife, Clair. Quit church too. You shouldn't have done that, Billy. You probably wouldn't be in the shape you're in now."

Then a nurse brought a man into the room in a wheelchair. "Another visitor for you, Martin," she said.

"Ah, Reverend Brandon," Martin said.

Billy remembered Reverend Brandon, the preacher who had married him and Clair. He'd also assigned Clair to a very conservative Women's Church Circle when he thought her regular Rebecca circle was becoming a hotbed of liberalism.

Clair loved teaching Sunday school. Billy thought back to the first September of their marriage. The summer sun was warming the cornfields. Clair had brushed her hair to a luminous sheen and looked over her shoulder to Billy.

"Are my seams straight, Billy?" Her crepe, one-piece, navy blue dress buttoned from the neck to the waste. The dress had a scalloped white lace collar, long sleeves with gatherings at the shoulders and a pleated waist. She wore a narrow belt and buckle backed with the same material as the dress. Black patent leather high heels accentuated her silk stockings with the seams in the back. Billy drew her image all the way to his heart. Even her voice excited him.

"They're straight all right," Billy had said. "I can hardly take my eyes off you. Wow, you're really something. Stay there. I'll get the Kodak." Clair canted her head, striking a pose, and smiled, as Billy snapped the picture. A picture he could no longer bear to see.

Before marrying Clair, Billy had attended church only occasionally on Communion Sundays, when he felt a need to be forgiven for his sins; which mostly consisted of taking the name of the Lord in vain, having one or two too many beers, and some intimate activities with the Elsville girls. His sins didn't weigh heavily on Billy's mind, though he was quite relieved when, Reverend Brandon had pronounced the forgiveness of all sins. Billy was indifferent about communion now, and at times he was even ready to go to hell.

Nothing seemed fair to Billy, ever since he was a kid, he'd been taking knockout blows. Now booze and a stroke had him on the canvas. Why get up?

Chapter 26
The Hospital
October 1951

WILLIAM F. BARTEL rubbed the last of sleep from his eyes and bathed his face with the golden shafts of morning sunlight as it edged its way through the lace curtains on his bedroom window. He lifted his hand from Clair's basket-sized belly, slid out of bed, kissed her softly on the cheek, and dressed for work without waking her. Billy was convinced there was a heaven on earth and he had found his part of it.

"It could be today," Clair said. Billy was standing by the Brown and Bigelow calendar hanging on the west wall. She'd woke up of her own accord, and watched him quietly as he shaded over October 4th with a pencil. The 1st through the 3rd had already been shaded over and the days from the 3rd through the 9th were underlined in red.

"I've got a red pen all ready to circle the date when we become Mom and Dad," Billy said joyfully. "When it happens, I'm going to write in the time of day, what the weather is like, the weight of the baby, and just what I'm thinking. This calendar will become a cherished family heirloom."

"Come over here and kiss me," Clair said. "I think I'll sleep-in awhile this morning." Clair sat up in bed, they kissed, and Clair held Billy in her arms. "I wish you could come back to bed," she said, knowing full well that Billy had to go to work.

Billy knew it too. After the kiss, he reluctantly said goodbye and went downstairs, where he kindled a fire in the kitchen stove, heated coffee for his thermos, opened a can of Spam, and made sandwiches to take to work. With his lungs filled with the crisp autumn air, Billy walked from his house joyfully, even skipping a little on his way to the car. He picked up a handful of maple leaves from the lawn, drank in their vivid colors with his eyes, then crunched them in his hands and held them to his nose. Billy particularly appreciated the scenes of fall. His mind began selecting sounds from what most others might call 'country stillness'. Billy heard a crow caw, a woodpecker drilling at a tree, a rooster pheasant crowing, a blue jay and a squirrel scolding each other, and a cardinal whistling faintly in the distance. So Billy whistled the cardinal's song and waited for an answer. Within moments, the dazzling tuft-headed red bird flew to the elm in the yard seeking the caller. And Billy, on this dazzling October morning, savored another drink of life.

At two o'clock in the afternoon, Mr. Thurmond hollered from the shop door. "Billy, Clair's on the phone." Billy hurried to the phone. Clair's voice was cheery. "Are you ready to be a father? I'm getting the message from Mother Nature that the baby wants to be born today. Can you come home?" Billy felt Clair's concern, even though she spoke so cheerfully.

"I've been having cramps. The contractions are five minutes apart now. We've got plenty of time, but I might as well go into the hospital and make sure Doc Selkirk will be available."

"I'll be right there," Billy said and turned to Mr. Thurmond. "I better go. It looks like Clair will be delivering today."

Mr. Thurmond put his arm around Billy's shoulders, walked to the main entrance, and patted him on the back.

"Take the rest of the week off, and take good care of our Clair. Congratulations, Billy," he said. You're a lucky man."

Clair was putting the last of her toiletries in her gray canvas satchel with the pink-and-white pattern by the time Billy arrived from work. Everything else she needed for the trip to the hospital had been packed. Her face was flushed and moist with perspiration.

A momentary stab of fear, like a mild electric shock, poked at Billy's brain, but he pushed it aside as expectant father jitters. *I love you, Clair* floated through his mind, but he didn't think now was the time to say it.

"If you're ready, we better be going right away. You don't look very comfortable," Billy said, picking up the satchel and reaching for Clair's hand.

"There's a difference between comfortable and agile," Clair laughed. She waddled through the door with Billy. The edges of hair bordering her face were wet now. "I feel fine. I've been full of energy all day. Just these last few minutes I've started feeling a little unsteady."

It took only five minutes to get to the hospital and two more to find Doc Selkirk seated at the roll top desk in his open office. He looked over the top of the glasses that had fallen forward on his nose.

"Clair, Billy," he said. "Come on in." He nodded to Clair, then to an older dark-haired nurse in a uniform who was standing by the door. "Nurse Johnson here will take you to your room, Clair. Room six. I'll be there and check you over in a minute or two. Billy, you go to the waiting room. We'll let you know how things are going."

Nurse Johnson whisked Clair away from Billy before he had a chance to say *"I love you"* as he had been practicing for this moment. *I'll say it in a little bit*, he thought. *I'll say it when she's settled in her room.*

As he watched them walking away, Billy noticed a spot of blood had dripped to Clair's ankle. "Hey!" he started to say, and then realized Nurse Johnson had seen it too. Probably normal, Billy thought, but the nurse quickened her pace.

Alone in the sparsely furnished waiting room, Billy paced impatiently, figuring Clair should be settled in her room by now. Room six, he remembered Doc saying. So he walked down the hall to room six, intent on telling Clair he loved her, but the room was empty and it didn't look as if she'd ever been there. There was no one in the hall or in Doc Selkirk's office when he passed by on his way back to the waiting room. He paced a bit more, and then slouched on a couch. There was a strong smell of antiseptic and other hospital smells he hadn't noticed before. The couch didn't feel comfortable, so he tried the brown stuffed chair by the coffee table. Looking at the chrome ashtray on a stand, Billy thought smokers must have an easier time waiting. "Be easier if someone else was here too," Billy said aloud in the silent room.

It was an agonizing forty-five minutes before Nurse Johnson came back to the waiting room. "Clair is coming along much faster than we anticipated, Billy. We've taken her directly to the delivery room." Billy followed the nurse to the door.

"I've got to see her."

"Oh no," Nurse Johnson frowned officially. Her crisp white uniform was without a wrinkle starched to stiffness and clean as a whistle. Billy noticed how she nervously hunched her shoulders before she spoke. "Men are never allowed in the delivery room! We'll let you know how things are going. We don't know how long it will be, but Clair is making a full effort now. The baby should be born soon," she said, and hurried away. *Those shoulders of hers are as broad as any man's at the foundry*, Billy thought.

Then Billy paced in the waiting room until he recognized the sound every board in the floor made when stepped on. His pacing often slowed to a stop near a picture of an old man sitting, hands folded, at a table with a loaf of bread. Printing on the gold metal clip at the base of the frame said *Grace*.

At 7:30, when Doc Selkirk finally came into the waiting room, Billy was shaken by the worn and worried look on his face. Doc's weary eyes dwelt too long on the picture on the wall and avoided Billy's eyes when he spoke to him.
"We're having some problems," Doc said. "The baby doesn't seem to be in the right position. We've given Clair a sedative and something for the pain. We're going to have to try to manipulate the baby's position." Doc's mustache and goatee were soaked with sweat and he struggled for words. "It's going to be difficult, but be patient. Things will work out, I'm sure."

The old doctor talked as though things were fine, but he fidgeted with his glasses and his head jerked occasionally with a nervous twitch Billy had never noticed before.

"Do you know her blood type?" the doctor asked.

A jolt of electricity zinged through Billy's brain.

"No. Why? Why? Does she need a transfusion? Is she bleeding?"

"There's no emergency. Just a precaution."

Billy knew the doctor was lying.

"Sometimes these first births can be difficult with older women. I wanted to let you know just in case, that's all. Don't worry. Everything will be all right. I'd better get back to her now," Doc said, and hurried off.

During the next three hours, Billy came to know there were four cigarette burns in the slipcover on the couch, a variety of food stains on the chairs and twenty-three small cracks in the plaster on the ceiling, and he had died many times worrying about Clair. When the doctor came back, he didn't look at Billy and seemed to be talking to the picture on the wall when he spoke.

"Very serious difficulties have arisen," he said. "The baby is breach. Clair is losing a lot of blood." Doc turned full face to Billy and put a hand on his shoulder. "We aren't equipped for this kind of emergency. We should have moved her to Northfield, but I'm afraid it's too late. We can't move her now. I'm going to have to try real hard and use a lot of force to help that baby be born. Otherwise, both the baby and Clair are in real trouble. I don't want to alarm you, but we have to move fast. You should know within the hour." Doc left abruptly.

Stark fear and anxiety filled Billy's mind. He prayed all the prayers he had learned from church and bible class. He desperately needed to talk to someone, so he called Ruth from Doc Selkirk's office.

"Ruth," he said. "I'm at the hospital with Clair. They took her from me as soon as we came here. It's been hours now. Doc Selkirk told me they're having problems. He wanted to know Clair's blood type. Do you know what it is?"

"For heaven's sake, Billy, why didn't you call before now? Her blood type is O positive, the same as mine. My god, Billy. You sound awful. Tell the doctor I can give blood and I'll be there right away. "

Ruth arrived at the hospital at 11:30. Billy was running his hands through his hair. He had a disheveled look. His cheeks were hollow and his eyes were streaked with red.

"Have you heard anything more?" Ruth asked. At that moment, Nurse Johnson came in.

"Billy," she said. "You have a fine baby daughter."

Billy beamed, "Oh, thank God," he said. "Is she okay?"

"Yes," said Nurse Johnson. "Your little girl is fine."

Billy's face softened in relief. "Can I see them now?" he asked. The stiffness of the nurse's uniform had wilted and there wasn't the lift to her shoulders or crispness in her voice as earlier when she spoke.

"Not yet. We're not sure when Clair will be back in her room. I need to go to her now. I'll be back shortly." Nurse Johnson hurried away. At 12:45 Doc Selkirk came to the waiting room. His mouth was turned down. He was fidgeting again, folding and unfolding his arms and hands.

"What's wrong, Doc?" Billy asked, and Ruth clutched Billy's arm for support. Doc Selkirk wiped the sweat from his eyes, and Billy noticed his hands were shaking and his lips were quivering as he led them to the couch where he motioned for both of them to sit down.

"Billy, Ruth." Doc's voice was low and strained. "Clair had a very difficult birth. There were complications. We couldn't stop the bleeding. She passed away about ten minutes ago. I'm sorry, Billy," he said.

Billy slumped forward, near collapse, unable to speak. His hands fell to the floor. His breath caught and stopped in the lump in his throat.

Ruth's hand flew to her mouth. "Oh no, oh no, it can't be!" she shouted. "It can't be, oh no." Ruth began kicking the couch and shouted "No!" with each kick.

Doc Selkirk wiped his brow with his sleeve and looked sadly at Billy and Ruth.

"I'll be back in a little bit. I'll need some more information. Do you want a sedative or anything, Billy?"

Billy sat and stared blankly into space without responding. For a moment, he saw the doctor, then a mental picture of Clair in his mind before he turned it off. The off switch in his brain turned everything off. He didn't think. He didn't hear. He didn't see. Temporarily, at least, he'd succeeded in escaping reality. He didn't see Ruth wad her tear-soaked handkerchief and clench it in her hands. He didn't see or hear her when she told him she was going to call her husband Al. He didn't respond when she tugged at his sleeve and lifted his chin with her other hand and implored "Billy, Billy, Billy what shall we do? Shall I call Reverend Brandon?"

The reality switch clicked on in Billy's mind, he retched and vomited into the ashtray. Then prayers asking God to make this a dream kept repeating over and over in his mind. Twenty minutes later, when Al Krankus arrived, Billy hadn't spoken a word as yet. With glazed eyes he looked at Al, then at the picture on the wall. "Amen," he said. His voice came from deep in his chest. He rose from his chair, and shuffled like a zombie and went out through the main hospital entrance, toward the darkness. He'd heard Ruth and Al following behind him, imploring him to speak.

"I'll need to know … which funeral home you wish Clair to be taken to?" Ruth had asked.

Chapter 27
The Funeral

RUTH TOOK CHARGE of funeral arrangements. Mr. Thurmond told her he had three men out scouting for Billy. She knew Mr. Thurmond and many in the community were thinking the worst.

Ruth slid a chair over and sat by Al when he came in for breakfast. "Oh, Al," she said, putting her hand on his arm. "What's to happen with the baby? Do you think we could take her? Even if Billy comes back, he won't be able to care for her. The nurse said she's healthy and doing just find. They'll have to know something very soon."

Al's expression was noncommittal, but Ruth thought she saw a flicker of light in his eyes when he looked up at her.

"It's okay with me," he said. "I'll go along with whatever you want to do."

Ruth and other relatives were assembled at the church by 9:30. But no Billy.

At 9:50 a.m. a scruffy-looking Billy Bartel arrived at church. He wore a rumpled shirt and tie, his eyes were red-streaked, his face was cleanly shaven but drawn and tired, and he spoke to no one. Ruth watched as Pastor Brandon walked over and put his hand out to Billy.

"Billy, we have been so worried about you. You've been in our prayers. Our sympathy goes out to you. Let us help you. Life must go on. Clair is with the Heavenly Father. She is at peace, now and forever."

Billy stared at nothing. Ruth sat down by him and put her arm around his shoulders.

"Billy, we'll be going upstairs now. We'll want to close the casket before the service. You want to view Clair for the last time, don't you?" she asked.

"No," Billy said.

"Billy, you've got to pull yourself together," she said, feeling suddenly irritated. "We've been worried sick about you. Where have you been? Have you seen your daughter?" Billy turned and looked at Ruth, his eyes in addition to the red streaks, were milky and hard.

"Yes. I stopped by the hospital before I came here. Ruth, will you take her for a while? I'm going to be gone again after the funeral. I'll be back, but I just can't stay around here now."

Ruth patted his hand. "Of course we'll take the baby. What do we call her? Did you have a name picked out? Billy didn't answer, and Ruth closed her hand around his fist as the organ music began. Billy just stared through the funeral service, then drove alone to the cemetery where Clair was laid to rest. At the conclusion of the services, Billy came to Ruth.

"Nancy," he said. "The baby's name is Nancy." Then he was gone.

At six o'clock that evening, Ruth's phone rang.

"Ruth," Billy said. "I'd like to come over tomorrow and talk about Nancy. I'll need to know how to provide for her care."

"Oh, thank God. Where are you, Billy?"

"Home."

"Oh yes, come over anytime," Ruth said. "Are you better now? I'm so sorry. Please Billy, take care of yourself. Come over as soon as you're ready."

"I'll see you tomorrow."

The following day, Billy and Ruth made arrangements for Ruth and Al to care for Nancy.

Chapter 28
Winter

RUTH ADAPTED TO mothering like a wildflower in the Spring—growing and blossoming with every new day; and Nancy thrived.

At first, Billy visited Nancy two or three times a week. She was born with a full head of black hair and sharp little fingernails with which she had already scratched her face by day four of her life. This all seemed to puzzle Billy until the hospital nurses assured him the hair wasn't all that unusual, and fingernails and scratching were customary with new babies. But it was her eyes that everyone noticed. She had searching, inquisitive, blue cloudy blue eyes.

Billy held Nancy when she was awake, but gave her to Ruth when she began to fuss. Often he sat in the old, gray upholstered chair in the parlor with her and they'd both drift off to sleep.

Ruth delighted in Nancy's care. She loved the baby's smell when she'd powder her and apply baby lotion after a diaper change. Ruth liked nothing better than to wrap Nancy in a soft baby blanket, sit in the rocker with her, and give her a bottle. She found something hypnotic in Nancy's inquisitive blue eyes, just like Clair's.

At months old, Nancy was regularly sitting at the table in a high chair for meals. Ruth noticed that Billy often hadn't shaved when he came to visit. And it appeared he'd been drinking. Almost immediately he began to look old, and Ruth noticed he'd begun to shuffle when he walked. His shirt and trousers were always wrinkled and soiled looking, as if he'd worn them for a week. Ruth wondered if Billy even washed his hands after work.

Soon, and too often in Ruth's opinion, when Billy arrived and Nancy was sleeping, he'd have a few beers with Al. They'd just sit silently at the kitchen table drinking from their bottles and glancing at each other occasionally, like two institutionalized slow-witted men looking blankly in whatever direction they faced. Ruth didn't outwardly express her disgust, but one particularly frustrating day, when she was out of Kotex and had to resort to old rags, she looked at the two sour faced men at the kitchen table drinking beer—blankly gazing off in space, apparently without comprehending a thing.

"*Bat dung,*" Ruth muttered to herself. "Their lives are nothing but bat dung, but it's not going to happen to me. I won't allow it. Not as long as I have Nancy, and, for me, that will be forever."

Chapter 29

WHILE NANCY WAS working on Billy, Ruth was working on herself. She thought about the word ADVICE that was penciled on her list. Buster Tiken, the owner and editor of the local weekly newspaper, came to her mind. She'd heard his first wife and daughter died in childbirth. He had remarried and had two more children, both boys. One was severely retarded and lived at home. The other was killed December 7th, 1941, in the Japanese attack on Pearl Harbor. His second wife, whom he adored, had been crippled by polio in 1938.

Hesitantly, Ruth picked up the phone. Her conscious mind said, "You don't do things like this."

"To hell I don't," she said loudly, just before the call was picked up on the other end. "Hay-lo," a male voice said.

"Mr. Tiken?"

"Speaking."

"Mr. Tiken, this is Ruth Krankus. I've just moved into a house on Oak Street -"

"Yes," Mr. Tiken interrupted. "What can I do for you? Do you want a subscription to the paper sent to your house? The rate is seven dollars and fifty cents a year."

"No," said Ruth. "I mean … I mean that's not why I called. I'm sorry; I just wanted to talk to you about something. Could I come down to your office at the paper tomorrow or sometime and just talk for a little while?"

"Are you Al Krankus' widow?"

"Yes, I've only been in town for a short while."

"I know. I'm sorry but we're not hiring anyone right now if that's what is concerning you, but I may be able to help if it's a job you're looking for. I'll be glad to help, but it's awfully noisy down at the shop and a lot of interruptions; I'm usually pretty busy too. I go home for a couple of hours at noon to look after my wife and son; you could stop by then if you like."

"I hadn't thought about a job yet, but if you don't mind, could I stop by around noon at your home tomorrow to visit with you?"

"Okay, fine by me." Buster then hung up the phone and busied himself getting the weekly paper to the press.

"Come on in," Buster Tiken hollered, in response to the knock on the door the following noon. "Come on in. I'm in the kitchen here with Emmy and Phil."

Ruth entered the white wood frame house from the cluttered screened porch, with the obviously homemade wheelchair ramp. She walked towards the sound of the voice through a front room with beige wallpaper, high ceilings, and dark-stained woodwork. There was a sanitary, almost antiseptic, fragrance to the house, mixed with aromas of cabbage and corned beef boiling on a stove. Entering the kitchen, Ruth saw a weathered, wizened looking man, about five-foot-six, lean and clean-shaven. His eyes were quick and squinty. His frame was slightly bent and he looked rumpled in every way. Dark, unruly hair stuck out in every direction on his head. Traces of printer's ink stained his clothing, hands, and face. He removed a bib from an obviously disabled man -maybe thirty-five years old.

A dark-haired, sprightly looking woman, about the same age as Mr. Tiken, was seated in a wheelchair, next to a yellow-and-white checkered oilcloth-covered table. A cardinal-red rose was in her hair. The kitchen was painted brightly with light blue walls, white trim, and blue and white curtains pulled back by sashes to the side. Sunlight seemed to be everywhere. Fresh-cut flowers were on the table and the work counter. Potted plants and hanging, flowering plants were placed and misplaced throughout the room.

"You're Mrs. Krankus, I take it." Buster said. "This here is Phil," he nodded toward the disabled man. "My son. I don't know what he comprehends. Only he does; but I'm sure it's something and that's okay by me." He turned to the woman in the wheelchair. "This is my wife, Emmy."

Emmy struggled to respond. Her voice and her head shook as she replied haltingly. "It's good to meet you."

"Thank you both for inviting me in," Ruth said.

"Can Buster get you some coffee?" Emmy asked again speaking with difficulty.

"Sure, I'd like some coffee, but let me get it." Ruth saw the coffee pot on the stove, found a pink-flowered cup in the kitchen cupboard, helped herself to the coffee and sat in the cane wicker chair offered by Buster.

"I'm afraid I've come here mistakenly," Ruth said. "It's embarrassing. Would you mind if I just had my coffee? It's nice to make your acquaintance. I'm sorry to have interrupted you. I shouldn't have come."

"You're an awfully apologetic young lady." Buster said. "Should I be glad you're not going to do what you came here for?

Did you wish us some harm and you've changed your mind?" Buster's squinty eyes looked directly at Ruth's. "Young lady, you came here with a purpose. I can see it in your eyes and on your face. We seldom get visitors here, especially at noon. Now, don't be embarrassed. Emmy and I and Phil have experienced a lot in life, and hope to experience a lot more. Now just relax and share with us your reason for coming."

"Well," Ruth said. "I thought I was having a lot of troubles and I didn't know how to cope with them, so I made a list of some of the things I could do to make things better. One of the things on my list was to try to talk to someone who really has had trouble and surmounted their adversity. I thought of all the troubles you and your family have had, Mr. Tiken." Ruth was too embarrassed to look at any of the people in the room, so she stared at the vanilla-colored linoleum floor. "I thought maybe you could give me some ideas about life and handling my problems," she said.

Buster squinted his eyes again and walked nimbly to the back of Emmy's wheelchair and put his hand on her shoulder.

"What do you think, Em? That's quite a compliment and good thinking, except that her supposition may be wrong. But I guess we can try to help her see things in a few different lights. There are many ways to look at things, you know. We get a lot of choices. Think we should try to help her, Emmy?"

"Sure," came the struggled reply from Emmy. Ruth twisted in her chair. Her face flushed.

"I feel just coming here and seeing you may be enough," she said.

"I'm going to call you, Ruth, from now on, young lady, and I want you to call us Buster and Emmy, and when you're talking, I want you to include Phil in the conversation and I want you to call him Phil. He won't answer, or even look at you, but we know he's listening." Buster paused and rubbed his forehead with both hands. "Ruth, first off, I'm not coping with my troubles." He spoke forcefully and sternly. "You know why? Because I don't have any troubles. I want you to take a good look at me. I can see reasonably well for a man my age. Watch me." He got up and walked around the kitchen.

"I can walk, all of my limbs are working, and I can hear, touch and smell. I don't have much of any aches and pains. So I figure if I have any troubles they must be conjured up in my mind. I have the ability to conjure up most anything, including trouble. But why do that when I can conjure up things that aren't trouble? You see, sometimes I think Em here has trouble and I think she just assumes Phil has trouble and who knows what Phil thinks. So it all comes down to what you're thinking. Can you see how difficult it is for me to think I have troubles, when I'm sitting here with Emmy and Phil?"

Emmy smiled; her chipped front tooth left a wide gap between her teeth, adding character to her smooth, tanned face. Her dress was black, with a white lace collar. A crocheted cream-colored shawl was draped on the back of her chair. When she spoke her words came from her mouth like they were being pulled up from her larynx on a knotted rope.

"What is trouble?" Emmy asked. "Oh, I know I can't walk, but every day I learn more and more about life. I have learned to travel in my mind; I can see seashores and valleys. With my imagination, I can be at the shop with Buster or any other place I like or want to be. Learning to do this has been a great adventure and I still have so much I can learn before I leave this earth. I have some difficulties, yes. I have difficulty controlling this old body of mine. But with Buster's help we get out, we go to concerts, and ball games and such. I study and live a fascinating life. The mind is not limited by space; I can be in Hawaii before you leave here. This old body is my home, a place to come back to."

"We better give her a rest," Buster said. "I'm continually trying to learn what this marvelous mind can do. I know this for sure. The mind can kill you or the mind can make you well, and all things in between. So you have to give the mind direction. It's lack of direction that's the root of most personal problems. What has been put into our minds, from the time we are born, is what makes most of the differences. At some point, I know we have the ability to decide what stays in the mind. We also have the ability to reconstruct thinking that we no longer agree with. Oh hell, forgive me Ruth. Somewhere along the line here you must have touched my go button."

Emmy ran her tongue across the ragged edge of her tooth. "It looks like old Buster here has found an audience. You better beware, Ruth, he can go on for hours. Then sometimes, you can't get a word out of him for days because all he seems to be doing is thinking." Buster fidgeted in his chair embarrassed for all his talking.

"Talking," he said. "Why she talks just as much or more now than she did before those vocal chords got kind of crippled up. It just takes her longer and sometimes she's harder to shut up than me." Buster laughed, the excitement in his voice a delight to his audience.

Ruth glanced at the frozen face of Phil who hadn't moved. His eyes were unfocused and he hardly ever blinked. A feeling came over Ruth that Phil was smiling inside.

"Now Phil here," Buster said. "I can't communicate with him much, but that's probably my fault. The doctors tell us he won't be with us much longer. We'll share and care for him as long as we can. Emmy has found a way of communicating with him that I don't understand, but I can see it on both of them."

"That's right." Emmy said. "But I don't know how to explain it. He's let me know, in his own way, that it's okay to talk to him or about him; but he doesn't like anyone to act like he isn't here. I talk to him a lot, mostly without saying a word."

"Emmy says God is in the mind," Buster continued. She says everyone ever born shares the same God. The God within you acts with all of the power of the universe. Ours is the free choice to avail ourselves of as much or as little of the power of the universe as we choose. God is love. Fear is an opposite of love. We shouldn't look to organized religions, or the church to be God in the game of life. God is within everyone. Life is thinking. Emmy has taught me that I have the ability to think what I want, and that I can control and modify what I think at any time. Emmy's an artist. She knows the art of thought-killing. Maybe all thoughts that have ever been thought, since the beginning of time, are running around loose in the universe.

"When tormenting thoughts arrive in your mind, they need to be killed for all time. For love to survive and be dominant, the art of killing unwanted thoughts must be attained. The law of substitution is a way of doing this. With the law of substitution, you have a team of about six to eight uplifting thoughts at your disposal. I can think about the day Em and I got married, how happy we were and what a wonderful day it was and all of the wonderful things it has led to. Or I can think of the time I caught a big lake trout up in Canada, or of one of the best editorials I have written at the paper. Specific pre-determined thoughts, just have a few of these ready to go into the game of life for you, when the unwanted, tormenting thoughts light in your mind. Be ready with a thought fly swatter. Swat tormenting, unwanted thought like you would a fly. Then before another, unwanted thought-fly lands on the same space in your mind, put in one of your substitutes and keep it there until your mind is ready to behave. You must control the thought process."

"Yes," Emmy said. "There are perhaps as many thoughts as there are stars in the sky. Ninety percent of them are good. We can expel and eliminate forever those that want to cause us more difficulties. It takes practice and effort to learn this art."

"Emmy can be a great teacher for you," Buster said. "You'll need patience with her though."

Emmy looked at Ruth. "Why don't you come back tomorrow afternoon, if you like. We can discuss some thinking options. Buster will be at work and won't dominate our conversation." A throaty laugh bypassed the stiffened vocal chords. "Don't let fear, guilt, and shame play in your game of life anymore. Put a couple of those bench-warming thought substitutes into the game. The negative thoughts have fouled out, they don't get to play anymore."

"Oh, thank you." Ruth said. "I'd like to come back. I feel like I'm imposing on you, but I feel so much better just having come here." Buster stood up, reached for his hat, and prepared to leave.

"Got to get back to work," he said.

"Thank you, Mr. Tiken, I'll be leaving too. Can I give you a ride back to work?" Ruth said.

"No, it's just five blocks to the shop and I need the exercise. You come back and talk to Emmy tomorrow, if you like. Visitors are good for her. As Buster walked out the door, Ruth said softly, "Can you skip Mr. Tiken?" Buster turned.

"What was that, Miss?" he said.

"Oh, I'm sorry, nothing, sometimes I talk to myself out loud."

A half a block from his shop Buster's mind ran a thought by him. *Skip? I haven't skipped in forty years.*

Clarence Dalton motioned for his three companions at the Rebound Inn to look across the street. "Well I'll be a son-of-a-bitch, look at that little old buzzard." They all watched as Buster Tiken skipped and laughed the last fifty feet to his shop.

"What the hell do you think has gotten into him?"

"I always thought he was a little daft."

The next day Ruth brought apples, oranges, and chocolate stars with her to share with Emmy and Phil. She came to their home twice the following week and busied herself about the house cleaning dishes and making the noon meals. Later, Nancy came by and they washed windows and clothes along with listening to, talking with, and learning from Emmy.

Saturday, three weeks after her first visit, Ruth and Nancy were pan frying trout for the noon meal when Buster came home.

"Look what we caught this morning!" Nancy said. Buster looked in the fry pan. He loved trout. They were rolled in flour and cracker crumbs and frying in butter. The aroma put him by a campfire near the stream.

"They're wonderful. Where'd you catch them?" Buster asked.

"The day hole in the Rock River," Nancy replied. She was at that smart age where her first inclination was to say, "In the mouth," but she didn't know Buster well enough for this yet. When the meal was over, Emmy thanked them warmly. Her eyes sparkled when she looked at Nancy and Ruth. Buster pushed his chair back and wiped butter from his mouth with a napkin.

"Can you type, Ruth?" he said.

"No."

"Can you write?"

"My handwriting is pretty good and I'm a good speller."

"Ever written anything?"

"Not that I recall."

"Think you can learn?"

"If you'd asked me this a few weeks ago, I would have said no, but today with all I've learned in the past few weeks; the answer is yes. Yes, I can learn. I'm going to keep on learning until the day I die. Why?"

"I could use some help at the shop; sending out statements, paying the bills, ordering supplies and the like. I can't pay you much at first, but maybe you could set some type too. Put some ads together for me. If you could learn that, I could spend more time with Em and Phil. Want to give it a try?"

"Buster, you know I'm expecting a baby. I would love to try until the baby comes. Then, maybe we could see what would work out for us afterwards."

"If you want, you can start Monday morning. You're feeling okay, aren't you?" Ruth handed Nancy the dishtowel.

"What do you think, Nancy?"

"You can do it Ruth, you're smart."

"Okay I'll give it a try," Ruth said.

Chapter 30
Dec. 15, 1980

RUTH WAS AT her desk at the *Norwood Journal*, opening the daily mail.

There was a letter postmarked Portland, Oregon. Ruth knew it was from Nancy. She cleared a place for the mail and leaned back in the worn, straight-backed chair.

It had been several months since Ruth had talked to Nancy on the phone. They usually talked at least once a month. She always looked forward to Nancy's Christmas letters. She had saved them all since Nancy's second year at St. Olaf College when Nancy had left home for good. It had been seven years now since Nancy had spent Christmas at Norwood.

Merry Christmas, the letter began. *Here's another letter for your collection. It's been a very restless year. I've resigned my job at the hospital. I haven't been able to advance as I thought I should and the job was not fulfilling. Maybe my expectations were too high after I got my RN degree. It seems the doctors and management are locked into traditional self-serving medicine. They are more concerned about the patient's morning meals being completed by seven a.m. and the window shades drawn in their proper places than they are about the health of the patients. We're understaffed and underpaid. Nursing should be more rewarding.*

Maybe I should go back to the Peace Corps, or try communal living again. I even thought of getting married this year, but some strange things happened on the way to the altar. In March, James, the doctor I have been living with since last January, asked me to marry him. I agreed and we were thinking of a date in November for the wedding. I didn't tell you because I wanted to wait until we got an exact date. Funny, how when you're living together, the days just go by and you don't notice the little changes. I knew I loved James, but something was holding us back.

At first, I thought he was just restless, like me. I always went to work before he did and normally he was up and had breakfast with me before I went to work. Then, he began coming home late from work and oversleeping in the morning. He became irritable and fidgety on weekends. I began to suspect he was using drugs, but I didn't say anything. In September, he just disappeared for a week. The hospital where he works kept calling; they had no idea where he was.

When he came back, he acted like he was never gone and wouldn't talk about it. He said he had gotten things back together and he was okay now. For the next month, he was like his old self again, but by Thanksgiving, he was sliding back into his strange behavior patterns. The Tuesday before Thanksgiving, I couldn't get him awake before ten in the morning. Out of concern, I took Thanksgiving week off from work. He was up early on Thanksgiving Day and went in to work. He seemed quite happy. He was scheduled to be home by three. Dinner was to be at six and I had it all prepared, but he never came home.

On Monday, I received a short note in the mail. It was postmarked San Diego. It just said, "Nancy, I won't be back this time, ever." He didn't even sign his name. It's been nearly a month now and no one has heard from him. Not the hospital or any of his friends. I had a classmate in high school that did something like that one time. He left a note at the Mobil station where he worked after school. "Gone far, far away for a long, long time," it said, but he showed up three years later.

I feel lost and I want to come home. Maybe I can help Daddy in some way. I hope he doesn't have to spend the rest of his life in a nursing

home. I'd like to come home for Christmas and stay with you until I find what I want to do again. Please think this over and give me a call.
Ruth smiled and wiped a tear from her eye.

Two days before Christmas, Nancy parked her Mazda in front of Ruth's house. She had never been one for things—and all the belongings she felt like keeping were packed into the car. The snow was four inches deep and the wind chill twenty below. Nancy looked from the car to the brick front of the two-bedroom rambler. Two eight-foot spruce trees, one on each side of the walk, were strung with blue, red, orange, green, and white Christmas lights. The front eaves were lined with tiny white lights that blinked. A red-felt sash with sprigs of holly lined the outer border of the door. But Darryl, the snowman, with his faded, scotch-plaid scarf; the one she'd given him years ago, was there to greet her. His old brown felt hat was cocked Irish fashion on his white head, and his coal briquette eyes had a sparkle of snow on them. His carrot nose had an icicle drip and his cranberry lips held a frozen smile for her. She couldn't remember why, but the snowman had always been Darryl. She shuddered as the icy winds found their way down the back of her neck.

"Damn cold here, Darryl," Nancy said out loud and walked over and gave a little more tilt to his felt hat. "Top of the mornin' to ya," she said, and pretended the frozen lips replied "Welcome home, Nancy."

Then the front door opened and Ruth, coatless, ran to Nancy, hugged her and kissed her. Ruth then held Nancy at arm's length, the better to look at her. "I love you," she said, then led the way inside the house.

A warm fire was blazing in the fireplace. A whirl of memories ran through Nancy's mind, triggered by the scents of pine from the Christmas tree, along with cinnamon and cloves from cooking ham. And, as always, there was the fresh fragrance of cedar from the green-cut, cedar log near the fireplace. Ruth took Nancy's coat and hung it in the hall closet. She had sold her other house five years ago.

Things had gone well for Ruth the past few years. In 1964, Buster told her he needed to spend more time with Emmy and wanted Ruth to take over the paper. By then, she had been doing most of the publishing and journaling for the paper anyway. With a thousand dollars down on the purchase contract, she bought the *Norwood Journal* from Buster. He continued working with her nearly every day, but never accepted any pay.

In return, Ruth spent a good amount of time on Fridays after the paper was out and on weekends making things comfortable for Buster and Emmy at their house. Buster enjoyed making meals and providing company and care for Emmy, who was now quite arthritic and in the first stages of Alzheimer's. Buster just didn't seem to know how to clean up around the house or put color in things. Ruth saw to the color. She enjoyed the warmth and light that Buster and Emmy showed her whenever she came to the house. She dreaded knowing that soon Emmy would need more care than Buster or she could provide.

"Nancy, there's no lining in this coat," Ruth said. "You can't go through a Minnesota winter in a coat like this. We'll go shopping tomorrow and get you a new one for Christmas."

Nancy found her way to the beige recliner by the fireplace, and settled down with a sigh.

Ruth brought eggnog, brandy, an assortment of cheeses, crackers, pickled herring, and cold cuts, and put them on the coffee table.

"Now, let's settle in for a good, long evening of old-fashioned jawboning," she said.

Nancy asked about her father. Ruth said he would be in the nursing home for at least another month and maybe much longer. The prognosis was uncertain at this time. Ruth hadn't seen much of Billy before this last episode at the hospital. Once in awhile, she used to catch a glimpse of him shuffling by, across the street from the office. Buster used to report on him too. He'd seen Billy in The Red Bird tavern once or twice a month when he'd stop for a coke. Billy was always there, sitting on the same bar stool drinking beer and not talking to anyone. Just sat there, drinking beer and playing "Return to Me" on the jukebox about four times every night.

"We can't just give up on him," Nancy said.

"I think I'm through trying," Ruth said. "He's been to the jag farm—you know, the place they take the drunks—at Willmar, he's had a light stroke and the DT's, and now he's gone from the hospital to the rest home. If he ever gets out again, I expect he'll go back to drinking."

"I know," Nancy said. "You wrote me all about that. I should have come home when he had the stroke."

"I gave up on him when he ran from me at the hospital after Burton was born," Ruth said. "I couldn't understand it. We had just gotten acquainted again and were getting along fine. He's only sixty-three or four now," Ruth said.

"I know," Nancy repeated. "There must be something I could do to make him think young again. He could easily live thirty or more years. I suppose he must resent me something awful for just leaving after high school and never coming back."

"I've been thinking on some ideas for you Nancy," Ruth said. "That might include something for your dad. But let's plan our Christmas and New Year's first, and then we can look to the future."

"Dianne and Lilla Mae built a new house over on Rice Street," Ruth continued. "Dianne still teaches at Norwood and Lilla Mae drives to Northfield to teach."

"Dianne never got outed?"

"Oh, there was an incident the year after you left home. Principal Grant told me about it. One day, a guy who looked big enough to kick start a B-25 bomber came into his office in a rage, demanding that he fire Miss Russy. His name was Randy Rung. He said his daughter wasn't attending any classes taught by a lesbian. If Grant didn't fire her, he was going to the school board. Principal Grant told him Dianne had been elected area teacher of the year, had a long record of excellence, and was sought out for advice by students and other faculty. Randy said he didn't want any excellent education for his kid that taught her to be a queer. Principal Grant and the man continued back and forth for nearly an hour. Finally, Principal Grant ushered the big man over to a picture on the wall. "You like horses, Mr. Rung?" the principal asked.

"You damn right. What about it?" Rung asked.

"This is a photograph of the greatest race horse of the century—Whirleygig."

"Yeah, I sure know of him," the man said.

"They couldn't get him excited around mares, so he never had any offspring, but he was never taken off the track because of it. Are you going to tell me Whirleygig wasn't a great racehorse because he was gay? Would you have stopped Whirleygig from racing because he was queer?"

"Christ, man. I never knew that," Rung said.

Principal Grant said they had a good talk after that, and before he left Mr. Rung said he was going to forget the whole thing. He told Principal Grant that Merford Thrane had put him up to it. "Merford can carry his own damn water," Rung had said.

"Nothing more was heard after that. Oh, there's always talk, but Dianne and Lilla Mae are accepted in the community as excellent teachers," Ruth said.

"How about Christmas plans?" Nancy asked.

"Let's celebrate it here at my house," Ruth said. "Just you and I on Christmas Eve and let's take some food and gifts over to Buster and Emmy on Christmas day."

"That's great," Nancy said. "Then let's have Dianne and Lilla Mae over for dinner on New Year's Day."

Chapter 31

BUSTER PEERED THROUGH the kitchen window, the gently falling snow reminding him of the snow ball fights, sledding, and snow angels of his childhood. He was abruptly jerked back to reality when he saw Nancy and Ruth clamber onto the porch. He could scarcely recognize them with their snowmobile suits on and their hoods tied snugly under their chins. Frost, whipped like cream, covered their eyebrows and lashes. They stomped the snow from their boots. The blizzard's winds rattled the storm windows in their easements so intensely that Buster feared the glass might shatter.

Buster opened the front door and shouted, "Get in here, you two! Take those suits off inside!"

Stepping through the open doorway, Nancy noticed the slack in Buster's shabby sweater sleeves and thought his neck had withered considerable since she last saw him. She couldn't remember how many years it had been.

"Merry Christmas," Buster said warmly.

"Merry Christmas," Ruth and Nancy chimed back.

"Emmy's in here," Buster said, leading them to the kitchen.

The kitchen didn't have the warm baking smells that Nancy remembered. Instead, the air was stale, there were rust spots by the water faucets and the colors in the curtains had noticeably faded.

"Haven't had a storm like this on Christmas day in many years," Emmy said.

"It's tough going out there. I'm glad we only had eight blocks to walk," Nancy replied. But she'd rather enjoyed the walk, challenging the whining storm. She and Ruth turned away from the wind several times and walked backwards to stave off the stinging drive of the frozen snow pellets against their faces, which were now cherry red and glowing in the warmth of the room.

The Christmas tree, a sort of "Charlie Brown" tree with sad dry needles, was in the kitchen. "'Cause that's where we spend most of our time," Buster explained.

Buster looked older to Nancy, but it was Emmy who had changed the most. Her gray hair was all white and had lost what had been its rich, full body. The strands were short, fine and fuzzy, reminding Nancy more of rabbit fur than hair. It seemed Emmy even struggled to hold her head up. Her voice was weak and even her bright eyes seemed to be flickering like a candle flame in a draft.

Ruth and Nancy prepared and served Christmas dinner, filling the kitchen back up with the warmth and mouthwatering smells that Nancy remembered from years ago. As soon as they finished eating, they passed around Christmas gifts and conveniently opened them on the kitchen table. Ruth played Christmas carols on the upright studio piano while everyone gathered around and sang. Emmy nodded off to sleep before they were through.

Late in the afternoon, when the storm subsided, Nancy and Ruth walked towards home, filled with Christmas spirit, Nancy in front breaking trails through the snowdrifts for Ruth.

"I'm going to want to spend more time with the Tikens in the coming months, if I stay around," Nancy said.

You don't know it yet, Ruth thought to herself, *but if my plans work out, you sure will be staying.* "Yes, they are showing their age and the pressures of their life. We need to give them more of our attention now," Ruth said out loud.

Dianne and Lilla Mae spent New Year's Day with Nancy and Ruth. Dianne was as slim as ever. Nancy thought Lilla Mae had put on some weight since the last time she saw her, but her personality had the same bubble, and her salty language had kept pace with the times. However, Dianne seemed more reserved than before. Her eyes nervously shifted back and forth, like she was searching for some sound from her mind.

The first week after New Years, Nancy kept her Christmas resolve and tidied up the Tikens' house. Emmy had nodded off to sleep after the noon meal. Buster hadn't shaved, his eyes were bleary, and his clothes were soiled and rumpled. Nancy thought of asking him to change in order to wash the clothes he had on, but she hesitated, fearing to embarrass him by asking.

"I've been awfully tired lately," Buster said, looking for Nancy's attention. "Must be too much lead in my veins from working with the typesetter." When Nancy reached for the last dish on the table, Buster whispered to her, "How about staying with Emmy for a while this evening? I've something I need to talk to Ruth about, private-like. Maybe I'll take her out to dinner …" he trailed off.

Nancy put her hand on Buster's shoulder. "Sure, anytime," she said.

A week passed. Nancy thought it was strange that Ruth had never shared any information about her dinner with Buster, even though they had been together at the newspaper office every workday. And Buster had been mysteriously absent from the office since.

Nancy pondered the mess she made of herself. Even with the leather apron on, she'd burned a hole in her jeans and blistered her leg with hot lead. Her hands, face, and hair were splotched with printer's ink, and she was exhausted, but the weekly edition of the paper was printed and ready for mailing before she sat down to rest.

"You're quite a worker," Ruth said, and came over and patted Nancy on the shoulder. "You deserve a bonus. How about dinner tomorrow night? Ryan's Inn, okay?"

Nancy figured there must be some special reason for Ruth's asking, but decided to wait her out. "Sure. Why not? I hope they have finger bowls for these dainty fingers of mine!" She laughed, swirling her ink-covered hands in the air.

Ruth and Nancy were ushered to a table at Ryan's Inn. Being out for dinner caused Nancy to think of Dr. James, and the times they had been out for dinner. She was surprised to realize that she hadn't thought about him in days, and had nearly forgotten about his disappearance. It was a fleeting thought that changed quickly to questioning Ruth's motive for inviting her out to dinner. Nancy knew Ruth had something up her sleeve, because when they left the house Ruth said she had a proposition for her. Ruth ordered a bottle of white wine and offered a toast. "Here's to strong women," Ruth said.

"To strong women," Nancy repeated, clicking her wine glass with Ruth's. After a short pause and another sip of wine, Nancy said, "Okay, Ruth. I'm wondering if you haven't been smokin' something. What's up?

"Remember when you worked at Vesta's when you were a teenager?" Ruth asked.

Of course Nancy remembered. She'd been fourteen when she started working after school at Vesta Clemon's old folks' home in Norwood. Vesta spoke Norwegian fluently and

English with a heavy accent—a good-natured, robust woman in her early sixties. She preferred print housedress with old worn slippers. Her "old folks' home" was a large, ten-bedroom, turn-of-the-century house. Vesta's place invariably smelled of cakes, breads, and old people. The living room, filled with couches of mismatched sets and small tables and chairs, served as a visiting area. Coffee and an assortment of baked goodies were always available.

"Okay, I remember. So what?" Nancy asked.

"First, another toast," Ruth said. She raised her glass again. "'The future belongs to those who believe in the beauty of their dreams'— Eleanor Roosevelt."

Nancy drank to the toast and raised her glass. "Here's to whatever's rattling around in that addled brain of yours."

Ruth reached for Nancy's hand. "Well, Buster and I have been chatting. He can't take care of Emmy properly anymore. He has inquired about placing her in the nursing home. They have a place for her, but she'll have to share a room. Buster can't stand to be separated from Emmy and wants to live in the room with her. The three doctors who own the home won't allow it. They don't think it has been done and they don't want to break tradition. Their administrator, Mrs. Yorkland, is a stickler for tried and proven procedures; she agreed with them."

"How does this have anything to do with me?" Nancy asked.

Ruth laughed. "Well, you know, when Buster couldn't take care of both the newspaper and Emmy anymore, he sold the paper to me on contract, and I took over for him and immediately I kind of changed things from the old traditions. Well, we heard the docs would like to sell the nursing home. Buster and I thought maybe you might like to buy it—be the manager and change some traditions, like allowing a husband to be in the room with his wife."

"You been drinking something strange too, Ruth?" Nancy asked. "Even if I was inclined to think about what you said, I don't have the proverbial pot to piss in or the window to throw it out."

"We know that, and we've talked to the docs about a contract. Buster and I would put up the down payment. If you agree and the price is okay with you, we can have the deal done and you can take over March 1st."

"Mother of God," Nancy said. "You and that old lead-ladling print setter are about as conniving a pair as I have ever heard of."

"Adventure, my dear. Never pass up an adventure." Ruth raised her glass for another toast. "To the warm feeling," she said. "Now, let's enjoy our dinner and not speak of it until tomorrow. The lamb here at Ryan's is excellent."

Nancy thought of her school days. She recalled walking the eight blocks to Vesta's at four o'clock, when school was out, bringing a change of clothes with her, unless she'd previously left a change at Vesta's. Her main job had been washing the dishes, pots and pans from the noon meals. Nancy became a favorite of most residents, who began looking out the windows at four o'clock to see if Nancy was coming up the street. When they caught sight of her, frowns turned to smiles.

"Look at her," Biddy Lester said standing at her walker. "Just like California sunshine making its way across the desert."

Those able to do so greeted her at the door. "Hi Nancy, have a good day at school?" Martha asked.

"Need any help with the dishes?" asked Lucy. "Even though I'm in this wheelchair, I can dry for you."

"Sure," Nancy said. "But watch the breakage, Lucy. It's getting so I'm just about breaking even some days with your help."

"Bullshit," Lucy replied. "That was just that one night and I paid you back."

"I know," Nancy said. "I was just kidding. But you do kind of scare me. Sometimes you shake in that chair like a dog shittin' peach seeds."

"Oh, watch your mouth," Lucy said, "Where do you younguns come up with such language?"

Nancy remembered walking down the hall, past Lars Kettelman, who was crutching laboriously back to his room, returning from the toilet. There was only one bathroom in the home. Lars stopped and turned his head toward Nancy who was approaching him warily.

"Keep your hands on those crutches, Lars. You always try for a feel of my butt when I come by, you old fart. One of these times you're going to fall on your head instead of your ass when you try that. It won't be worth the pain."

Lars made a playful swipe at her with his crutch as she went by. "You'd be surprised what I can do, Nancy. I'm not dead yet," he said with a laugh. "Have a good night, you young little fart," he said.

Vesta's closed when state health officials began enforcing more stringent regulations, and the area doctors began to think of a larger, more centralized old folks' home where they could come regularly and practice medicine. They thought they could treat more patients in an hour if they had forty or fifty old folks in one place rather than several places where only one or two people needed their help. So, in 1971, the doctors from the small towns of Norwood, Black Falls, and Hiller joined together and built a new 80-bed nursing home in Norwood.

Chapter 32

ORSON BACON WIPED his wedge-like nose on the sleeve of his tattered, tan suit coat, and then continued pushing the dust mop across the green and white speckled linoleum floor. He stopped in front of the nurse's station.

"I hear the docs sold the home, Mrs. Yorkland," Orson said. "Why didn't you buy it? You still gonna work here?" Orson wiped his nose again and looked directly at the stern-looking nurse.

"None of your damn business, Orson. I didn't even know the place was for sale. Now you get back to work or I may see to it you lose your job even before the new owner takes over." She turned on her heel and went to her office.

Adele Yorkland was miffed. She had worked for and sucked up to those three doctors for over ten years and they didn't even offer her the courtesy of letting her know that the place was for sale. Even though she had no intention of buying the place, she was still pissed off at their lack of respect for the professionalism she had shown through the years. And she was thinking, *who the hell is this young woman—who's supposedly bought the place?* All Adele had heard was that she was a west coast nurse just back from Oregon. For Adele, being a west coast hippie nurse didn't qualify anyone to run a nursing home.

Mrs. Yorkland doubted if she would stay on and work with such a person, but many patients needed her protection. She'd have to stay until she could make sure they would be cared for, or convince them to go to a different home. Adele Yorkland had plenty of places where she could work, but it might be difficult to find one where she could be totally in control as she was at this home.

Nancy consulted with Dianne and Lilla Mae at their house, questioning whether she should go ahead with the proposal to buy the rest home.

Lilla Mae said, "Go for it. You only get one go-around in life. Take a chance. You haven't got much to lose. Let the tail go with the hide."

Dianne thought it would be a great opportunity. "You have a great variety of experience and you've always been compassionate," Dianne said.

Lilla Mae said, "Forget it if it's just going to be the same old shit of warehousing people for a few bucks profit till they turn up their toes and croak. Instead, make it a place of freedom where a couple of old dykes like Dianne and I in a few years could stand in the hall and kiss each other without the whole community having a shit hemorrhage. Give the old duffers a real chance to live like they want to, not like the preachers or a bunch of ass-twitching, puckered-up professionals want them to."

The next evening, Nancy lit a tall white candle left over from Christmas and put it in the east window of Ruth's house. She had never lit a candle like this before and didn't know why she did it now. Something her Catholic friends might do, she thought, but they never use big candles like this. Between her thinking and coffee drinking, the candle had already burned a quarter of the way down. She took a deep breath and then examined her fears and her breath came out in a whoosh. The candle flickered and died. Nancy knew what she had to do.

The next day, Nancy went to visit her father for the first time in ten years. She was skeptical that he would even recognize her, his own daughter, and she angrily thought back to the many times in her childhood that he let her down.

But suddenly, all these thoughts were banished upon seeing the man, grown old before his time, lying in the bed. The old man who in a flood of tears, exclaimed "Namphy! Namphy!" when she walked into the room.

Nancy wanted to reach out to him, but she hesitated, wondering if there was anything that could be done to bring daybreak to Billy's vacant eyes.

"Daddy," she said. A rather sinister-looking old man with one drooping eye, sitting fully clothed on the second bed in the room, interrupted her.

"Deadbeats," he said. "Just a bunch of deadbeats around here."

Nancy observed that the man had peed his pants and brought a strong smell of urine to the room; a situation not unfamiliar to a nurse.

"What's your name?" Nancy asked.

"Peter the fisherman," the main said, while looking at a booger he'd picked from his nose.

Billy muttered something incomprehensible, though a trace of a smile came to his face. Billy tried again and Nancy chuckled. She was sure Billy had said, "He never catches any fish," referring to Peter on the next bed.

Not the best of room pairing, Nancy thought. Then she sat on the bed, next to her father, and held his hands. "I'm going to help you get well," she said.

"I'm tho thory," Billy mumbled.

Nancy helped Billy to sit up in bed. "There is no need or time to be sorry," Nancy said. "We have a future together, Daddy. I'm back in Norwood for good." She held her father in a long embrace, feeling his sobs shake his wasted frame.

Doc Glassrud arranged for Nancy to spend two weeks at a nursing home in St. Cloud, to mix with management and staff and acquaint herself with the day-to-day responsibilities of running a nursing home. The thought of being so responsible for so many people sent shivers running down Nancy's spine all the way to her feet, which began growing cold. *And the name 'nursing home'- there has to be a better name*, she thought.

The two weeks in St. Cloud, though informative, only made Nancy more determined than ever to make the last few miles of life a little more tolerable for as many people here on earth as she could. She kept an open mind about finding a descriptive name for her new facility. She felt the name would be a great deal to the well being of the people in her care. She was convinced that if they thought it was the end of the line for them, then that was exactly what it would be. Nancy imagined a far different kind of place than the one she experienced during her two weeks at St. Cloud. She pictured a place of peace, dignity, respect, full of learning, and even adventure. *People should be given the opportunity to approach death as if it were a curtain call*, Nancy thought. *If there are risks involved, let them choose for themselves as much as possible. Every opportunity of independence rightly theirs should be given to them. Every ounce of independence should be honored, that independence would be respected, as long as there is a heart beating in the chest*, she said to herself. Then she thought she was sounding a bit like a preacher and wondered if she had the guts to carry out these lofty ideals.

Ruth's kitchen was a remarkable place of comfort for Nancy.

"Mind if I have a beer, Ruth?" Nancy asked, while opening the refrigerator door. "I'd like to get a place of my own now, so I can slop around a bit. I'm not as tidy as you are."

Ruth ushered Nancy to the beige recliner by the fireplace. "I know you can be comfortable, or even sloppy around here, but I agree, you should have your own place. I'll help you find a place, when you're ready. How are things going at the new 'home'? When do Buster and Emily get their room?"

"All I've done so far is check out the bookkeeping system and try to size up that Mrs. Yorkland. I need an excellent business administrator to work with, a person who is not a bottom-line, for-profit administrator. So far, I'm not impressed. Mrs. Yorkland is an organization–plus type. She's so cold, a fly on her would freeze, even on a hot day."

Ruth poured herself some black coffee, pulled a chair up alongside Nancy and sat down. Nancy sipped her beer.

"Do you know how old Mrs. Yorkland is?" Nancy asked.

"About forty-five. She's a widow, you know," Ruth said.

"I think she resents me. Her voice gets as thin and sharp as her features, when she speaks to me. In her mind, she knows how things should be done and expects them done her way by everyone employed at the home. With the staff, she's commanding; but when the doctors are around, she's a condescending, twentieth-century nurse. She gives them a strong dose of 'Yes Doctor, Nurse Goodness will take care of everything for the wonderful doctors.'"

Ruth patted Nancy on the knee. "I think it's time for you to just be yourself," Ruth said. "Show her your style and see if she adjusts. You will learn quickly if she's too rigid and too old to learn."

Chapter 33

SEVERAL WEEKS LATER, Nancy bought an early-thirties, two-bedroom, wood-frame house on Snake Alley, next to Rock River. It seemed a quiet house. This morning, in her frigid bedroom, she listened to the gurgling rush of the river downstream from the 'day hole', one of her favorite girlhood trout fishing sites.

After using a combination of meditation and self-hypnosis to energize her body, Nancy brought herself to full conscious awareness, preparing her mind for the coming day. Nancy often employed these mental exercises along with yoga, and the law of substitution, which she had learned from Ruth, to enrich her daily life. When testing the effectiveness of the processes, Nancy had found she was able to increase or decrease her heartbeat and her blood pressure through thought control.

She opened her hands, which were cupped over her face and eyes. The bedroom walls were painted off-white and bare of other decoration, except for the west wall, where a round thermometer, the size of a pie plate, hung in the center of the room near the ceiling. It had a blue, metal border and its half-inch red dial pointed up to thirty-nine degrees. "CAWS FEED MILL," in two-inch red letters, decorated the crest of its upper semicircle.

Nancy pulled the top flannel sheet tightly around her neck and hugged herself for warmth under three layers of covers. She momentarily wished James were snuggling next to her. Nancy had meditated the previous evening. Just before she slept, when her mind was clear of all thought, she made a request of her subconscious mind to come up with a fitting name for the nursing home. Consciously, she hadn't been able to think of anything appropriate. She had learned meditation from an Indian Yogi while in the Peace Corps. Leaving messages for her super-conscious, as a rule, worked well for her.

The next morning, before she was fully awake, a very distinct voice along with a printed message came to her. Inside Nancy's forehead, where pictures of the mind are made, were the words HOLIDAY FOREVER, five inches high and just more than a foot long, they appeared in a dark Irish green color, seemingly suspended in the air. The picture was to the right of the center of her face, at eye-level. A voice said clearly, "Holiday Forever".

At first, Nancy questioned the connotation of "Holiday Forever". Then she began perceiving a totally different concept, regarding care and consideration of people who, for whatever reason, weren't able to fully manage their lives without assistance.

She thought of her own eccentricities. What would happen if she were in a supervised home and attempted to sleep in the buff in a cold room with the windows open in the middle of winter? Like she was now. It would be *tranquilizer time*.

She wondered how she could change institutionalized care, with all its traditions, that resulted in warehousing people, tranquilizing them if they were independent, and merely placating them till they were gone?

"Who am I to question or argue with my super-conscious mind?" she said aloud. "The guests in the new place will be treated as guests ... 'on Holiday—Forever'."

Nancy threw back the covers. "Yeeeowww," she said, her naked body engulfed in a blanket of icy air. She leaped from the bed, ran down the hall to the bathroom, turned on an electric auxiliary heater, slipped into a white terry cloth bathrobe, and brushed her teeth while waiting for the room to warm up.

After showering, putting on her undergarments, and draping her robe across her shoulders, she called Ruth.

"Ruth, I've thought of a name for our new venture. I thought I'd better run it by you. I don't want to lose my funding source over a name. The name is 'Holiday Forever.'"

"Did I hear you right? Holiday Forever? Holiday Forever what?"

"Just 'Holiday Forever'. Do you like it?"

"Goofy, like you Nancy. Where in heaven's sake did you come up with that name?"

"My super-conscious gave it to me last night."

"Oh, that's different!" Ruth laughed. "We aren't about to argue with the super-conscious, are we? Sure, go ahead, Nancy. I think it's quite refreshing. You do know, however, that this conservative community is going to give you a bad time about it, don't you?"

"Maybe for a while, but it'll catch on when people who live and work there get new ideas and change some of their thinking habits. How could you expect creativity if it continued as the Norwood Nursing Home? When you get old, do you want to end up in the Norwood Nursing Home, or do you want to go on 'Holiday Forever,' Ruth?"

"God, Nancy. Just think. You're all settled down, right here in town, where I won't have to worry about you anymore. I raised a pretty good girl, huh?"

"Don't put your worry cap away just yet. I don't know if the state and community will adjust to some of the freedoms I have in mind for people at Holiday Forever. They're special, you know. Not all laws and rules and regulations apply to anyone at Holiday Forever. We're going on a new trip, Ruth. Get ready for the ride. Don't be afraid to haul back on the reins, if you think I've gone too far. And thanks, Ruth. I love you. Bye."

"Bye Nancy," Ruth said.

Nancy poured herself the second cup of coffee. Two stints in the Peace Corps, a couple years of commune living, and a nursing degree didn't necessarily qualify you as a care facility administrator. She had learned how to be free, and now she had to show elderly and infirm people how to enjoy more freedom now than at any other time in their lives. And teach them that it's never too late for adventure, especially for those who have been held back and victimized by time, place, and culture. And she intended to allow individuals to dictate their own morality, as long as there was no harm or danger to others.

By 8:00, the unbridled March winds had blown in a snowstorm. Frigid northwest winds played string music with every twig and branch on the trees. Temperatures were near zero. Snow swirled into five-foot drifts around Nancy's car.

Nancy, dressed in her snowmobile suit and boots, stepped out into the storm, which had silenced even the crows. Instead, she heard only whining wind gusts and the clap of loose shutters on houses.

When she entered the rest home, her cheeks were wet and red, and her eyelids and eyebrows were caked with frost. Mrs. Yorkland was there to greet her. *Twentieth Century Miss Efficiency*, Nancy thought. Mrs. Yorkland's white uniform was neat and crisp. Not one of the shiny black hairs on her head was out of place.

Nancy unzipped the suit, pushed back her hood, and shook out her long sandy hair. "Good morning, Adele," she said. Mrs. Yorkland looked annoyed. "This blizzard has me so refreshed and full of energy that I'd like to begin getting acquainted with all of the staff and making some changes I have in mind. I'll meet you in your office, after I've had a chance to see my father."

"Hi Daddy," Nancy said. Billy was sitting up in bed when Nancy came into his room. Peter the Fisherman was sleeping.

"Namphy," Billy said and flashed a one-sided smile.

Nancy gave him a hug, straightened his pillow and combed his unruly hair. "I'm going to assume your mind is working better than your body at this time."

Billy nodded.

"So, okay. Today we begin to use your mind to help your body get well. I also expect it may have been the abuse of your mind that got you here in the first place.

Billy made a one-eyed frown and twisted the side of his mouth that he could control. Peter the fisherman, though asleep, passed a drumbeat of gas.

"Daddy, are you ready for some mind exercises that might put you well on the road to recovery?"

"Yeph," he said, and reached for Nancy's hand.

Nancy held his hand in both of hers. "We can begin with what is called the Law of Substitution. Here is what I want you to do. I'll get a large note pad for you to write on, and a way to secure it, so it will be useful. Your first task is to write down five or more of the most pleasant memories of your life—experiences, places, happenings you'd like to revisit. We'll take this step-by-step. Okay? I'll check back with you later. Mrs. Yorkland is waiting for me now."

Mrs. Yorkland was pacing about the room with a deep frown on her stony face, as Nancy entered her office.

"Well, here goes," Nancy thought. "If there are going to be changes around here. We might as well start now."

"Adele," Nancy said. Nancy observed the same stiff reaction as the first time she called Mrs. Yorkland 'Adele.' "I would like you to organize a summary of each resident here at our facility. Not a medical summary, but your thoughts about them. When you're through, we can survey from room to room. I like to meet each resident personally. I'd like absolute frankness in the assessments you give me."

A look of apprehension and puzzlement crossed Mrs. Yorkland's face. "Yes, Miss Bartel," she replied curtly. "Most of the information you request is already in my files and memory. I can have it ready for you in a couple hours."

Nancy appraised Mrs. Yorkland and with a sly, friendly smile, and decided to push her luck in order to analyze the response.

"You know," Nancy said. "I kind of think if folks around here hear me referred to as Miss Bartel, they might get the idea that I'm some kind of crotchety bitch. Now, let's take the name Nancy. Ever heard of a Nancy bitch? Even if you say it sternly it doesn't sound crotchety, does it? Now, so everyone understands, I'd like to be called Nancy, except when I'm being a crotchety bitch. Then anyone who likes can call me Miss Bartel. This will be a simple way of communicating and it will let me know the mood I'm projecting, okay?" Nancy thought Mrs. Yorkland looked mildly flustered, and perhaps a little amused.

"Yes, Miss Bartel." Mrs. Yorkland looked at a picture of Florence Nightingale on the wall and gruffly cleared her throat. Her features softened, then she turned, offering Nancy a pleasing smile. "I mean Nancy," she said.

Maybe there's more to this stiff old broad than I thought, Nancy mused. *She's definitely clever and might even be more adaptable than I thought.*

Nancy lowered her voice and added warmth. "Adele, I want to get started here on the right foot," she said. "I don't know much about administering a facility of this nature. I've been told that you're a very efficient and loyal administrator. I'd like for us to work together. We need your skills here. I believe I know a lot about people, and I have my own rebellious ideas about life and how people should be treated. We'll be making some radical and controversial changes that will be shocking to traditionalists, moralists, and a few other 'ists'. I'm hoping we can work together and enjoy it."

"Miss Bartel—ah, Nancy. I've worked at this home since its very first day. I can tell by your expressions and your eyes that you've got a preconceived notion of what I'm all about. I've a responsibility to the residents of this home. I'll stay on for six months, perhaps more if we get along. If you're up to the responsibilities of your job, I'll give it a try."

"When I was in grade school, I was first taught arithmetic and the alphabet with flash cards," Nancy said. "I'd like for you or someone to get all the pictures available of everyone who works here and as many residents as possible. Then I hope you would spend at least an hour each day with me, using the pictures as flash cards until I know every person by their first and last name. I want to know everyone by their first name within a week."

"Yes, Miss Bart—ah, Nancy. I think I have a picture of nearly all the employees in my files and most of the residents have photos they're very proud of. It won't be a problem at all. We can have your first session any time after noon today," she said.

"Perfect. Now, how about if we go for a tour of the facility and you can introduce me to the employees," Nancy said.

Adele walked out of the office. The first employee they met was Orson Bacon, a portly handyman, janitor and a retired farmer. Orson could fix anything, sometimes not for long, however. He was five-foot-three and pear-shaped with a head of thick brown hair, evenly trimmed at mid-ear level, which accented his round face and evenly spaced round eyes. He had a low forehead and a broad featureless nose that spilled across his face.

"Orson," Adele said. "I want you to meet our new proprietor and executive director." She paused a moment before continuing. "This is Nancy Bartel. She wants you to call her Nancy, and later on, when you get to know her better, if you think she's a crotchety bitch, you may call her Miss Bartel. That procedure goes for me too."

Orson blinked his grape-like eyes and ran his coat sleeve across his nose. "Well, Jesus H. Christ! What the hell is going on here? Glad to meet you, Nancy." Orson flashed a toothy grin, which puffed his cheeks out much like a gopher.

Nancy took note of the style of the new Adele, who had changed her demeanor without exhibiting a hint of emotion. Nancy liked Orson's face. Humor seemed to be hidden in it. "May I call you Orson?" she asked.

"Sure as shit," Orson said.

"Orson!" Adele said.

Nancy received the same kind of introduction from Adele wherever they went. Some people were amused, some offended, and some puzzled.

Mrs. Yorkland, the bitch, likes to play games too, Nancy thought. She was thoroughly impressed, and admitted to herself that

Adele was quick on her feet—not afraid to take a risk—a woman of tremendous confidence. Nancy thought this old girl might be all right. As her Uncle Al used to say, "She might do to ride the river with."

Their first flash card session was after the noon meal, in Nancy's office. Adele, a "Miss Efficiency", wasn't wasting any time. She had an explanation with each picture that she flashed.

"This is Ruby Workman. She does general cleaning in residents' rooms and bathrooms. She's very quiet. Her husband beats her. He's a drunk. She's thirty-three years old; they have six kids. She works at other part-time jobs when she gets the chance. She's extremely considerate of the residents, and they all like her."

"This is Hazel Wyseth, classified as a health care worker. She works hard and gets her job done. She's somewhat of a moralist. She is liked or disliked; depending on the personality and opinions of those she is in contact with. She's married, has a couple of kids—has henpecked her husband for twenty years."

"This is Katey Long, our chief cook. Good person—doesn't socialize very much with the other help or the residents. Usually has a bottle of Jack Daniel's whiskey close by somewhere—kind of nips away at it all day, sometimes gets a little social and unsteady just before she goes home. She's a widow. Probably will retire in a couple of years. We need to be looking to train someone to replace her. Says she would like to stay on part-time or when needed after she retires."

"This is Jason Drew. Works in the kitchen after school. He's a junior in high school. Comes from a poor family, needs the job for spending money. Smart kid, a real joker. Plays a few practical jokes on the help or the residents from time to time.

Katey doesn't say much about him, but she thinks the world of Jason."

"This is Lucille Wand. She's twenty-eight. Likes men. Men like her, women generally don't. She's a health-care specialist. Goofs off more than she should. Takes good care of men, neglects some of the women. She's married, appears to be a good mother to her children. She likes other men and loves them whenever she gets the chance."

"This is Susan Pelt, forty-three, a registered nurse. Lives on a farm with her husband and three children. She doesn't need to work for money, and her work here doesn't seem to interest her all that much either. I think she needs an escape from home-life where she's treated as a second-class citizen. Suffers from servant, wife, and mother syndrome. Laughs a lot at inappropriate times, otherwise very pleasant."

The editorial comments impressed Nancy. She viewed the staff as acceptable, but wondered if they would be able to break from the rigidity of the place. She hoped their attitudes would change, with the dose of liberalism she was planning to administer. To Nancy, the sharp-featured Mrs. Yorkland appeared to adjust to her surroundings like a chameleon. *She might be just what I need around here*, Nancy thought. *She likes her job and I think she'll do what's needed to keep it.*

Chapter 34

NANCY LOOKED UP from the desk when Adele, ready for a flash card session, entered the office. Nancy wondered how many black sweaters Adele had. She always wore black sweaters, like they were her own private uniform. The sweaters always looked as if they had just been purchased or picked up at the dry cleaners.

"Good morning," Adele said. "I have a complete set of pictures for you now."

"Would you please shut the door?" Nancy asked. "We need to have a talk."

Adele shut the door, pulled up a chair in front of Nancy's desk, and sat down.

"Before we start with the flash cards," Nancy said. "Tell me what you think of my new name for the home. It's Holiday Forever."

Adele paused and shifted her posture in the chair. Her shoulders sagged and she half closed her eyes.

"If I didn't need this job for the money, I'd quit," she said, twisting in her chair, as if trying to screw it into the floor. "The way introductions went last week was enough to last me for a week or two. Now this. Why don't we just call it 'Surprise a Day Home'?"

"Oh, come on, Adele. It's not that bad. You can live with it awhile, can't you?"

"Yes, Miss Bartel." Adele's lips had thinned and she threw her shoulders back.

"Oh, so now you're using the term 'Miss Bartel' to express your disapproval of something you feel you have to go along with. You're a crafty bird, Mrs. Yorkland—I mean Adele."

Adele took her eyes off Nancy, rose from her chair and walked to the window, gazed out and without turning around spoke. "If I knew you better, I think I might be enjoying this exchange. All we're doing is sizing each other up and vying for position," she said.

Nancy stepped from behind the desk. Something in the tone of Adele's voice was comforting.

Adele turned from the window and faced Nancy. "I haven't decided if I want to work for you or not, yet. You're quite the challenge. You've seen a lot in life I've never had the opportunity to see. I've experienced a lot of things you have little or no experience in. It's going to be tough for you around here without my cooperation."

Nancy walked by the window and stood near Adele.

"Adele, one of my goals in life is to be a smarter person tomorrow than I am today," she said. "And that means being a different person." She looked Adele straight in the face. The two women were almost the same height. "I call that learning," Nancy said. "If we are exposed to something new or different and don't change, we haven't learned anything. Learning without change is impossible. Now, if you're going to insist on holding to all of the old ways around here, we're going to have a tough time getting along. So far, I am very impressed with your flexibility, your honesty, and ability to be straightforward. If you think you can help me change this place for the better, I'd love to have you stay on." Nancy knew the key to her success was a caring staff. Adele had put together a good staff, and during the last week, Nancy had also seen her caring side.

"Change!" she said. "I'm not against change, but if I'm here, I'd like to be a part of the change. Maybe I've some ideas too. I have a real and genuine interest in the people here. Oh, I'm sure you've heard all about the 'rigid Mrs. Yorkland," and you've formed your opinions. If I stay, I'd like for you to take your pre-formed opinions and stick them where the sun doesn't shine." Her voice was loud and high pitched and she walked back and forth in front of Nancy. "Before this week, I had some pretty solid opinions about you, too. I formed them from what I had heard from others. I wasn't going to like you. Maybe I don't have to like you, but I'd like to try to work with you. I'd like to be a part of the decision-making process and work together, make this somewhat of a 'we' operation. With all of my experience, I think we could make a good team. I want to be part of the process and have my thoughts and experiences evaluated before major decisions are made. If that's okay, count me in on this 'Holiday Forever'." She shook her head. "Oh Jesus—Holiday Forever!" She chuckled.

Nancy thought Adele was enjoying the session. She was surprised, but she liked the new Mrs. Yorkland.

"You're right," Nancy said. "I've been thinking too much like I could run this place alone. I'm glad you brought it to my attention. I won't be making decisions in a vacuum. I need your help. Thanks for offering. Let me know who else you think can be brought in on the team."

"If you're open for some advice, let me give you some," Adele said. "You're going to be making a lot of changes and rocking a lot of boats around here. I can see that already. I've got a few boats I'd like to rock, too. You're going to be challenged in many ways—by the staff, the residents, and the community. Have you thought of legal advice?"

"You mean old Loophole, the lawyer? He's a patient—er, guest here now, isn't he?"

"No, I was thinking of Andy Curtis," Adele said. "He lives out in the country. He comes up here once in a while and helps some of our residents with their business. He never overcharges and does a lot of work pro bono. The folks here like him a lot. Besides that, he's not married—good looking and about your age."

Nancy laughed at Adele's efforts to be matchmaker. Then she remembered working in the hospital in Portland. The head nurse wasn't the best looking and often she was a bitch at work. Some of the nurses thought if they could get her laid, she'd be all right. Could this be Adele's strategy?

"They say lawyers are always screwing somebody," Nancy said. "Are you suggesting something, Adele?"

Adele's lips thinned again with embarrassment. She didn't know if she was quite ready for all of the frank brashness of the new owner of Holiday Forever.

"Let's forget the flash cards for today," Nancy said, deciding not to push the issue. Instead, she brought up the subject of a room for Buster and Emmy, and she was pleasantly surprised when Adele thought it was an excellent way to start breaking tradition.

"You take care of the bureaucrats," Adele said. "I'll have a room ready for the two of them in a few days."

Their meetings with people began at the main nurses' station in the lobby. A staff person Nancy hadn't seen before stood behind the counter. Her face looked sun baked, with more creases than a fifty-year-old cowboy. Her bare elbows showed through the worn fabric on the sleeves of the faded pink sweater that she wore over her starched white nurse's uniform. An abundance of kinky brown hair was tied in a tight perm that matched the craggy look of her leathery face.

"Zona Kovich—head nurse," Adele announced.

"So, you're the new boss around here," Zona said. "You're quite a looker, aren't you?" Zona intoned with a gravelly voice. "It's going to take more than looks to run this place. I've heard some good things about you though. Knocked around pretty good in your time, they tell me, and made some mistakes along the way. Hope you learned from them. I'll just wait and see. Seems as if you've gotten off to a good start. I understand you've got Mrs. Yorkland here," she tilted her head towards Adele, "being an Adele. That's good for her. Mrs. Yorkland can be a pain in the ass once in a while."

Adele smiled, and Nancy knew she was going to like Zona Kovich. When they shook hands, Nancy noticed how strong, warm and weathered Zona's hands were.

"You look and act like you might have knocked around a little yourself, Zona," Nancy said.

"I've got two grown sons who have turned out okay and a husband who has stuck with me for some thirty years, but you're right. I have knocked around a little in my day. Seen a lot of life, you might say. Well, I've got work to do." Zona leaned over and tied the white laces on her black tennis shoes. "Nice meeting you, Nancy Bartel," she said. "I hope we work well together. It'll be that way or it won't be at all."

The first three rooms, those closest to the nurses' station, were occupied by elderly women, two to a room, all widows and all incontinent. Three of them weren't able to hear. Of the three who were ambulatory, two talked mostly to their dead husbands, and another chattered in a language which no one understood.

Mabel Torgerson, in the next room, was a sprightly, smoothed-faced, blue-eyed lady in her eighties. She liked to talk and had a fun-loving manner. Six weeks ago, her neighbor had found her, passed out, in her farm home. She spent a week in the hospital at Northfield. The doctors said it was her heart—prescribed some medication, and referred her to the rest home, where she hadn't had a reoccurrence since. Her area of the room was orderly and clean, as was that of her roommate's, Edith Chase.

Edith was a raw-boned woman, also in her eighties, whose stern look and deep-lined face showed her age. Edith's gnarled hands gripped the black rubber top of the wheels on her wheelchair as she listened to Mabel and Nancy's conversation. Her right leg, just below the knee, was missing. Nancy introduced herself. Edith merely said "Oh."

"How long have you been here?" Nancy asked.

"Nearly a year now. I couldn't take care of myself after my brother died." The stoic look remained on her face. Later, Adele told Nancy that Edith was diabetic and arthritic. She had never been married and had spent her adult life as a homemaker for her bachelor brother on the farm where they had been born. A Norwegian Lutheran, she had lived a sheltered, judgmental life, dictated by strict orthodox religion.

Mabel, however, was free-spirited and outgoing. Her husband had died in this very home six months earlier. On Saturday nights she and her husband often enjoyed the evening out with a few beers.

Edith had never had a beer or any alcoholic beverage. To her, a person who took a drink was a drunk and a sinner against God. Her judgments, however, didn't extend to Mabel. She rather liked the stories of the rowdies at the Gables tavern. As roommates, they got along well.

Cloudy Slowcome, in the next room was fifty-nine, dying from natural causes: emphysema from a lifetime of smoking, cirrhosis of the liver from a lifetime of drinking, and worn and painful arthritic joints from a lifetime of hard menial labor which began when he was too young and his body was still growing.

Cloudy was a local legend for telling tall tales, as well as being in and out of trouble. Only his eyes and husky voice retained signs of life. Cloudy rolled his eyes in Nancy's direction, and asked Adele to prop him up in bed and tidy up his wild red hair.

"Holy shit," he said. "You're the new boss around here. Well I'll be God-damned. Imagine that. Let me get a good look at you. Jesus, woman, you're something else—fine as frog hair. Why … you're built like a brick shithouse. It sure as hell won't be bad dying here if you're going to be around. Just lookin' at you makes me think I've already died and gone to heaven."

"Thanks for the compliments, Cloudy," she said. "We have to be going now, lots of people to meet. See you later."

"God, I hope so," Cloudy said.

Before entering the next room, Adele cautioned Nancy. The guest, the Reverend Chris Overland, had been the pastor of the Evangelical Norwegian Lutheran Church at West Prairie for twenty-five years, living and preaching righteousness throughout all his years at the church. His personal life was exemplary. A devout family man, he was much admired by the entire congregation, as were his model wife, two sons, and a daughter.

"About a year ago," Adele said, "he began having an unusual amount of headaches and began acting peculiar and unconventional. Swearing began to be a significant part of his language, even though he had never been known to swear, even to his close family. His bizarre behavior might last for ten or fifteen minutes, or even a half hour, after which he would be near normal and not recall that he had acted abnormally. He was forced to take a leave of absence from the church, and went through exhaustive medical examinations. An inoperable tumor was found on his brain. There is nothing a hospital or medical facility can do for him. He's fifty-seven. His condition is progressing rapidly. We are doing our best to care for him here. Don't be surprised by his language.

"Good day, Reverend Overland." Adele said. The Reverend had on a brown suit, a white shirt, and a paisley tie. He sat in a straight-backed wooden chair, his head bowed and his hands folded in his lap.

"Bless us, Lord. Amen," he said in a clear, deep voice before looking up.

"I want you to meet Nancy Bartel," Adele continued. "Nancy, this is Reverend Overland." His thin brown hair grew long on one side of his head and was combed over a bald spot. He was tall, slim-faced, and well groomed.

The Reverend looked at them solemnly and in a gentle voice asked, "Oh, are you two from the Ladies Aid?" He looked down and wrung his folded hands.

"Fuck the Ladies Aid," he said. "Come in, come in. Don't stand there in the narthex, you assholes." He stood up, smiled, and bowed. "The Ladies Aid meets in the church parlor at nine," he explained. Then his eyes glassed over. "Now what was it you pussy-breaths wanted again?" he asked.

Nancy hunched her shoulders and stared at the man, at a loss for words.

Adele's composure was intact. She clasped the reverend's hands in hers and said, "We came for the Lord's blessing and to be of assistance in your ministry."

"I'll be here full time now, and I wanted to meet you and see if there is anything we can do to make your stay here more pleasant," Nancy said, regaining her composure.

"God damn it, I don't know. Sometimes I know something, sometimes I don't. Tits, tits, I know you got goddamn tits. Come over here to the font. I'll baptize them and give them a proper name. I can tell they have never been baptized. We'll need godparents for them. Where are the godparents?"

Suddenly, Reverend Overland's eyes cleared. He stood, silent and still, staring into space, as if in a trance for a moment. He walked to his bed, perspiring profusely. He propped himself up on his pillow, in a sitting position and then looked in surprise at his guests.

"Oh, I didn't notice you two come in," he said. "Who's your companion, Adele?"

"This is Nancy Bartel. She and I will be working here together on a regular basis now." She spoke as if the previous conversations had never taken place.

"That will be wonderful. A fresh new face always makes for good atmosphere. I have a brain tumor, you know. I had to quit the ministry. However, for the most part I think I could continue. I certainly can minister to those here in the home who feel the need of the word of the Lord. Be sure to call on me. I'll be glad to help any time. The Lord be with you both."

"Well, thank you very much," Nancy said. "I'll keep that in mind. We have to go now and meet our other guests."

On the way to the next room, Adele told Nancy that the Reverend sometimes had as many as three or four quite normal days in a row. "We never know what to expect," she said, "but don't think ill of Reverend Overland, Nancy. He has been a good man during his life. He needs our compassion and understanding." Adele wiped her eyes.

Nancy found that about sixty percent of the guests were women. Fifty percent of all guests had difficulty with verbal communications. Her guests represented a cross section of society with unique individual needs and reasons for being at Holiday Forever. Words couldn't express the challenges that Nancy had seen.

When the last tour was completed, she walked silently with Adele to the office. "We've a lot of work to do, Adele." She said. Nancy wondered if she was up to the tasks that lay ahead. Momentarily, she questioned the wisdom of even trying.

"It's been a while, "Adele said, "since you've been around people warehoused to die. If you get callused to that, it's time to quit. You better decide now what you're here for, and whether it's worth it, or forget it."

Nancy walked slowly to her desk and shuffled papers near the typewriter. She felt indecisive and knew Adele sensed it. *Thank God for this strong woman*, she thought.

"I'll share some feelings with you," Nancy said. "I've some doubts right now that I need to get over. I'm thirty-one years old; I've got a lot of life ahead of me. I have lived a varied, exciting, and mostly carefree life. Am I ready to make this place and its people my life's work? If I am, I need to know why. And right now, I'm not sure I know why. Can you tell me why, Adele?"

"No. You have to be able to answer that for yourself," Adele said. "But I asked that same question of myself for quite a few years. Then I quit asking and just existed day by day. After you showed up, I started asking again. I thought I almost had the answer. After all these years, I looked at you and your expectations, and thought maybe you could make a difference. I thought this might be my chance of changing things and making the lives of a few people a little better. I thought maybe you were someone with enough courage to let these people live until they die."

"You saw how easy it is to take their personalities away, to make them docile and wait patiently until they die," Adele continued. "If they don't fit into our view of how they should act, we give them Valium. Some of these people have lived their whole lives with families they couldn't stand, with standards that didn't fit their personalities. Now we force our standards on them. Some have lived with social restraints their whole lives and are literally begging for a little freedom, if only for the last few days of their lives. Then we shackle them with our social mores and enforce them with prescription drugs and tranquilizers. It's made me sick and turned me into what you saw when you came here on your first day. Nancy, you don't know me. You only know what I have turned into. Now, you, Nancy! If you're what I think you are, I've got my answer. If you're not, I'm ready to find work somewhere else in a different field. You're scared as hell, aren't you?"

"I'm scared," Nancy replied, "but not for me. I'm scared *of* me. Failure I can deal with. It won't be only me that's punished for my failure. Financial failure can be a learning experience. I could take that, but failure with this home can hurt a lot of people. Continuing with the status quo at this home would be failure. Is it only you and I who really know that?"

"That's the risk you have to be willing to take," Adele said. "It's rumored around here that you play a mean game of poker, Nancy." Adele pulled up a folding chair, tugged down the bottom of her black sweater and sat down across from Nancy.

"At another time and place," Adele said, "when I was younger and more daring, I played a few hands of poker myself. I was in a game one time with this big war veteran about eighty years old, tougher than a boiled owl. He talked mostly in single words, not sentences. I was making a bet one time and showed hesitation. He looked at me with a hostile face. Only his eyebrow rose as he squinted down at his cards and then looked back at me. 'Don't let the shit crowd your liver, lady,' he said. That was about the only sentence I had heard him say the whole night. I made the bet. Without hesitation, he raised. I raised back. He straightened up, smiled broadly, folded his cards, and nodded his appreciation, as if to say 'you've learned your lesson well'. He didn't say anything, but enjoyment was written all over his face. You see, he played poker for more than the money. So I guess, if you don't know why you're in the game, Nancy, and you don't like the stakes, you better fold tent."

Nancy started laughing. "Shit," Nancy said. "You made that all up, didn't you? Or did you just hear that story from Cloudy or something? You don't look like a poker player, but you're sure starting to act like one."

Nancy paused a moment and took a deep breath; then, she continued, firmly and forcefully.

"I've made up my mind. Can I count on you for the long haul? I certainly can't make it here without you."

"Promise me one thing, and I'm in," Adele said.

"Okay, what?"

Adele fidgeted. Then she said to Nancy, "I've decided it's time for me to change my personal life, too. I've never had a date or dinner out with a man since my husband died many years ago. I want you to help me get a date."

Nancy put her head down on the desk, her shoulders shaking. She looked up, and Adele could see she was laughing so hard she was crying. "I'll find you the best-damned date you've ever had," she said. "You might be interested in a keeper, even though I haven't kept one yet. I'll know a keeper when I see one. I'm still doing catch and release."

The next morning, when Nancy met Adele at the entrance, she threw her arm around her shoulder and they walked to the office together. A few minutes later, they returned with a tag board sign, hand-lettered in forest green, and posted it behind the nurse's station:

Holiday Forever
A Guest Home

Chapter 35

BILLY'S LEFT HAND and his mind were working okay. Orson had fashioned a sturdy place for his paper so he could write. Billy was having difficulty learning to write with his left hand. On the second day after his assignment from Nancy, he was crying when she came to his room.

Nancy sat on the bed, put her arm around her father, and wiped the tears from his face. Billy handed her the note pad.

Nancy,

My memorable thoughts all centered around your mother. This tormented me and caused me more of the same problems I have been going through all these years.

Nancy patted her dad on the back and laid the note pad on the writing stand. "We're not going to give up," she said. "The mind can be like a clamp. It gets a hold of a thought and won't let go. The only way to get rid of that tormenting thought is to put another in its place. It's the Law of Substitution." Nancy pointed to the notepad. "Now, write down some pleasant memory that does not involve Clair."

"Canph."

"Can."

Billy stared out the window. He saw some horses on a distant hill and his mind left the torment of Clair and he was thirteen, cultivating corn with the team. He smelled the earth he loved so much. He saw and heard the songbirds coming for unearthed seeds and grubs. The wind was fresh in his hair. The sun was warm on his back.

Nancy felt the tension leave Billy's shoulders and watched his face relax as he began to write.

Cultivating corn—with team—silly!

Not silly at all, Daddy," Nancy said. "I saw you go there. It's a place you can go whenever you choose. You will be surprised how many new things you will feel and see each time you go there." Nancy wrote a "1" on Billy's pad. "Tomorrow I'll expect two more thoughts to use for substitution,' she said.

"Phlank you," Billy said.

Chapter 36

NANCY WAS FEELING very good about Adele and the rest of the staff at Holiday Forever, but more innovations were in order. Nancy asked Adele if she'd like to take two weeks off—one to just get away for a while and one to visit other nursing homes around the state so she could bring back new ideas.

"Setting me aside, already?" Adele asked.

"No. Not at all," Nancy said, "but you know, anyone can fall into a rut. Just think of how much fun it is to get out of a rut you didn't even know you were in. You aren't above that, are you Adele?"

When she left, Adele made sure that all assignments would remain the same until she returned. Nancy assured her that things would be *mostly* the same until she got back.

Nancy called Ruth on the phone. "I've got the room all set for Buster and Emmy to move in. We could do it this weekend. Want to help?"

"I've been wondering about you. You've all but abandoned me since you took over that home. You hardly ever call, and you haven't been to see me."

"I've been awfully busy, Ruth. You have no idea what that scheming of yours has gotten me into."

"You don't fool me. I can tell by your voice that you love it."

"Oh, you're right, as usual. Are you going to help with the Tikens or not?"

"I'll go up Friday night and start getting them packed. We can leave most of their house as it is until Buster and Emmy get accustomed to your place. Buster wants to keep on helping out down here, as soon as Emmy is acclimated and all."

By Sunday morning, Buster and Emmy were in their room at Holiday Forever.

In Adele's absence however, Nancy had become quite concerned about her guests and staff. She seldom heard laughter. Everyone spoke in hushed, subdued tones, as if in a monastery. The doctors all acted like monarchs. The only thing that anyone looked forward to, it seemed, was the next meal, or the chance to go to sleep, or the end of the work shift. Nancy couldn't wait for Adele to return. She needed change quickly.

Nancy went out of town on Saturday. Early Monday morning, she summoned Orson for help when she arrived at work. He helped her to carry a large cardboard box from the backseat of her car to the front counter where Zona Kovich was in charge. Nancy asked Zona to assemble all of the available staff for a meeting in the recreation room as soon as morning tasks were completed.

"Have as many of our guests as possible attend also," Nancy said.

At ten-thirty, all available staff members and nearly half of the residents were assembled in the rec room. Nancy asked Mrs. Kovich to help her with the box.

"Be careful now, Zona, keep the box level, and be gentle," she said. It was wet on the bottom and smelled of urine. A rustling movement came from within, accompanied by mild yips.

"For Christ's sake, Nancy, do you have dogs in this box?" Zona asked.

"Not just dogs, but registered Golden Retriever puppies, Zona."

"What the hell are we going to do with them?"

"They are joining us as part of the staff."

"Part of their staff? What's their job going to be?"

"Their job is the same as yours and mine: to make people here feel better and to make life more interesting and comfortable."

"But you can't have dogs in a rest home!"

"Who's going to throw them out? If people can have puppies in their own homes, they should be able to have them here. We're going to give it a try, see what happens. Even if they only last for a few days, it will be well worth the effort. We need changes."

Nancy tugged at the box. "Come on, help me bring them to the rec room, and let's turn these two loose."

Zona rolled her eyes. "Lord, woman. I don't think you have any idea what you're getting into."

They set the box on the floor near the center of the rec room. Nancy spoke to the hushed group.

"I've had the opportunity to meet most of you by this time. Now I would like you to meet two friends of mine who have agreed to join the staff as full time volunteers. I know they'll love all of us."

She reached into the box and pulled out a cuddly red ball of fur. "This young lady's name is Fats," she said. Holding Fats in one hand, she reached into the box and brought forth the second puppy.

"This young man is named Sloan. He and Fats just met each other yesterday. They're from separate litters. They're for all of us to cherish and care for. Resident volunteers wishing to assist in their care may come to my office any time during the day."

She set the puppies gently on the floor. Silence followed, then a murmur, then smiles, giggles, cheers, tears, and applause.

Sloan walked slowly and cautiously to Fats, sniffed all around her, playfully slapped her on the face with his paw, then jumped in the air and yelped at her. Fats looked bewildered, shook, and piddled on the floor. Sloan sniffed and licked the feet of the people assembled in wheelchairs. Fats lay down on her stomach and covered her face with her right paw.

Immediately the staff went into action. The first to reach Fats was Katey, the cook.

"Come on, Fats," she said, picking the puppy up from the floor and holding her closely. "That old Sloan had no business slapping your face, even if he did think he was just playing. You just wait! We'll get him back. You're ok; we'll take care of you. You're going to need this old cook to make sure you get plenty of good food."

Orson cleaned up the piddle, then picked up Sloan and held him up for all to see. "Great puppy, huh? Couple years from now, he and I will go pheasant hunting and bring back a few birds and we'll have Katey cook them up for us."

Orson waddled into Nancy's office at noon, carrying Fats and Sloan.

"Now what am I going to do with these goddamned dawgs?" he said with a smile so broad he needed more face for it to fit on.

"It appears you are volunteering to take responsibility for the dawgs," Nancy mimicked.

"Not really. They're your dawgs."

"No, I gave them to Holiday Forever. They're part and parcel of this organization."

"What do you plan on doing with them?"

"I don't plan on doing anything with them. We have any number of intelligent people around here who aren't used to thinking and assume they're not allowed to think. Let them decide. I haven't thought it through, on purpose. I'd like the residents to decide. Just let it happen. Those two little whelps can't hurt anything around here no matter what they do, and I'm sure nobody around here is going to hurt them. You don't fool me, Orson, you like 'em too. Now why don't you just take them back and see whom amongst our residents might have some ideas on what they would like to do with them. It will get them thinking about something other than aches and pains and dying."

"You mean, just let them decide what to do with these puppies? Some of them are crazies. You know that, Nancy."

"Orson, you still have a little to learn, don't you? You watch. There are no crazies when it comes to puppies."

"Well, I'll try, but I don't want anybody hurting these two. They should be left alone for a while now. They need a nap by themselves. Where'll I put 'em?"

"Take them back. Let the residents figure it out. If they don't come up with something, you do it. I'm sure you won't have to make any decisions. Just help them accomplish what they think is right and will work."

The dogs spent the night in a big cardboard box in Mabel Torgerson and Edith Chase's room. The two old ladies demanded that they stay with them. The two puppies slept soundly all night, without a whimper, all cuddled up and exhausted from their day. It was a restless night for Mabel and Edith though, as staff members continued to sneak into their room to check on the puppies, some two at a time, whispering and giggling.

The next morning, guests in the home were up unusually early, dressed and ready for the day. Sparks of life flickered across faces which had been lifeless masks of boredom and defeat the day before, imploring of anyone who'd listen, "where are the puppies?"

By noon, an uproarious argument erupted in the rec room.

"Don't feed these puppies any of your table scraps. They'll get sick!" said Foster Clant, an eighty-six year old man sitting in his wheelchair with one leg in a cast from ankle to hip. Sloan struggled in his lap, making every effort to find uncovered skin or a face to lick. Finally he was satisfied licking the hand that was petting him.

"We are all going to have to get together and agree on what these puppies should be fed," Foster continued. The room erupted in a din of guests all talking at once, each with an opinion, or a story of how they had taken care of their pet at home.

Foster rapped a crutch sharply on the table.

"Quiet down and listen, you guinea hens," he said. "We're going to have to find a way out of this. Let's see if we can do it the right way. Let's one of us call the county agent and have him prescribe a diet for a puppy this size and age. Or we can call the vet. Let's just do what one of them says and there won't be any argument."

Mabel said she'd go along with what the county agent said, but she was afraid the vets might be just like the doctors. "They'd like to feed them some pills and give them all kinds of shots and things. Doctors—they don't have the foggiest idea about nutrition and health if you're not sick," she said.

The group argued and fought, discussed and compromised, before coming up with a plan and an agreement by suppertime.

The plan was for Orson to keep the puppies in his tool storage area at night for a while. Foster was to contact the county agent. A volunteer fund was to be administered by Edith Chase to purchase food and other necessities. Pat Ogrant was to contact the local vet for advice, but it would have to be approved by the advisory committee. Foster would chair the puppy's advisory committee. All guests, so inclined could be members of the committee.

An infectious feeling of excitement and anticipation swept through the home like a breath of fresh air. Within two weeks, the puppies rollicked at will throughout the premises. Bored old men and ladies who used to sit in their wheelchairs with their heads down, day after day, couldn't help but to react to the puppies chasing their tails and each other. Submissive guests raised their heads and smiled when Sloan or Fats attacked their stockings or slippers. Some of the guests mocked outrage at missing slippers from their rooms. Legitimate complaints of damage were paid from the volunteer fund that was always adequate, even without solicitation.

When Adele returned to work after a two weeks leave, she deftly hung up her black cape, smiled, gave Orson a cheery morning greeting, and proceeded to her station at the front counter, whereupon she stepped into an unseen pile of dog shit. After removing her shoe for inspection, she bellowed at Orson, who happened to be slowly ambling towards his supply room.

"Orson! This looks and smells like dog doo! Who is responsible for this?"

Orson surveyed the scene. He suppressed any show of amusement. On his full-moon face appeared a smile as wide as the rim of a saucer. "Matter of fact, we're all responsible. We better get it cleaned up right away. You take care of your shoe."

"Orson!" she said, standing stiffly with her hands on her hips. "Orson, this is no time for insubordination. How did this get here?"

"Sloan or Fats, I suppose," he said. Just then, the two little crimson whelps, like elongated balls of crimson yarn, careened around the corner, Fats with a slipper in her mouth chased by Sloan, who caught her in front of Adele's counter. A tug-of-war ensued with both dogs heading down the hall, each tugging at the slipper.

Orson thought Adele, with her wide eyes and tight skin, looked like a starved owl. Coughing and wheezing, Orson couldn't control his fit of laughter. Tears streaked his face as he tried to talk.

"Adele, you look like an owl-faced Statue of Liberty with a dog-shit-laden shoe for a torch!" Adele, stock still, holding her shoe high in the air with her right hand, looked on incredulously at Fats and Sloan.

"Orson, this is not funny," she said.

He looked up from his bent over position in the midst of another cough. "To hell it isn't. You should see yourself! Ha-ha!"

"Where do you get off talking this way to me, Orson? You have never done this before!"

"Oh, I just forgot, Mrs. Yorkland. You were gone all last two weeks, weren't you? I forgot about that. Funny the effect these damn little dawgs have on a person. You don't know about Fats and Sloan, do you?"

"You mean those two little mongrels? Who let them in here anyway? Whose are they?"

"They're ours, Adele. And they sure ain't mongrels. Nancy brought them in and gave them to us. Aren't they a stitch?"

Fats and Sloan turned around in the corridor and came back, in overdrive, toward Adele. They went by, put on the brakes, and came back.

"Ours!" Adele exclaimed. She stomped away to Nancy's office.

"Miss Bartel! I've been gone for two weeks. I visited many care facilities. I never saw anything like this. What is this, anyway?"

"Looks like dog shit on a shoe to me," Nancy said, straight-faced.

"Dog shit on a shoe …" Adele stammered angrily. "I'm not talking about dog shit on a shoe."

"What are you talking about?"

"I'm talking about this zoo. This place is like a zoo and everyone acts nonchalant, like it's a normal place. Orson thinks it's funny and gives me no respect."

"Come over here, Adele. I want to show you something. I want you to look at it real good, in every detail." Nancy put her arm gently around Adele's shoulder and ushered her to the office door. On the back of the door was a full-length mirror. Nancy positioned Adele directly in front of the mirror, raised Adele's arm, left her there and went back to her chair.

"Now look at that, and tell me it's not funny," Nancy said.

Adele looked herself over. Her straight black hair was all askew. Her eyes lifted to the sullied shoe. Adele tried with all her might not to laugh. She even thought of wiping the shitty shoe on the tittering Nancy. Then a laugh burst from her lips. Nancy laughed too.

"God, I can't take any more of this." She guffawed and snapped two tissues from the box to wipe the tears from her eyes. "I would have choked to death if I held my laugh back any longer."

Finally, Adele placed the offending footwear on Nancy's desk. "I might just as well join the crowd and act like other people around here. Why don't you clean my shoe up for me, Miss Bartel?"

"Why, I will be more than glad to, Mrs. Yorkland." Nancy gave Adele a sweeping bow.

Adele retreated to the stuffed leather chair, sat down, and let out a long breath.

"Oh Lord, I know I can get a job at any of those other, normal care facilities at better pay, and I'm working in this nut house!"

Nancy walked to Adele, faced her squarely, and put her hands on Adele's shoulders. "But you see, you're part of this place now, Adele. You're one of the nuts. You saw yourself in the mirror, didn't you? Where else would you fit? You're one of us. Now quit bothering me. I've got this shoe to clean up. I'll have it back to you in a minute."

When Nancy left the office, Adele was sitting slouched in the chair, plucked of energy but renewed in spirit.

Billy now had five substitutes to put in his game of life when tormenting thoughts began to squeeze down on his brain. He could cultivate corn. He could see and hear the riffles in the stream, watch the muskrats swim, and catch the five pound rainbow trout he'd caught when he was fourteen, or talk to Ernie Blair and come to an agreement on buying his farm. With so much of the tension gone, and with constant practice, he was able to pronounce Nancy's name. Billy also thought he noticed some sensation returning to the right side.

Nancy taught him methods of relaxation and self-hypnosis. Billy was a good student. He learned how to clear his mind and recognize the alpha state that occurs just prior to sleep.

Zona Kovich stopped by Nancy's office before leaving for work for the day.

"Not much new under the sun," she said, "but you can always do things just a little bit different, can't you? Miss Bartel, if you would have told me that having a couple of puppies around here could make this kind of difference in the staff and guests before it happened, I would have called you a damned liar. I've never seen anything like this in all my years of work in the health field. People have changed. Their attitudes are different. This place has a totally different atmosphere than a few weeks ago. It can't just be those two damned little hound dogs, can it? Why, this is a fun place to work! Adele used to act like she had a hot poker up her ass. Now she's mostly human to everybody, she loves those mutts, and is acting like she loves everybody else."

Nancy came from her chair and sat on her desk facing Zona. "The puppies didn't do anything much, Zona," Nancy said. 'They just didn't try to adapt to our ways. When new people come here, whether it's staff or new guests, they kind of wait around and watch and see how they are expected to act, and then everybody tries to do what they think is expected of them. When this happens, everything stays the same, year after year. Sloan and Fats didn't wait around to see what was expected of them. They just acted like themselves, and little by little, the real people around here started acting like the selves they used to be or really are. Oh, I know there is more to it than that, but we don't have to figure out everything scientifically when we know it's working. Like you, Zona. What's kept you from talking to me like you are, until now?"

Zona smiled. "I like your style, Nancy," she said. "Why don't you come up to the Vet's Club with me and we'll have a beer or two?"

"Sounds good to me. I'll get my jacket, and I'll be right with you."

By two-thirty in the afternoon, Susan Pelt, the forty-three-year-old farm wife nurse, was completely frazzled.

I don't know if I can take this place much longer, she said to herself. *There's no predictability. This so-called 'new freedom of expression' has infected all the guests. George Rudnik—who everyone thinks is a shell-shocked veteran—in room twelve is acting like he's in a nudist camp. The only time he is shell-shocked is when he has to put his clothes on. Then he doesn't speak. He refuses to wear any clothes in his room and once in a while, he stands in his doorway naked.*

But he's not the worst. No, that's Mrs. Tenman in room twenty-three.

Bonnie Tenman, a widowed farm wife in her late eighties, was diagnosed with dementia ten years earlier, after her eldest son found her wandering outside the house because she thought she'd locked herself out the day before; when her son came around the back to pry open the kitchen door with a crowbar, he saw that it was wide open.

She has been stuffing everything she can get a hold of in her room up her vagina—pop bottles, lipstick tubes, bananas, and carrots from the kitchen. Disgusting! This has to be stopped!

Susan went to find Nancy. She was in one of the corridors, whistling "Dixie".

"Miss Bartel, I must speak to you privately."

"Sure, but idle down a little, Susan. You look like your motor is in overdrive and your transmission's not engaged. You can burn something out that way, you know. Come along to the kitchen and we'll have a cup of coffee."

They sat at a long worn table in the kitchen and Katey, the chief cook, brought them coffee. Katey's face was flushed and she had an "all's right with the world" look, which only added to the frustration of Susan Pelt.

Susan collapsed with her head face-down on the table. "I don't think I can take this anymore," she muttered, without lifting her head.

"Oh, it can't be as bad as all that," Nancy said.

"Oh, yes, it can." Susan straightened up and looked directly and disgustedly at Katey, then glanced back at Nancy and shook her head. Then she told Nancy about Naked George and the problem with Bonnie Tenman.

"What do you think, Katey?" Nancy said loudly.

Katey turned to Nancy. "About what?"

"About what Susan and I have been talking about. What would you do about it? You've been around here for many years. What's your advice?"

"I know what they'd do about it if you weren't here, Miss Bartel. I know what they used to do about things like that. They'd get the doctor in and tell him how terrible things were and they would drug the patients up some way, make 'em kind of like zombies 'til they died. Do everything they could to keep them alive, so the patients or the welfare could keep paying the doctor bills and the nursing home. They'd keep them alive, but they sure as hell wouldn't let them live."

"Okay. What would you do in these cases, Katey?" Nancy asked.

"I'd probably get Bonnie a dildo or a vibrator. If she's got an itch, let her scratch it with something that might work. If she had a good-sized dildo up there, she wouldn't have room for all that other junk she keeps sticking up there. All they have done now is take everything out of her room. Every time she finds something to use, they take it away from her." Katey ambled over to the table, and stood by Nancy with her hands on her hips.

"Naked George," she said. "I'll go talk to him. He's an intelligent man. Maybe he has good reason for wanting to be naked. I know he's not nuts; he's just not conventional. Nakedness is no big deal. Why are we making such a fuss about these things, anyway? This isn't supposed to be a cathedral, is it?"

Susan, aghast and speechless, wrung her hands nervously. "Can't we talk privately, Miss Bartel?" she asked.

"Oh, relax, and don't call me Miss Bartel. Katey has some ideas. I would like to know what you think about them. Let's discuss it with her; later we can have our private conversation."

Susan, obviously embarrassed, hesitated before she replied. "I'm not sure I know what a dildo or a vibrator is. I've led a very sheltered life, Nancy. I've heard other ladies talk in public bathrooms about devices for masturbation. Is this what you're talking about?"

Nancy responded. "That's it, Susan. The dildo you operate manually, and a vibrator is a motorized dildo."

"Oh, God help us. What is this world coming to?" Susan cried.

"What do you think of drugging her up then, to keep her from masturbating?" asked Nancy.

"No. I don't think we should recommend that."

"Then I say we take Katey's suggestion, get her a dildo, and see how that works. I'm going to the Twin Cities tomorrow. I'll pick up a couple of dildos and a vibrator. We can have them on hand for emergencies like this."

Nancy nodded to Katey. "I like your suggestions. I'll talk to Naked George. Susan, you can help Bonnie with the dildo when I bring it back. If Bonnie wants to use it, make sure it's well lubricated. See how things work out and report back to me."

Susan thought she might faint. "I couldn't do that," Susan managed to choke out.

"Why not? You said you didn't want to see her drugged up, didn't you?"

"Yes, but isn't masturbation sinful? I can't participate in sin."

"Susan, if it's sinful for you, that's rightfully your decision, but we have no right to decide for Bonnie or anyone else what is sin here at Holiday Forever."

"But things are so different around here. I, I just don't understand sometimes."

"Just think of it as furthering your education and de-sheltering your life a little." Nancy walked towards the exit. "I'll go have my talk with Naked George. Thanks for the advice, Katey. And slow down on the grape, it's kind of early in the afternoon."

"Come on, Susan," Nancy said, "We have work to do." She helped Susan upright, and started whistling the tune of "In the Summer Time".

Susan got up slowly. "I guess we don't need our private talk, Nancy. There's nothing private around here anyway. We get advice from cooks, janitors, and dogs. Now I can go home and listen to my husband and my kids tell me what the world is all about. I feel like a repository, a depository, and sometimes a suppository. Look at me! I'm a registered nurse ready to give shots with a dildo. I have arrived! This world is not at all like what I expected when I grew up."

"Try looking at the world as it is, and say 'how fascinating'. I'll bet it will change your outlook."

Foster Clant was in the corridor in his wheelchair, trailing a piece of leather on a long string behind his chair. Fats and Sloan followed, alternately pouncing on the leather and shaking it. He wheeled into the rec room, which was full of residents and visitors. Many of the visitors were little children. Nancy had posted a "Children Welcome" sign outside the building. The children squealed with delight at the presence of Sloan and Fats. Nancy liked what she saw. Three and four-year-old children were talking intently to old men and ladies. The puppies, all tuckered out from their chase with Foster, lay stretched out on the floor, sleeping. A red-haired girl and a blond boy were petting them.

Nancy tarried for a half hour talking to the guests and playing with the children and puppies. As the children left, they gave hugs and kisses to old men and ladies. The room was a-buzz with activity, even though some of the guests were sleeping soundly in their chairs.

Foster Clant taunted Bert, who was lighting a cigarette by the far wall.

"Tobacco is a dirty weed," Foster said. "It was the devil that planted the seed. It dirties your pockets and smells your clothes and makes a chimney of your nose."

Nancy had overheard Foster talking to some of the older children. In a singsong voice, he had vocalized for them. "The raccoon has a brushy tail. The possum's tail is small. The rabbit, he comes running by, and he has no tail at all."

Then Nancy skipped her way to George Rudnik's room. George was lying on top of his bed naked. Nancy sat down and sipped coffee from her cup.

George was seventy-nine and over six-foot tall. His eyes were bright and alert. His room was orderly.

"George," Nancy said, "I'm sorry I haven't had the opportunity to meet you before. I'm Nancy Bartel, the proprietor of Holiday Forever. I'm glad to meet you and welcome you as a guest to the home, but we do seem to have a slight problem. Some of the other guests and members of my staff are having a problem with your apparent aversion to wearing clothes. Do you have any suggestions?"

"Sure."

George propped himself up on the bed, swung his legs over the edge, and sat facing Nancy. He was never going to try explaining his aversion to clothing. No one needed to know of his experiences as a medic on the front lines in the war. Blood and guts—blood and guts; he'd been covered in blood and guts day after day. There were no showers on the front lines and the bloody mess had dried on his hands, arms and on his legs. It was nobody's business that he had cracked up and was pulled off the front. And nobody's business that he showered up to fifteen times a day after that. Nothing had let him break free of the blood and guts feeling on his skin. It was nobody's business that he got a section eight discharge from the service, and nobody's business that now, in order to survive, he needed to spend a good share of his time naked—so he could see there was no blood and guts on his skin.

"I've only been here a few days, but I've heard a lot about you. You like to be called Nancy, right? Well, Nancy, my suggestion is, just let everyone get used to me. After a few days, nobody will even notice or give a damn.

"I knew a lady once, a particularly pretty lady. One of her eyes was put out in an accident. When you first saw her, that empty eye socket was about all you would see. She never did anything cosmetically about her damaged eye. She never covered it up as most people do. She worked as a waitress in a small town restaurant where most of her customers were regulars. A few days after she came back to work, no one seemed to notice the eye. She was just the same Lil, and the regulars teased and flirted with her like they would any pretty girl. Once in a while a stranger would stop in and make a comment about Lil's damaged eye. The usual response was—'What eye? Oh, Lil's eye. I had forgotten about that; nobody around here ever notices it.'

"It will be the same if I walk around here naked. In a few weeks, no one will care or notice the difference; but I'd be handling the situation."

"How about a compromise, Mr. Rudnik?" Nancy asked.

"Aren't' I compromised enough just being in here? And don't call me Mr. Rudnik, I'm George."

"Okay, George. How about you just be naked in your room? We will screen any potential roommates to make sure they don't object."

"Now look, Miss Bartel. I'm not off my rocker, just a little eccentric. Just eccentric enough to keep my sanity in a place like this. I just plain feel better when I'm not fettered by clothing. If being naked causes a problem; time will take care of it."

A lady visitor walked past the open doorway.

"Oh my God." she gasped.

"There. You see, George. That's the kind of problem we have."

"Don't you understand, Nancy? It's their problem. It comes from bad upbringing. These old codgers and the staff people around here should get their thinking straightened out. Nudity is not about sex, nor is it sensuous except in the mind of the viewer. Neither should it be repulsive. Objection to my behavior is just another method people have used over the years to control and exert authority. I'd like the chance to demonstrate my theory to you. If we continue with the problems after a couple of months, I'll be a good boy and have my clothes on all the time. I'll bet you, if I do this right and go kind of slow about it, within two months I could appear nude almost anywhere here in the home and the regular people here, staff and others, would take no notice. Look at yourself, Nancy. You're sitting there in your chair communicating with me. I'll bet you've forgotten that I don't have clothes on."

George fluffed his pillow and rested his back against the headboard.

Nancy quietly drank the last of her coffee.

"Okay, I'll give it a try George," she said. "I'll alert the staff and assist you with the others, but the full responsibility is yours."

"Thank God for you, Nancy," he said. "When I first heard about you, I was afraid you might not have enough chalk in your backbone to whitewash a billiard ball, but you've got chalk, lady, and a lot of it. You're not afraid to live, and you're not afraid to let us old people live, are you?"

"Well, I'm willing to see if you can pull this off. No pun intended, George."

What's next? Is there anything on my agenda to top this? Nancy thought.

Chapter 37

"WHAT'S NEXT?" BECAME the norm rather than the exception during the following months. Many new policies were instituted and old policies eliminated. And some fresh new characters emerged from former docile patient-guests of the home.

Flowers and a vegetable garden flourished, in what was formerly a well-manicured back yard. The spaces between the rows in the garden were wide enough for wheelchairs and guests with walkers could get between them. Guests fashioned all kinds of tools to work in the garden, such as old spoons and table forks taped to the end of a cane. Old broom handles taped to short-handled garden utensils served those who had difficulty bending over, and the garden never lacked for attention.

Within two months, Naked George walked the halls of Holiday Forever and visited with staff and guests, and everyone appeared totally oblivious of his nudity. George dressed for dinner and the other meals. Otherwise, he was just one of the guests: Naked George.

The dildo had satisfied Bonnie's itch, but she passed away of pneumonia after six months. Several of the other guests, made aware of Bonnie's treatment, left a note along with some money for Nancy to make a similar purchase for them. All requests were handled discreetly.

When he was a year old, Sloan committed a grave error. One of the children in the rec room gave him some food, and then tried to take it back. Sloan snarled and growled at the youngster, and that was the last of Sloan at Holiday Forever. Nancy found a good farm home for him; with the provision that she could bring Fats by once a year for breeding. Fats continued to be the perfect pet. She allowed herself to be roughed up by the youngsters and babied by the old folks.

On Friday afternoons, at three, the rec room was converted to a make shift barroom for happy hour. Guests brought the beverage of their choice. The staff provided the ice and mix. Often old folks in wheel chairs, accompanied by two or three others, some barely able to walk, and chattering like partridges in heat, made their Friday pilgrimage to the liquor store in preparation for happy hour. The eight-block round trip to get the supplies was a happy trip in itself, taking over an hour: one less hour of potential boredom.

Off duty staff and visitors often joined in the festivities. With a couple beers under his belt, Foster Clant was a raconteur in a wheelchair.

"Here's a poem for you," Foster said.

"You see that tree grows near our house?
It must have been there quite some time,
It's nothing but a slippery elm and very hard to climb.
The other day a woodsman came to chop that refuge down,
And carve it into kindling wood to peddle round the town.
I says to him, I pray thee stop, refrain as is, and stop
Lay down that forest razor, man, chop not one single chop.
You better make your ax behave,

That slippery elm you've gotta save,
Cause it's the only one my wife can't climb,
So, woodsman, spare that tree!
You see that hole up near that old treetop?
I've got five dollars there, it's yours if you refrain the chop.
I'll throw that five spot down to thee,
Just like I promised thou,
But you better make your ax behave,
That slippery elm you've gotta save,
Cause it's the only one my wife can't climb.
So, woodsman, spare that tree!
And I can't get up myself, unless my wife is a'chasin' me.
So when my wife trots after me, up in that tree I roost.
So bring her here, and I'll call her a very naughty word,
I'll give an imitation of a bird,
And I'll go up like a healthy squirrel and never need no boost.
But you better make your ax behave.
That slippery elm you've gotta save,
Cause it's the only one my wife can't climb,
So, woodsman, spare that tree!
You may not know where to go when my wife comes around.
But remember this if I'm not on the ground.
I'll throw that five spot down to thee,
Just like I promised thou,
But you better make your ax behave.
That slippery elm you've gotta save.
Cause it's the only one my wife can't climb.
So, woodsman, spare that tree!"

Last call, at Holiday Forever on Friday nights, was at 6:30.

Chapter 38

ON A WARM, muggy morning, Steve Grench trudged up the long, wooden stairway to the apartment above the drug store on Main Street. The door was ajar. His father, Burt, sat at the kitchen table. He'd cleared off a space among the mess of dirty dishes, silverware and cereal boxes at the end of the table. This allowed him enough room for resting his forearms and opening a can of beer. Steve's mother slept on a urine-soaked couch near the back wall.

The ammonia-laced air stung Steve's nostrils. Old newspapers and empty beer bottles littered the floor. Steve brushed newspapers from the seat of a chair and sat down. He closed his eyes, and held his head in his hands, before struggling to speak.

"In all my years, with all of my experience, I can't comprehend this. What's going on here, Dad? How did it come to this?"

"Little by little, I guess." Burt slurred his words.

"This is unimaginable." Steve waved his arm across the room. "You can't take care of Mom anymore. We have to get her out of here."

"Where can we go that will be any better?"

"Any place is better than this, Dad. Maybe you and Ma should apply at Holiday Forever, the rest home over in Norwood."

"Rest Home! You want to put your mother and father in a rest home? What kind of life would that be? Might as well be dead! I'm still in good health. I'm only eighty years old. I've got my car, and I still drive. Why the hell do you want me to go off and die somewhere?"

"Better to die anywhere than here." Steve went to his mother on the couch, brushed the matted hair from her face, and attempted to wake her. Her creased eyelids opened. Gray eyes, with motionless pupils, stared as if into nowhere.

"She's been that way for a full day now," Burt said. "She's got that way on me a couple times before. This is the first time I couldn't get her to the bathroom."

"Dad, I've never tried to tell you what to do in my whole life, but I'm going to tell you now, and you'd better listen."

Steve tramped to the stove, emptied the syrupy remains from the coffee pot, and began making fresh coffee. "I'm going to get some breakfast and coffee down you, then I'm going to call and make an appointment to see about getting Ma into Holiday Forever. If you don't like that, you'll have to come up with a better idea. You know I live three hundred miles from here, and I'm not going to go back there and leave my mother in these circumstances."

Steve called Holiday Forever. After the phone conversation, he turned to his father.

"I just talked to Nancy Bartel, the proprietor at the home. She said she'll see you at two this afternoon. Now, goddamn it, you eat, get yourself cleaned up, and keep this appointment. I'll take care of Ma while you're gone."

Burt was back at the apartment by three-thirty. Steve had given his mother a bath and put a clean nightgown on her.

"Quite a place up there," Burt said. "That Nancy is quite the character. They got a golden retriever there with eight pups. Remember the golden retriever we had on the farm, Steve? They got a room where Ma and I could live together. I would be able to care for her as much as I could. Nancy said they need somebody like me that could drive. I could keep my car up there and everything. I told her about the garden we used to have on the farm. She thought it was a hell of an idea. She got a spade from a caretaker named Orson, took me out in the yard, and be damned if she didn't dig up the grass and put a shovel full of good black dirt right in my hands. How does that look to you, Burt?' she asked. "Then she showed me the garden and said I could help with that or have one of my own. She was real sincere, acted as if we had known each other for a while. She put her arm around my shoulders, walked me to a garden hose over by the tool shed, and held the hose while I washed the dirt off my hands. Then she doubled back that hose, pinched off the flow, took a drink, wiped her mouth off with the back of her hand, and flipped the water off like an old farmer. If we can get the paperwork done, we can move in by Monday. Will you help me with the paperwork, Steve? They don't call it a rest home; they call it a guest home."

It only took three weeks at Holiday Forever, with the special attention of Zona Kovich, to get Burt's wife to full recuperation. Zona put her on a balanced diet and saw to it that she took her blood pressure and heart medications at the proper times.

Burt, being busy and helpful to others, found that this was a good substitute for all the time he had previously spent drinking beer. Not that he quit entirely. After three months had passed, Burt and his wife were ready to be discharged, and were looking for a place to live in Norwood. Then, one morning, Burt's wife didn't wake up. She had died during the night of a heart disease.

On the day after the funeral, Burt—sad-eyed and wearing the same suit he'd worn to the funeral—came to Nancy in her office with his hat in his hand.

"I'd like to thank you, Nancy, for all you've done for us," Burt said. "I'll get all the stuff out of the room tomorrow."

"You have already paid till the end of the month, so you can stay till then if you'd like," Nancy said.

Burt twisted in his chair, and said, "I've kind of found a home here, Nancy, what with helping Orson with things, and the garden. I'll sure miss doing my part in that garden."

"I understand you're a pretty good carpenter," Nancy said.

"Used to be, that's for sure. I've laid block in my day too, and done all kinds of fixin' when it comes to plumbing."

Nancy got up from her chair and paced back and forth in front of Burt.

"What are your plans, Burt?" Nancy asked.

"No plans, Nancy—just kinda wish I could stay here, but I ain't sick and I don't need nursing care."

"I've got a few plans rattling around in this head of mine, some that you might fit well with. You interested in hearing them, Burt?"

Burt straightened up in his chair and some of the sadness left his face and yes.

"Sure as shootin' I am, Nancy," he said.

There were a few silent moments before Nancy turned to Burt.

"You have become acquainted with my father, Billy, haven't you?" she asked.

"Oh yes, I've even helped him out a bit on occasions."

"He has improved tremendously. He can walk with a walker now. Here's what I'm thinking. He's got this little farm just on the outskirts of town. He's let the farmstead get all rundown, including the house. I think within a week, Billy will be able to walk with a cane. His right arm is slow, but he's learned to use his left arm pretty well. Do you think you could take him out to the farm and you two could start to straighten things up and make it livable again?"

"Why, that's right down my alley. I'm eighty and still active, maybe a little slow, but what's the hurry." Burt said, pushing himself up from the chair.

"I think we might get Dad out of here and back home. He's beginning to be bored. Both his body and mind need exercise."

"I could find plenty for him to do—even in his shape—out at the farm," Burt said. "We'll have to see if he gets along with me, though."

"I don't think that will be a problem," Nancy said. "At the beginning, I see this as a two-month project. Then we can assess the situation and go from there."

Plans were growing in Nancy's mind like mushrooms in May. She saw her father living independently again, she saw him and Burt continuing to help and volunteer at Holiday Forever, and she saw the two of them helping her on a bigger project. A number of guests at Holiday Forever were mentally handicapped since birth. Nancy thought they could be integrated back into the community through a foster care program, such as the one in Geel, Belgium, that she had been researching recently.

"Nancy," Burt said.

"Oh, I'm sorry Burt. I got to thinking too deeply and kind of went into a trance. Where were we?"

"We were talking about fixin' up your dad's place. Should I talk to Billy about it, or do you want to first?"

"I'll talk to him and tell him you're coming to see him. Then I think the three of us can take it from there."

Buster had fallen to sleep in his chair behind his office desk. Ruth was reluctant to wake him. Buster had insisted on helping with the paper each week, but the strain on him from Emmy's deteriorating health was evident. When it was time to close the shop, Ruth jiggled Buster's shoulder.

"Uh-huh," Buster said as he was startled awake. Not realizing he'd gone to sleep, he needed to look around before he knew where he was.

"It's time we close now," Ruth said. "How's Emmy doing?"

"Oh, she's not so bad physically, she gets wonderful care, but that Alzheimer's is mean stuff. There are parts of days she doesn't recognize me at all. She woke up the other night and demanded I get out of bed, thought I was a stranger that had wandered in during the night."

Ruth took Buster's sweater from the coat rack and brought it to him. "Maybe you should think of moving back to your house, Buster," Ruth said.

"Nope. When I signed on with Emmy, I signed on for the long haul. I'll be with her until one of us passes on." Buster took the sweater from Ruth. "This is the sweater I bought when Burton was born," he said.

"How about you going up to Holiday Forever, say hi to Emmy, shave off those scruffy whiskers of yours, and you and I and Nancy can go out to dinner?" Ruth asked, steering deftly away from any mention of Burton.

"Great." Buster said.

Chapter 39

IN THE CLASSIC sense, Les Morig was an itinerant drifter. At fifty-three years old, he had a hawk-like nose, his skin was smooth and soft, powder-puff white in the winter, and now in mid-October he was only slightly tanned.

At the crack of dawn that morning, he climbed out of a semi-tractor-trailer on the highway near the Conoco station, with a small brown suitcase and a duffel bag. The truck continued on, the diesel smoke cleared away, and Les hoisted his duffel bag to his shoulder and walked unsteadily down the street. He needed to rest, so, near the park, he sat on a bench and rolled a cigarette. When he lit up, the smoke was thick, dark blue, and heavy. He smoked slowly, inhaling deeply, and then rested for twenty minutes. When he got up, he was more energetic and walked a straight line to Holiday Forever. He sat on the curb until eight o'clock then asked to see Nancy Bartel.

"My name is Les Morig," he said. "I've been reading about you and this place in the *Norwood Journal*. I have glaucoma and multiple sclerosis. Drifting as I do, it's difficult to medicate myself, and my eyesight is progressively worsening." He leaned forward and squinted. "I have the means to pay for my care if I were allowed to stay here."

Nancy leaned forward and appraised Les, thinking him rather abrupt. "Are you under the care of a local doctor?" she asked.

"No," he said. "I consult with doctors, but I'm an independent person. I don't always take their advice. I'm nontraditional. I believe in herbs and vitamins, like aloe and ginseng. I take a lot of vitamin C."

Nancy moved nearer to Les and sat on the edge of her desk. For a drifter, Nancy thought Les had a fresh smell about him. His clothes were worn and old, but clean—a brown wool pair of pants, a faded gray shirt over a white t-shirt which showed at the neck, and an olive-drab military jacket. "US Marines" was stenciled above the upper left pocket. His clothes fit him perfectly; Nancy guessed that he must be a veteran.

"Will you want a private room, then?" Nancy asked.

"At first—at least until I get to be known." A flush came to his face. "At some point, I might need someone to read to me."

Nancy told him a room would be available within two weeks. "I'll take it," Les said, and he gave Nancy a telephone number in Madison, Wisconsin. "Let whomever answers know when the room is available. I'll be here the next day."

When the room became available, Nancy called the number in Madison. A woman, sounding very young to Nancy's ears, took the message.

"I'll inform him," she said.

Les arrived at Holiday Forever the next day.

Six months later, Les paid his monthly rental a full year in advance. He told Nancy his mail would be delivered to a rented box at the post office. He stored a large metal box with a heavy combination padlock in the clothes closet of his room. He kept the door to his room mostly closed, and he had a large portable electric fan by the window.

Nancy noticed that he had made special efforts to be friends with Orson, Burt, and Katey the cook.

Katey was flattered by the attention. At Christmas time, she found a full bottle of Jack Daniel's hidden in the kitchen. Les just gave her a knowing smile when she asked about it. Often he'd sit and visit with her at the end of the day. She discovered that Les was very intelligent, a man wise to the ways of the world. He had an inquisitive mind and asked her all about her life. Katey felt like he was really interested. He asked if she had taken risks in life; and told her he had been somewhat careless of his mind and body in early life.

Katey thought his adventurous lifestyle had created within himself a state of mind that suited him, which he kept secretly stored away and didn't reveal to many other persons. She wondered why Les tried to engage her in philosophical discussions about life, though he rarely had thoughtful conversations with others at the home. He told her he was winding down toward life's end at an early age, but he sure wasn't worried about it. He didn't drink, but said he had experimented with a few mood-altering chemicals in his day.

Hearing this, Katey exclaimed, "Oh, my, no!" and took a long swig of the half coffee-half Jack Daniel's mix in her cup.

Les asked Katey if she could keep a secret. Upon her affirmative reply, he then confided to her that he smoked marijuana for medicinal purposes.

"Medicinal purposes," she scoffed. "About as medicinal as my booze."

But Les showed her several articles and documented testimony concerning the medical properties of marijuana. He gave her publications to take home and read, one of which contained the published opinions of a federal administrative law judge.

After learning that Les was smoking pot in his room, Katey began to fear for what else he might be doing. Thereafter she made herself real busy when Les came by to visit. Soon, however she sorely missed the time spent visiting with Les.

One evening, Katey stopped by Les's room before going home. The door was closed. She knocked. Les asked her in and she sat down.

"Why have you been telling me all these things about yourself and marijuana?" she said, and pointed a chubby finger at Les. "I don't think you've told anyone else. Why me?" Katey demanded. "I want to know."

"I'm glad you do," Les said. "Do you trust me?"

"Well, yes. You've been here beyond six months now. You've given me no reason not to trust you, except I find it a bit strange you have zeroed in on me. I expect you have a purpose."

"Yes, I have a purpose, but I also have come to appreciate you as a person. I like you, Katey, and I trust you."

"Then I think it's time I know your purpose."

Les proceeded to his closet, twirled the combination on the padlock and opened his metal box. He showed Katey a plastic baggie containing a dry, green substance.

"This is the exact amount of marijuana that I need to have boiled for twenty minutes in a gallon of water with a half-pound of butter. The marijuana should be in cheesecloth when you boil it. It then needs to be cooled and the butter collected after it floats to the top." There was intensity in Les's voice.

"What's the butter for?" she asked.

Les faced Katey, bent over and whispered.

"Katey," he said. "I'm a contact person for patients with cancer who are receiving chemotherapy. They become very nauseated after treatment. Sometimes even the smell of food makes them sick, and they have no appetite. Marijuana offers them relief, but there's no place for them to legally get marijuana. It's still illegal, even for medicinal purposes. There are two young cancer patients who have an aversion to smoking."

Les stepped back and cleared his throat. "I would like for you to use the butter to make cookies and brownies. One of the mothers of the patients will be here Monday. She's afraid to have anything to do with marijuana because of the law, but she thinks it would be safe just to take the cookies from me. It's been tried before and we know it works. I need a cook. You could do it at home and bring me the cookies."

Katey stammered and shook her head. "No," she said.

Deeply disappointed, Les shrugged and closed his eyes. He then took the baggie, placed it on the shelf in the metal box, and closed the door.

"Wait a minute. What if I should get caught with it in my purse?" Katey said. "I don't want to go to prison. They send people to prison because of marijuana. I might have an accident on my way home. I drink, you know."

Les patted her shoulder in understanding. "That's okay, Katey. I can find another way."

"I want to help. Is it young girls who have cancer?"

"Yes."

"How about if I get you the cheesecloth. You put in whatever you have, call it herbs. I don't want to know. You put it in the cheesecloth and tie it up. I'll have a gallon of water boiling and the butter ready. You've got a phone in your room and I've got one in the kitchen. I'll call you when I think it's okay, and you can come, and drop your cheesecloth in the water. We could do it tomorrow. I'll bake the cookies for you here in the kitchen."

The first of many batches of Katey's special cookies and brownies found their way to cancer patients in the following weeks. And Les began having more visitors, many of whom were bald and wore scarves on their heads.

Billy's right leg dragged a bit when he walked and his lips appeared unusual when he talked; but he and Burt had fixed his farmhouse up, put in a new sidewalk, and painted the inside. Billy hired a housepainter to do the outside painting. Billy painted and used the handsaw with his left hand. He'd moved home now. At first, some haunting memories bothered him, but through the law of substitution, he overcame them and now he thought only of the wonderful memories he cherished. In his mind he was even able to be with Clair again.

They'd fixed up a room for Burt. And Nancy stayed overnight once in a while. He and Burt had cooked for themselves while on the fix-up project, and now Billy even fixed a meal for Nancy on occasion.

Life was, for Billy, surprisingly good. Sometimes he could almost feel Clair's presence by his side, kinda like the way he'd seen his dad after his dad had died, and somehow he could sense that she was glad he was finally happy.

Chapter 40

"KATEY FROM THE nursing home sent me down here for a package," Jason Drew, Katey's high school kitchen helper, told the pharmacist.

"What's she going to do with these?" the pharmacist asked.

"I don't know. What is it?" Jason asked.

"Empty capsules. A whole carton. What's a cook going to do with empty capsules?"

"I sure wouldn't have any idea," Jason said. When he got back to the home, he gave the package to Katey and asked her what the heck she was going to do with the capsules.

"Now, Jason, that pharmacist had no business telling you what was in that package," Katey said. "You just forget it and go about your dishes."

Jason went about his business, but continued with thoughts about the capsules. After Jason went home, for the day, Katey brought the capsules to Les Morig's room. She also brought with her a pound of butter she'd skimmed from the top of a kettle she'd boiled marijuana in.

"I want you to stay and watch this," Les said. "If something should happen to me, I want you to be able to pass this information on."

Les melted the butter in a unit used in restaurants for serving drawn butter. Then, with the use of an eye dropper, he filled the capsules with the butter. Katey placed the capsules in the camper-sized refrigerator Les had in his room.

Katey, mesmerized by the process, asked. "Now what's this all about?"

"It's a capsule form of medical marijuana for those who can't smoke or who are so sick they can't stand the smell or taste of food. We make pinholes in the capsules and they are used as suppositories for very young children."

"You're going to get us in big trouble, Les Morig," Katie said. "And I'll be up the river right along with you."

Unknown to Les and Katey, Jason Drew was eavesdropping right outside the door.

Nancy wasn't aware of the cookies and capsules, but Les had shown her, in private, articles about using marijuana for glaucoma and multiple sclerosis. He told her he was using it in his room and said if it were to be problematical he would leave the home. Nancy told him she wanted a home where people's rooms would be as safe as their own homes. She would respect everyone's right to privacy. Les thought it would be better if Nancy didn't know about the cookies. She'd probably approve, and that would put her in a very compromising situation. Les was having problems obtaining enough quality marijuana to meet his customers' needs; another problem he did not share with Nancy.

Les ingratiated himself with both Orson and Burt and became a volunteer assistant in the garden project. He asked for a separate section in the garden for his special herbs.

"We can plant this variety at the same time that you plant the spuds," he told Orson, showing off a packet of seeds.

"Burt's got the spuds. We plant them first of the week," Orson said. "We'll get some twine and mark off the other rows this week yet."

"Hey Orson," Les said, one day after the garden had been completely planted. I got a few packets of seeds left. You got Saturday off?"

"Yeah, why?" Orson asked.

"How about if I give you some money to buy a few beers? We can take Fats along and you drive us down to the river. You can fish while I plant a few of these seeds on the river bottom land by the river."

"What's so special about them herbs?"

"Just some health herbs," Les said.

Saturday afternoon came by sunny and lazy. Vultures circled above the river in a cloudless blue-backed sky. Orson sat by the river's edge, fishing and drinking beer. Fats slept at his side. While Orson and Fats slept, Les planted a packet of seeds in a thick wooded area and another in a grassy area between the river and the woods.

In late July, three large weed-like plants were growing tight against the far wall of Orson's tool shed, obscured from the view of the roads or entrances. They were nearly six feet tall, shaped like Christmas trees, with dark-green, long, slender leaves with variegated edges. Orson found the plants, and was about to pull them up.

"Hold on there, Orson. What the hell are you doing?" Les yelled, rounding the corner of the building.

"Gonna pull these weeds," Orson said. "Didn't notice them here before. Must have grown like hell the past two weeks. You told me you were going to take care of the weeds along the buildings."

"For Christ's sake, Burt, don't pull those out! They're part of my herb garden. They have to grow near the building. They don't like many people around them or they don't do good. Now get away from them and leave them alone."

"Shit, I didn't know. You never said anything to me. What kind of herbs are they, anyway?"

"The leaves and buds have a soothing effect on you. You know, like the aloe plants we grow. Only you use them differently. I'll show you this fall, but for now just don't say anything about these plants to anyone. We're the herbal experts around here. If anyone asks, just pretend it's part of our herbal garden; then change the subject and show people our vegetable garden."

"What's the name of 'em?"

"For now, we don't call them nothing. They're just weeds that looked kind of nice along the building so we didn't pull them. We just wanted to see what they would look like if we let them grow."

"You're acting kind of queer about a couple of frigging plants, you know, Les."

"You old fart, haven't you been around long enough to know when to quit asking questions and just go along with the situation? Forget about these weeds, and I'll show you more about them if we make it through to harvest."

"Okay by me, Les. Don't get testy. I'm a hell of a lot older than you. I may be slow, but I catch on. You don't have to worry about me. If I ain't supposed to know about the god damn plants, I don't know about the friggers. Okay? And if I'm asked about the frigging weeds I'll just say, what frigging weeds? I don't know anything about the frigging weeds. They're Les's frigging weeds. He kind of likes them. Okay, Les?"

"Sure, that will be just fine, Orson. Now, come on and help me with the stakes for the tomato plants." Les tired quickly doing physical work and needed a long rest every ten minutes.

Chapter 41

WHEN THE GUEST home doctor told Minnow Grubbs his leg needed to come off, Minnow asked what the odds were of the amputation adding at least a year to his life.

"Two to one," Doc said. "Better odds than I've ever got from you. Without the operation, you've got two to three months at the outside."

"I'll take it."

Minnow was a brittle diabetic. He already had one leg off above the knee. Medication and massage had not been able to get circulation to the other limb.

"Now, tell me this, Doc," Minnow said. "I like to drink three, four beers a day and chew on cigars. I never light 'em. Let's say I've got two, two and a half years left. How much time is the beer drinking going to cost me?"

"That's a tough question. Who knows? In modern medicine, there might be a new breakthrough any day that will do the job for you."

"Without a breakthrough. Straight out, Doc. Don't hedge. I'm not into hedging my bets in this circumstance."

"Okay—with you, Minnow, I'll lay it on the line. I'll be guessing, but my best guess says laying off the beer might give you another month for every three months you got left."

The phone interrupted the conversation. Minnow's sure hand caught the phone before the second ring.

"Minnow here."

"Minnesota by three, over Iowa," the caller told him.

Minnow paged a battered, old bound book, to page twenty-one. "This is twenty-one, right? I got you on the sheet for 170. You okay by that?"

"Yup."

"Okay—go fifty more on Minnesota, plus three. See ya."

Minnow gave the phone a shove. It swung to a special metal pole and automatically locked into position. Minnow stuffed an unlit cigar in his face and picked up his pen with his round stubby fingers and made an entry into his notebook. As he closed the notebook, the phone rang again.

"Minnow here," he said. "eighteen, eh?" He quickly thumbed a tab and turned to page eighteen of the notebook.

"Minnesota by three, right? Okay, your sheet's clean." Minnow clenched his teeth on his cigar. "Okay, you're on for twenty, Minnesota plus three. See ya." He then turned back to the doctor.

"That's the best I can tell you Minnow," Doc said. "I'll be better able to give you the odds after we get that other leg off." He got up to leave. "I'll be going now. And put me on Iowa for fifty."

Minnow Grubs chuckled. He relished being Holiday Forever's resident bookie and was looking forward to Saturday's big game—the University of Minnesota vs. the University of Iowa. The Big Ten battle for the trophy pig, "Floyd of Rosedale."

"Got a letter for ya," Orson said, entering the room as the doctor was leaving it. He put an envelope on Minnow's tray. "We got twenty on Minnesota for today, Minnow. Put Ole, Glenn, and Katey down for ten each. The new guy in room fourteen, Clarence, wants five on Iowa. He used to be from Waterloo and he's sure Iowa's going to win. "

Minnow counted out the tens, fives, and ones from the envelope, and shoved the envelope under his pillow.

"Orson; have you got everything down so we know how to settle up?"

"Yeah." Orson replied. "I'll be able to settle up right after the game."

The phone rang while Minnow was transcribing the information to his notebook.

"Minnow here."

"Hey, how you doin', Minnow? I want to put fifty on Minnesota. What's the line?"

"Minnesota, plus three," Minnow said curtly.

"Okay, put me on for a fifty. I think I'm up to three seventy-five on you, now. Is that right?" Minnow paged through his notebook.

"That's right, eight. You're plus three seventy-five on the sheet. You've been luckier than a two-peckered goat lately, but don't get too cocky now; the sun doesn't shine up the same dog's ass forever. Being a veterinarian, you should know that. Okay, you're on Minnesota for fifty."

"Rustle us up a couple of beers, Orson," Minnow said.

Nancy arrived at the print shop just as Ruth finished the run on the weekly paper.

Ruth took off her leather apron, poured a cup of coffee, and hunched down behind her desk.

"Been a long day, Nance," she said. Then she noticed Nancy had a funny look about her. "Oh God, you're up to something, aren't you, Nancy?"

"It's like you think you can read my mind," Nancy said. "That's a little sick."

"Sick! I've been watching that face of yours since the day you were born. I know when you're up to something."

Nancy poured herself a cup of coffee. "Okay, so you're on to me," Nancy said and sat down. "You're a real good friend of Sheriff Smith, aren't you?"

Ruth frowned. *What kind of trouble is this girl in now?* She thought. "So, cool it with the bullshit and come out with it."

"Well, I know he's a widower and well-liked. I promised to get a date for Adele, and I haven't done anything about it. Do you think you could get anything lined up with the Sheriff for her?"

Ruth clapped her hand on her forehead. "How about getting yourself fixed up? You haven't been out with a guy since you got back."

"The sheriff is more Adele's age," Nancy said.

"I don't know. The sheriff stops in here maybe twice a week, pours himself a cup of coffee, and shoots the breeze with Buster and me for awhile. I suppose I could bring something about Adele up to him. Who knows what might happen, but I'd be a little careful about having the sheriff around your place if I were you."

"Why?" Nancy asked innocently.

"Oh, I understand you have a resident bookie up there now."

"You mean Minnow? He's not doing anything like a commercial business. He just takes a few bets for the staff, a few guests, some of the townspeople, and a few of the Doc's patients. It's just five- and ten-dollar bets, except for a couple of the Doc's. And a hundred for them is like five for the rest of us. Sometimes, on days when there's a big game, it's like festival time at Holiday Forever. Minnow's been a good addition to our place."

"Even so," Ruth said. "Rumors around town are beginning to suggest that Holiday Forever is a loose and wild place."

"We're liberal thinkers," Nancy said. "Our motto is—*'If you can do it at your home, you can do it at this home.'*"

"Why do I have the feeling that someday I will have to be defending you? Ruth asked. "In the meantime, I'll sharpen my matchmaker skills and see what I can do for Adele."

"And by the way, Ruth, I've been dating Andy Curtis. Didn't you know about that?"

"Andy Curtis, the lawyer that lives out in the country?"

"Yes, and for that matter, he's taking me to Ryan's Inn for dinner tonight."

"Well, for land's sakes. I guess I have been working too much. I haven't even kept up on the local gossip. That's no way to run a small-town newspaper."

Andy liked white wine, Nancy preferred red, so they each ordered their own choice. Nancy lifted her glass in a toast.

"Don't seek the answers, live the question—Rainer Maria Rilke," she said.

"Hear, hear," Andy said.

Nancy's knowledge, demeanor, looks, and business acumen impressed Andy. He liked her sense of humor, and recognized that she often used humor to veil her disgust with the orthodoxy within many professions. He also noticed that she usually brightened up once the business discussions were over. He remembered kissing Nancy on the cheek the first time they were out for lunch at Ray's Fine Food. "Nice touch, but don't push it, counselor," Nancy had said with a good-natured smile.

Andy looked at her now with her wine glass in hand. He truly liked Nancy. Women still kind of scared him though.

His first marriage lasted two years. And they had slept together only the first six months of that time. There was no hate or anything; it just happened. They grew to not like each other. It took Andy many months to realize the finality of it all, and nine more months waiting for the divorce to be final.

"You've been hurt," Nancy said abruptly.

Andy was a trial lawyer and didn't fluster easily; still, Nancy Bartel had a gift for catching and keeping him off-balance. *How the hell did she know?* he asked himself. "Well, yes," he replied out loud.

She nodded, and took one of his hands in both of hers. "I thought so."

After that, she drew him out gently and carefully. She drew his whole life story from him, including his disastrous marriage. She kept him loose-talking and poured his wine glass full. And it felt right and good.

All of a sudden Andy raised his hand in protest.

"Okay, enough of that, Nancy Bartel. How about you? Ever been married?"

"I think marriage might be only for those who can dedicate themselves to being married," she said.

Andy reflected on the pieces of Nancy's life story she had shared with him. Leaving home when she was eighteen, and protesting the Vietnam war in the late sixties along with her life in a California commune: beads, headbands, drugs, leather-fringed jackets; and her stint in the Peace Corps in Central America. She'd talked of seeing men and women, in many countries enslaved to the culture of traditionalism and drudgery, and kept from rising out of it.

"You're quite the rebel, aren't you, Nancy?" Andy asked.

"I don't consider myself a rebel," Nancy said. "I just want to keep an open mind and enjoy all of life's surprises, even if some are unspeakable."

Andy was amused. He'd found that when Nancy got wound up, she was hard to stop; what with all her philosophizing and questioning of life's purposes.

"At least for right now," Nancy continued. "I want to learn not to judge the folks at Holiday Forever, control them, make their life right or wrong, or change them to my or anyone else's views. They should have a chance to free their minds and clear any path they choose to follow."

"Hi, Jason," the chief said. "Want a lift the rest of the way home?"

Jason knew of the police chief, but he'd never been offered a ride in the squad car before. He thought it would be a real treat, something he could tell his high school buddies about.

"Sure," Jason said. The chief opened the door for him.

"How do you like the squad?" the chief asked.

Jason observed a shotgun locked in its holder between the seats and searched for the radio controls.

"Cool," he said.

"Got the time to take a cruise with me, Jason?"

There was nothing Jason would like better, but he was having a hard time figuring out what kind of luck had befallen him to get this kind of opportunity. *I'm not going to pass it up though,* he thought.

"Sure thing," Jason said and wondered where the switches were for the red lights and siren

"I'll take her out on the highway and show you what this squad can do."

Jason nodded his approval. In a short while, they were on the open highway. The chief turned on the rotating red light and the siren and was doing ninety in less than a minute. He slacked off, slowed down, and turned to Jason.

"Ever thought of being in police work?" the chief asked.

Jason had thought about it, but never real seriously. He thought it was something he could take pride in, though. The chief told him that the police were looking for good, patriotic citizens like him.

A week later, Jason was enjoying his second ride with the chief.

"Ever met a big-time federal agent, Jason?" the chief asked.

"Never," Jason said.

"I've got someone that wants to meet you,"

The chief drove to an alley behind the old stockyards, where the pens and corrals were abandoned and falling apart. The chief pulled up alongside a green sedan parked by a loading chute. A man in a dark suit and sunglasses standing by the sedan got into the backseat of the squad car.

"This is federal agent eighty-eight," the chief said. "He can't reveal his name—only his number."

Jason was riding as high in his mind as he'd ever been. He'd never excelled at sports and wasn't too hot with girls, but here he was in the company of the police chief and a secret agent of the U.S. government.

"I understand you're a good, patriotic citizen, a straight arrow," the agent said.

"Yeah, I guess so," Jason said. "I believe in our government."

"Well, how'd you like to do a little work for your country?"

"Is it something you think I could do?"

"Sure, Jason. You'll make more money than they are paying you at the home. And you can continue working at the home—at the same time. You'll be our eyes and ears."

Jason wondered how much better it could be. He could be an undercover fed. If that wasn't prestige, nothing was. He didn't think this job would last that long, but he was sure he'd be hot man—number one with the girls once he blew his cover.

"Count me in," Jason said. Then he suddenly began to wonder, why they had sought him out. He didn't think they had zeroed in on him accidently, and he began to worry.

"It's just a simple task we've got for you, Jason," the agent said. "All you have to do is keep your eyes and ears open and report to us."

Jason thought it must be something at school, but he didn't know anything other than that a few of the kids smoked a joint now and then. *Geeze, I hope I don't have to rat on them,* he thought.

"We think there is something funny going on at Holiday Forever," the chief said. "Ever see anything suspicious going on up there?"

Jason thought for awhile. "Only thing I can think of is one of the nurses, Susan Pelt, came by the other day."

Jason figuring he was an agent now, spiced up his language a bit. "She was crying to my boss Katey and having a shit hemorrhage about an old guy named Christian Blade. Said old Christian was eighty-six and recovering from his third heart attack, but he had this friend—her name was Monique—about thirty that came to see him. Susan said she thought Monique was a prostitute. I saw her one time myself—she's one hell of a looker. Susan said she'd told Nancy, the owner, about it, but Nancy told her that whatever was happening in Mr. Blade's room was none of our business.

"We're really not interested in that kind of stuff right now," Agent 88 said. "Can you think of anything else?"

Jason told them about the ten-dollar bet Katey had made with Minnow on the Minnesota-Iowa game.

"Anything connected with drugs?" the agent asked.

Jason said he didn't know anything about any drugs, but he'd keep his eyes and ears open.

With this new responsibility, Jason began watching all the cop programs on TV and became intrigued with the fast cars and hot women that undercover agents operated with on the programs. The chief gave him a little spending money, but told him he needed more solid information on drugs for it to be worth their while.

Katey boiled a batch of marijuana in cheesecloth, made the mistake of carelessly discarding the contents in the garbage.

The next day, Jason, the high school spy had something "worth their while", and planned on making them pay for it. That night Jason met Agent 88 and the chief at the old stockyards.

Jason told them he had found a bag of marijuana, and had taken a picture of it in the garbage can before he removed it.

"Great. Where is it?" asked the agent. Jason had watched cop shows most of the previous night, and put on the bravado of one of his TV idols.

"You guys haven't lived up to your bargain," Jason said. "The price has gone up."

"What do you mean, you little shit?" the agent shouted.

The chief intervened. "Wait a minute. Let's not get too excited here," he said. "Maybe we've short-changed Jason a bit. Let's see what he has to say. What can we do for you, Jason my?"

Jason puffed himself up as much as he could, like he'd seen on TV.

"I need a hot car and a hot woman. Get me that Monique that comes to the home."

Agent 88 did all he could to stifle a laugh and coughed into his hand. "We can't do that kind of stuff, kid."

Jason looked away, got out of the car and began walking towards home. He was nearly home when the green sedan pulled up alongside him.

"Hold on, Jason," the agent said. "I think we can work something out. We can't let you have a car, but how about we get you a hot girl with a hot car?"

Jason saw himself being driven around town where he could be seen by the high school crowd. His girl would be so hot, she'd steam a windshield—lipstick red as blood. She'd be wearing a miniskirt, and his hand would be on the bare skin of her thigh as she drove.

"Now yer talkin'," Jason said.

The state Bureau of Criminal Apprehension sent down one of the undercover agents they used on prostitution stings. She was busty, blonde, and drove a red convertible. White leather boots, miniskirt, tight sweater, blood red lipstick, the whole nine yards.

She picked Jason up at the stockyards. When Jason got in her car, she slid her hand over to his upper thigh.

"Where to, sweetheart?" she asked. "Or do you want some action right here?" Jason's leg was shaking, as she brushed her hand a little nearer his crotch. Jason squirmed towards the door on his side.

"We need to drive through town a few times," he said. "What's your name?"

"Frenchie, and I'm hotter than a fresh-fucked fox in a forest fire."

Frenchie put the stick shift in low, gunned the throttle and let out the clutch. They threw gravel thirty feet behind them and the tires squealed like banshees. Jason thought for a moment his neck had snapped.

"How do you like that for power?" Frenchie asked.

Jason's throat was like one big swollen Adam's apple. He couldn't get a word out. Frenchie made the next corner on two wheels and headed for Main Street.

Jason thought about putting his hand on the woman's leg, but the thoughts froze with fear. In fact, Jason had never had his hand on any woman's leg. He'd never been with a woman. He'd only been kissed twice, a couple of goodnight pecks, after the junior prom.

Frenchie screeched the convertible into a parking place on Main Street, got out of the car, and hiked her sweater up so her navel ring and tattoo showed above the waistband of her miniskirt. She strutted over to Jason's side of the car. When Jason got out she hooked her arm in his. They paraded up one side of the street, crossed at the corner, and strutted down the other. Frenchie's six-inch spike heels hit the sidewalk like tap hammers on a cement block.

"How'd it go?" Agent 88 asked Frenchie after she had dropped Jason off at home..

"The kid will never be the same. It will take him a week or two to put his nerves back together. The poor kid. He's about as virgin a territory as I've ever experienced. I know I wasn't supposed to do anything with him, but I had him going like a race car and couldn't resist. I tickled his ear with my tongue and gave him a French kiss. I thought that thing was going to break the zipper in his pants. I touched his balls with my little finger and his teeth began to chatter. Then the kid came all over himself. He was mighty glad to be home when I let him out of the car.

"How'd it go, kid?" Agent 88 asked Jason.

"Great wheels," Jason said. "And the babe, she was okay. Made her wait half the night before I topped her off."

Chapter 42

MONIQUE STRETCHED AND arched her shoulders as she walked. The still, warm evening air brought a feeling of contentment to her. She pulled open the front door of Holiday Forever and swished inside.

Nancy, working late, pushed her chair back from her desk, leaned back, and cupped her hands behind her head of sandy hair. She swiveled her chair, and gazed out the window where evening shadows on the lawn were fading in the twilight. A self-satisfied smile softened her face and her heart warmed thinking of the trials and circumstances she had overcome to create the harmonious community spirit in her guest home.

She noticed the gray van for the first time when its side door opened. A man in a blue-gray jacket and a stylish seed corn cap stepped out and hurried across the street. The letters "D.E." something was stitched to his cap. The man hurried to the entrance of Holiday Forever. Nancy rested at her desk, unconcerned, knowing the head nurse at the main desk would take care of whatever the man needed.

A moment later, however, her office door burst open. The man with the blue-gray jacket rushed in and closed the door behind him.

"Stay put," he commanded in a brusque voice. "I'm from the D.E.A. I have a search warrant for the entire premises. Are you Nancy Bartel?"

"Knocking before you enter out of style, sergeant? What's the D.E.A.?"

"I'm not a sergeant," he said indignantly. "I'm Larry Chute, central office director, Chicago District Federal Drug Enforcement Agency." He shoved the search warrant in the direction of Nancy's face.

Nancy took the warrant and rose from the chair. She saw a flurry of activity outside her window. The van was emptying a cargo of men onto the street. Some were uniformed men with handguns, rifles and shotguns. They all ran toward and around her building. Their jackets and caps illustrated their trade. B.C.A., F.B.I., Police, and D.E.A. Shouts were coming from everywhere, both within and without the home.

"Freeze! Against the wall", someone shouted.

Nancy ran for her door, but was brusquely stopped and shoved to her chair by the D.E.A. man. She steeled herself and gripped the chair to restrain herself from challenging the officer.

"What the hell are you crazy sons-of-bitches doing?" Nancy yelled. There was another scream and Nancy sprang from her chair. She tried to push by the officer again. He put an arm lock on her and threw her backwards. Her face hit the door jamb when she fell to the floor. Officer Chute put his knee in her back and cuffed her hands behind her. He slid her across the floor, sat her up and propped her against the wall.

"You're under arrest for resisting an officer," he said, and read her the Miranda Rights.

Nancy felt the blood run from her nose onto her white blouse. "You Nazi son-of-a-bitch. What's going on here?"

Director Chute replied stiffly, "This is a raid, in full cooperation with the United States Drug Enforcement Agency, the F.B.I., the Minnesota Bureau of Criminal Apprehension, and the Norwood Police Department. We are seeking evidence of illegal drugs, prostitution, gambling, bookmaking, pornography, and restricted sex paraphernalia. We will be searching the grounds and every room."

"You're completely out of your minds," Nancy said. She coughed blood from her mouth, and knew her nose had been broken.

"I'll need a favor," she said, addressing the officer in a defeated tone. "Pick up the phone, dial 777-2223, and put the phone to my ear. First, though, there's some cotton in the first-aid kit there on the wall. You do know first-aid, don't you, sergeant? Wad up a bit of the cotton and stick it up this bloody nose of mine."

"Why the call?"

"I think I'm going to need a lawyer, and when I'm through, you can use the phone, because I'm sure you're going to need one also. Seems to me, your ass will be in a peck of trouble for what's going on here."

Larry Chute frowned. "If you can act like a lady, I'll take those cuffs off and give you your first-aid kit. Then you can make your call."

"Act like a lady," really pissed Nancy off. It took all of her emotional and mental strength to control her fury and focus on what needed to be done next. *Fake some diplomacy perhaps.* "Maybe we both acted a little harshly," Nancy said. "Let's start over, okay?"

"Promise no funny business?"

When Nancy nodded, Chute unlocked the cuffs and held her arms, waiting for further reply.

"No funny business," she said. Chute gave her the first-aid kit and put the phone on the floor beside her and stood guard, soldier-fashion, at the door.

"I'd like to sit at my desk, wipe my face with some tissue, and make the call," Nancy said.

"Go ahead."

Nancy put the cotton in her nose and wiped her face with tissue. The blood in the back of her throat had clotted. She wiped her blouse the best she could, then dialed.

"Andy Curtis."

"Andy, this is Nancy. Can you come right over? We're being raided."

"Panty raid, Nancy?" laughed Andy. "You people are a little old for that, aren't you? What's with your voice? Got a stuffy nose?"

"It's stuffy, alright—its broken. Andy, I'm serious. We've got trouble. A real raid. The Feds, the Crime Bureau, the vice squad. One of the officers is standing right here. They've gone wild. They won't let me out of my office."

"Nancy, you can't be serious!"

"Oh, but I am. Are you coming over, or do I have to call some other parasite of your profession?" Nancy yelled.

"I'll be right there, but this better not be a joke."

Nancy hung up and turned to the officer. "Officer Chute," she said. "Would you post a guard and search this office later? I have guests that need special attention. I think it would be in your best interest if I were allowed to look after them."

"I'll walk with you until you find someone to assign the duties to, then you will have to come with me to the police station. When your lawyer gets here, they can tell him to come to the station."

Minnow sat upright in bed with his hinged telephone at his ear. He was wearing his favorite red, yellow, and blue Pendleton shirt over his pajama top.

"Ten on Wisconsin by three," Minnow said into the phone, as two uniformed men burst into his room. One of the officers swatted the phone to the side. Minnow lost his balance and tumbled from the bed. His overbalanced torso fell, almost like a weighted arrow, head first to the floor.

"What the hell is going on, Minnow?" a voice said on the phone. The BCA man picked up the phone. "Who is this?"

"Twenty-one. Who's this? Where's Minnow?"

"Twenty-one. That's a funny name. What's your real name?"

"Fuck you, ass hole!"

Minnow lay unconscious on the floor.

"Oh, for Christ's sake," said the DEA man. "Help me get this guy back in bed." Minnow's legless frame was difficult to handle. Finally, the officers slung their rifles on their backs and muscled the unconscious Minnow back to his bed.

The BCA Man checked Minnow's pulse and nodded his head to the DEA Man. "I think he just rung his bell."

"Christ, I hope that's all," said the officer.

Ignoring Minnow, the two began their search through the bureau drawers and the closet. BCA Man viewed the notepad from Minnow's bed and glanced at the last notation.

"Got it." He displayed the notepad to his partner.

Minnow groaned, and his mind struggled back to consciousness. His head throbbed and hot shooting pains knifed through his neck; then he vomited.

As his mind began to clear, and the pain in his neck began to subside, he rolled to one side and then the other, propped himself up on his elbows, and said in a deep husky voice,

"Evening boys. You did have an appointment, didn't you? I expect my line had been busy, or you would have called. You wouldn't mind helping a fellow sit up, would you? Is it the odds that's bothering you boys?" Minnow wiped the mixture of blood and vomit from his face with the bed sheet.

BCA Man shoved the notepad in Minnow's direction. "You're under arrest for engaging in illegal bookmaking."

The officers sat Minnow up in bed, read him his rights, handcuffed him behind his back, and leaned him against the headboard of the bed.

Minnow coughed, cleared his throat, and spat a direct hit between the feet of DEA Man, splashing the mixture of phlegm, vomit, and blood on the officer's mirror-shined shoes.

"I'm sad-assed sorry about that, sir," Minnow said, "but my aim is not too good, trussed up like I am. Now I'm ready to make a deal with you boys. A real bargain. However, there may be some risk in it for you, so think about it before you decide. Here's my deal. You take these cuffs off me and I'll promise not to run."

While the officers continued their search, Naked George came into the room, followed by a uniformed police officer.

"George, get me a doctor and a lawyer, in that order, will you?"

The officer spoke to his brethren. "Got a nut case here. I don't know where he belongs or what to do with him. I'm not touching this naked mental case"

"I resent your inference, uneducated slob," Naked George said.

The officers talked openly about Naked George, as if he were a nonentity.

"Find some attendant to take care of this crazy guy," said DEA Man to one of the uniformed officers.

Naked George ignored the men, got a washbasin, cloth, and towel from the bathroom and cleaned Minnow up.

"Tough game, Minnow," George said. "I'll take ten on you though; straight up, no points." The officers stared, without interfering,

"No bet, George. I'm betting on myself." Minnow felt faint again. He had been handcuffed before, but not since his legs were amputated.

Naked George picked up the phone. The officers just looked at each other. George called emergency at the Northfield hospital and related the pertinent information to the doctor on duty.

Minnow told George he needed insulin immediately, and at least some aspirin for the pain from the fall.

Naked George turned to the officers. "Would you frozen-minded Neanderthal military men please take these cuffs off my friend? Thaw out your brains and let some compassion enter your minds."

Minnow lost his balance and tipped precariously toward the floor. Naked George saved him from falling.

"We better take the cuffs off," said DEA Man. They removed the handcuffs and helped Minnow to a sitting position.

"I'll go see about the insulin and get one of the nurses to check you over," Naked George said. "I'll be your witness in court Minnow, even if I have to put my clothes on." The officers allowed him to leave.

In room 222, Monique pulled a chair to the side of Christian Blade's bed—kicked off her red spike heeled shoes and tucked her shapely legs, along with her black net stockings, beneath her on the chair. Her tight knit skirt was comfortably hitched halfway between her belt and thigh. The zipper on her undersized red wool sweater was at half mast.

Andy Jackson, on a folded twenty, seemed to be smiling as he peered above Monique's bosom-filled black lace bra. Christian popped open a chilled bottle of champagne; he and Monique clicked their half-filled glasses in a toast.

"Here's to drink, here's to hope. Here's to what's ailing my little piece of rope," Christian said. His cloudy, eighty-six-year-old eyes had brightened.

"Here! Here!" Monique said. She raised her glass high and had planted a kiss on Christian's forehead, just as the door burst open.

Monique jumped up and turned to the doorway.

"Freeze," said a young blue-uniformed officer carrying a rifle. "Aha!" The officer grabbed Andy Jackson from the lip of Monique's lacy bra—while simultaneously scanning her sumptuous body from head to foot.

Monique looked at the officer calmly, and sat down and curled her legs up beneath her again. A wholesome smile, which belied her part-time profession, blossomed on her face.

"What's so funny, sister?" the officer asked.

"You," Monique said. "You, standing there with your rifle in one hand and a twenty dollar bill in the other and leering as if you'd never have another chance to see a full set of boobs in your life."

"You're both under arrest on suspicion of prostitution," the officer said, and reached for his handcuffs.

Outside, Orson Bacon walked towards the tool shed with his garden hoe in hand. at his heels. Orson reached down, to pet the golden coat of his best friend Fats, following along at his side.

"Fats, old girl," he said. "I think it's time we call it a day. Come along. I'll put this blister-maker away and lock up the old shed. Then I'll be leaving you. I think I'll go have a couple of beers. Ever thought about having a couple of beers, Fats?"

Orson took one last look at the blue and white clouds in the western sky. His solitude was abruptly broken as two uniformed police officers approached him; one of them carrying a battering ram.

"Hi guys, what's up?" Orson asked.

"Hit the dirt."

"You guys aren't from around here, are you?" Orson asked.

"I said, hit the dirt."

"I've been hitting dirt all damned day with this blister machine."

The second blue coat grabbed Orson by the back of the collar, tripped him, and threw him to the ground. Pear shaped Orson flattened the earth like one big puff ball. He was choking and gasping for breath, as the tin badges pulled his arms behind his head and cuffed him.

Fats growled, showed her teeth, and sunk them into the cloth on the pants leg of the kitten-faced officer. Fats shook the pants leg, trying to free Orson. Kitten face drew his weapon, kicked at Fats, and shot. Fat's head dropped, before her whole body collapsed.

The officers pulled Orson, wheezing and coughing, to a sitting position on the grass. His body convulsed, and tears streamed down his face. Sitting off balance and handcuffed behind his back, Orson tumbled sideways and rolled onto his back.

The officers deserted Orson in that position and proceeded on their way to search the tool shed for marijuana. They poised their battering ram; ready to break in the door as a completely naked man approached them.

"The door's not locked," Naked George said casually from a distance. "No need to break it in."

They looked in astonishment at the arrow-straight, smooth-bodied, naked old man with a wineskin face. The officers put down their battering ram. To them, the naked old man acted as if he were on an ordinary, regular evening stroll.

Naked George continued his laconic approach, setting an even, nonchalant gait.

"Better look after old Orson over there," he said. "The guy with the dead dog at his feet. He's got bad heart trouble and it sure sounds like he ain't getting' his breath. If you boys know some first aid, you better look after him very quickly."

Naked George inched close by the officers and looked across the green yard to Orson.

"He could be a goner if somebody don't check him over; see that he gets some air. His lungs are all filled up. Dangerous thing when you have emphysema, being trussed up and on your back like that."

The wide-eyed officers looked from Naked George to Orson. Recognizing the danger, they hurried to Orson's aid, and helped him to a sitting position. They peered into his slimy, snot-dripping face, and then whacked his back a few times.

"Are you okay?"

"Goddamned stupid assholes," Orson said. "Why did you little piss ants have to kill a nice, gentle dog like our Fats? Someday, somebody will get you for that."

One of the officers looked back towards the tool shed. The door was open. The slack-skinned naked man was approaching them again. He carried a long-handled shovel and a large brown paper shopping bag. Each side of the bag was emblazoned in lavender letters with "Ebert's Fine Women's Wear".

"Wait right there!" shouted an officer.

Naked George quickly stopped as he was told.

"I'd like to bury the dog," Naked George said. He continued in an even voice without a touch of urgency. "Better get her buried before some of the old ladies see her out here. Some of them might go crazy, or have a heart attack, or try to put a butcher knife in you men."

He bent over and pulled what appeared to be an unending length of blue plastic from the bag. "I got this plastic to wrap old Fats in before I cover her with dirt. Is it okay to leave my bag and shovel here while I go get my shoes? Awfully hard to dig barefoot." Without waiting for a reply, he moved on, leaving the long-handled shovel and the shopping bag in the grass.

Minutes later, Naked George came back, picked up Fats, wrapped her in plastic, and carried her to the corner of the lot. Blood from the dog smeared George's side and chest. He was wearing only burnished black oxfords and black calf-length socks held up by black garters with red borders. He went back for the shovel and shopping bag, ambled over to the corner of the lot by the large stately elm, and began digging.

In room 234, Les Morig, feeling pain from the pressure on his eyes caused by glaucoma and jittery from the spasms of multiple sclerosis, prepared his homegrown herbal relief. Carefully, he sprinkled the dry, brownish-green substance from a baggie onto the paper and rolled the joint; he walked to the window, and looked out at the dim sunset. Men with rifles and handguns were guarding the building. Les immediately knew what was going on. As a roaming vagabond, this wasn't the first raid he had observed in his life. With calm resignation, he chocked his door open and sat down in his easy chair, leaving the plastic bag of marijuana and papers on his nightstand. Drawing a deep breath on his reefer, he held his uneven breath, and then exhaled, watching the blue smoke curl and rise toward the ceiling. As officers rushed through his open door, he took another deep drag and exhaled slowly.

They grabbed the cigarette. The dry paper stuck to the moisture of Les's licked lips. The joint fell apart and glowing embers of marijuana showered Les and the officers.

"Nice move." Les brushed the ash from his lap and picked the paper from his lip. Without being instructed, he arose and faced the wall, hands clasped behind his back, while they cuffed him and read him his rights.

One of the officers shoved the half-full bag of grass under his nose. "What's this? Marijuana?"

"Brownie mix," Les replied.

"We can take this smart ass right off to jail."

One officer struck Les alongside the head.

"He must think he's in pot heaven, look at him, he's old but healthy-looking. A few nights in jail and he might get some respect for the society that spends its tax dollars to keep him in a euphoria of smoke."

Les smiled defiantly, his head smarting from the blow.

Several doors down and across the hall, two more officers entered a room unannounced.

Ernestine Cusboard sat up in bed, gave her last gasp, expired and lay down. Her open, glassy eyes stared at the officers from her dried up wrinkled face. The officers looked aghast at each other, then back to Ernestine's open, now clouding, eyes.

"Is she dead?"

"I think so. This is the wrong room. Let's get the hell out of here."

In another room, Sharon Hanford 84, and Lydia Barnhoff, 86, sat in their chairs, awestruck and embarrassed. The officers searching their room confiscated a couple of dildos, a graphic book on how to use them, and a mail-order catalog of sexually explicit material.

"We'll deal with you ladies later," they said, leaving the room with their booty.

Susan Pelt, the duty nurse, ran up and down the hall shouting.

"I knew it! I knew it! I told you so. I told you so. Oh, my God, what am I going to do?"

Adele, unmolested by the police, scurried from room to room trying to make order. Her professional composure intact, she made the rounds, reassuring the excited and confused guests. At Minnow's room however, fear and heartache swept over her.

"Are you okay, Minnow?" she asked.

"I think so. A nurse just looked me over, gave me a shot of insulin and something for my pain. Naked George called for the doctor. You go help someone else now." Adele reluctantly stepped out and looked down the hall. Naked George, with shoes, socks, garters, and a bloodstained chest, was about to leave the building. She ran to him.

"What happened to you? You crazy coot, what are you doing?"

"They shot Fats. I'm burying her over by the big elm tree in the yard."

Adele couldn't hold on any longer. Her resolve melted to tears. Her face and body went soft and mushy, as if there were no bones in her structure. A voice within her told her she couldn't let this happen. Then her face and body tightened, as if a wire drawstring pulled every feature together. She became taut—stiff as a hickory stick, and continued her rounds, inspecting every room systematically. After finding Ernestine, she returned to her office to call the undertaker. A blue-uniformed officer was searching her desk. He looked up as she came in.

"This your office?" he asked. "We have a search warrant for the premises. We're searching for illegal drugs, pornographic materials, and evidence of bookmaking." A self-satisfied smirk crossed his young face.

Only Adele's piercing eyes moved. The cold rays of her steely sight settled on the bloodstained, torn cuff on the pant leg of the officer. Her lips were so tightly compressed, a crowbar couldn't have parted them. Adele didn't waiver when the officer stared into her face.

"You're the one that shot our dog, aren't you?" she asked.

"That bitch attacked an officer in the performance of his duty," he said with all the officialdom of his office.

Adele reacted instinctively, reverting to her days in the military. She kneed him hard in the groin, gave him a quick judo chop to each side of his neck, and bloodied his nose with her knee as he fell. He was down and out. She took his gun from its holster, emptied the shells from the chamber, put them in her pocket, and laid the empty gun on her desk. *"I should stick it up your ass and twist it,"* she muttered. Thinking better of it, she merely took the cartridges from her pocket, pulled his pants down and shoved them up his butt. When he began to moan, Adele left him and continued on her rounds, caring for her people.

It was after dusk when Burt, who of late had begun showing his age with slowness of mind and body, drove his old, well-kept Pontiac carefully towards the guest home. He was returning from an errand down by the river for Les. Officers stringing colored rope across the street blocked him from his destination. Leaving his car in the street, he stooped under the rope and strode toward the home.

"Get out of this area! Get back in your car!" shouted a police officer.

"Has there been an accident? Is someone hurt?" Burt asked.

"Nobody's hurt. We're conducting an investigation. We don't need onlookers or sightseers. Now get back in your car, old man, and get out of here."

"Everybody okay? Nobody hurt or killed?"

"No. Now get."

A mental picture of the lush green weeds Les grew by the home and down by the river swam slowly into Burt's mind. He had the tops of some of them in the trunk of his car. He was to put them in Orson's tool shed for drying.

"Don't just stand there acting like one of the patients here. Get the hell out of here!"

Burt ambled back to his car. He drove very carefully and later stopped at a small, white frame house five blocks away. As he knocked on the door, a huge gray cat rubbed on his leg.

Marvin Gastner, a bald man, about seventy, answered the knock. He looked at Burt, then at the giant feline. Marvin's eyebrows were as stiff and long as the cat's whiskers.

"Randolph, where have you been?" He nodded to Burt and back to the cat. "Cat's name is Randolph. Randolph Scott. He's been out drifting on the prairie for nigh on two weeks now. Come on in, Burt—you too, Randolph. What can I do for you?"

Marvin ushered them both into the kitchen of his bachelor quarters. Dirty dishes were piled high in the rust-caked sink. He opened the door of the small refrigerator. A leftover morsel wrapped in wax paper fell from a shelf to the floor.

"Randolph," Marvin said, picking up the morsel. "Look at that damned face of yours. I'll bet you can hardly see out of that left eye. Been fighting again, haven't you? Can't tell if you won or lost. You look better'n last time, though."

Burt squirmed, holding his rumpled brown hat in his hand.

"Let me get this old ruffian cowpoke some victuals, a little milk, and I'll be right with you," Marvin said.

"How's your ankle, Marvin?" Burt asked.

"My three weeks recuperation at the guest home fixed me up pretty good. That's quite a place over there. I made a lot of friends in three weeks." Marvin attempted to clear a space at the table and pulled out a chair and motioned Burt to sit.

"That Minnow Grubbs sure is quite a fellow, isn't he? I got to him for twenty bucks when I was up there. I called him up just a while ago. I wanted to put ten on Saturday's game. Something happened right in the middle of our conversation. A lot of commotion, then some smart ass got on the phone and demanded to know who I was. I told him to stick it. You know what's going on, Burt?"

"Marvin, do you know what D.E.A. stands for?"

"How's it used?"

"Well, I was on a little errand with my car. When I came back to the home, it was all roped off. Cops were all over the place. One of them ordered me off. Told me to get the hell out of there. He had 'D.E.A.' on the back of his jacket."

"I've seen that on T.V. I think it stands for Drug Enforcement Agency."

"Well, what would they be doing up there?"

"You tell me, Burt. When I was up there, it seemed to me that you and Les were doing some interesting things with the weeds in that herbal garden.

Weeds? What do you mean, by weeds?"

"Marijuana."

"I wasn't never sure. Les told me not to ask. Les is big on herbs—aloe, ginseng. You suppose they'll be after me?"

"You got any of the weed?"

"We haul some in my trunk once in awhile from the river plot. Got a couple of the tops off the weeds in the trunk now. Les has some dried and in baggies. There's a big shopping bag from Ebert's more than half-full of it up at Orson's tool shed."

"You've got a river plot, too?"

"Marvin ... er ... I've known you ever since I came to town, a few years ago. Les and I, we've always bought our garden seeds and tomato plants from you. I would consider it a great favor if I could pull my car into your garage for a bit. Maybe you could help me clean it up, vacuum the trunk. Then maybe we could burn everything in your wood cook stove there."

"Sure. Pull that old Pontiac into the garage. I'll help you clean her up. Nobody will know but you, me, and Randolph Scott. Me and Randolph, we're as tight lipped as a Methodist old maid."

Nancy's message bothered Andy Curtis. He made a phone call.

"Cliff, this is Andy," he said. "Got a call from a client; have to cancel our tennis match. Let's reschedule for next week, same time."

"No problem."

Andy splashed his face with cold water, combed his hair, and put on his gray sweater. The one that Nancy liked. He patted a dash of shaving lotion on his cheeks, and reminded himself, *"Hey, this is business, not a date,"*

The cool, smoky haze of dusk had turned to darkness. A sense of urgency crept into Andy's mind. As he walked to his car, he heard what must have been a gunshot. The gunshot startled Andy out of a daydream about Nancy. The sound had come from the direction of Holiday Forever. Adrenaline induced shivers of anticipation rushed through his body. The red and blue lights of squad cars reflecting through the tree leaves further astonished Andy when he arrived at the home.

"For Christ's sake," he said aloud. "This is serious," and he jogged to the entryway, only to be stopped by a policeman.

"I'm Andy Curtis, attorney for Nancy Bartel."

"I'm not sure if Miss Bartel is here. I'll get an escort for you. First, show me some identification."

Escorted by a police officer, Andy entered the building, and found Nancy's office locked. Naked George, in the hallway, seemed to be the only person in charge.

"They took Nancy and Adele down to the police station," George said. "I've called the doctor for Orson and Minnow. He isn't here yet. They shot and killed our dog. Mrs.Cusboard is dead. What should I do about her?"

Andy observed Katey Long, glassy-eyed and unsteadily making her way from the kitchen, with a fifth of Jack Daniel's in her hand.

"You the guy that killed our dog—Fffaats," she slurred, and swung the whiskey bottle at the officer's head. The officer ducked and Katey missed. She twisted in a tight circle, settled to the floor as if in slow motion, and passed out.

Andy needing time to think, walked the five blocks to the police station, where he was recognized by a local policemen.

"Where's Nancy?" Andy asked.

Bewildered and meek, by the goings on, the young officer pointed to the chief's office.

"In there with the chief, the B.C.A., and the D.E.A.," he said.

Andy entered the chief's office without knocking. Blood had dried on the cotton in Nancy's nose. A bruise on her cheek had turned an ugly black and blue, and her hair was a matted mess.

"What the hell is going on here?" Andy inquired.

A tall man stood up and faced Andy.

"I'm Commander Schwartz, commanding officer of Region 5 D.E.A."

Andy looked at his crew cut and noted his name. "How appropriate," he thought.

Schwartz continued. "This is Officer Clayton of the B.C.A. and Chief Douglass, whom I believe you already know."

"They're all crazy," Nancy interrupted. "They hurt Minnow and Orson and ... and shot Fats. You can see what they did to me!"

"I'm an attorney, representing Miss Bartel. I'd like to talk to my client privately, please." Andy said.

The commander looked to the chief, who nodded toward Nancy. "Of course," he said. "Chief, can you find them a room?"

"There's a table in the fire hall," the chief said, and ushered them to the hall.

Nancy slumped in a folding chair by a card table. She put her hands to her face, amid a flood of tears. Then Nancy related everything she knew about the raid.

Andy shook his head in disbelief. When Nancy had finished, he went to the outer office and addressed the chief and commander.

"This stupid-assed raid has me more than pissed off." Andy's voice had a growl like a German Shepherd.

"I want to inform you at this time that I am representing all of the people under arrest of investigation in connection with your raid at Holiday Forever. I would like the names of anyone arrested or detained in any manner, and a list of the charges. Now." He exclaimed.

The officers assembled the list of names and charges. After looking them over Andy asked to use the phone.

"Certainly." Chief Douglass made room for the counselor. "Judge Norton, this is Attorney Andy Curtis over in Norwood." Andy filled the judge in on all the particulars he deemed relevant about his clients and asked to have them released on their own recognizance. The judge said to wait ten minutes and he'd call him back.

Judge Norton then called the sheriff's office in Norwood. "Sheriff," the judge said. "I just got a strange call from Attorney Curtis, over there in Norwood. He gave me quite a story about a police raid on the local rest home. What the hell is going on? You involved in it?"

"No. I've heard talk about it, though. I didn't think they would really do it. I think the B.C.A. and the narcs have gone a little nutty. They approached me a couple of months ago, wanted me to join in their investigation. I told them to back off and let me take care of it. I didn't like the way they were acting, so when they didn't back off, I told them I wouldn't have anything to do with their goddamn raid. They were acting as if an organized crime ring were operating the rest home. I never heard from them again. I sure didn't think they would do something as dumb as this."

"You know this Nancy Bartel, sheriff?"

"Sure, judge. She's a fine woman."

"Let me read you the names of the other people they have arrested. Tell me if you know them." The sheriff laughed when he heard the names.

"Yes, I know them all, except Monique. They're certainly not a threat to society."

"So you don't know Monique," chuckled the judge.

"Nope."

"See any problem if I ordered them all released on their own recognizance?"

"Not at all. I'd do the same if I were Judge. But do you have the authority?"

"Probably not. But if just some of what Andy Curtis told me is true, I think the law officers should be shaking in their boots. I'm sure they'll do as I ask. Thanks, Sheriff. See you in court."

Chief Douglass answered on the first ring.

"Chief, this is Judge Norton. I want all of those whose names Mr. Curtis gave me in connection with your raid released on their own recognizance, immediately. Now, let me talk to that state B.C.A. man."

"Officer Clayton, Judge Norton wishes to speak to you."

"Officer Clayton, this is Judge Norton over in Northfield. What the hell are you guys doing over there?"

The officer began a long explanation, but shortly, the judge interrupted.

"I want them all released immediately on their own recognizance."

"Your honor, this is highly irregular."

"Your raid is highly irregular."

"There may be federal charges beyond your control," Clayton said.

"Then you better make the charges now. This is my order. I want them released until formal charges are filed." Then the judge hung up.

"Screw the judge." Clayton said to the chief. "Let's get on with our interrogation."

Andy's patience was worn thin. He asked permission to call Judge Norton again.

"Okay, okay," Officer Clayton said. "Forget your call It's getting late. Everyone is free to go counselor." See you in court."

Chapter 43

POOT ARMSTRONG HAND-SIGNALED the boxcar's entry to the siding, while Squint Eye Johnson applied the rail-siding hand switch in the freight-marshaling yard at the B&N Railroad terminal in Seattle. With the cars positioned, Poot climbed atop the last car and set the brake. As he made the last twist of the brake wheel, his hat blew off in the wind. Squint Eye uncoupled the lead car and disconnected the air-brake hoses.

Poot didn't like diesels. He longed for the old steam engine that had a personality and knew how to dress. Ever see a diesel that knew how to wear a cowcatcher and make it look like it belonged? Hell, no. The old engines could shoot steam out of both sides of their mouth and hiss like a snake, and when they sat and waited, sometimes you couldn't hear a thing. But touch that throttle and a thousand horses came alive with a roar. No, they didn't sit there and purr like a bunch of goddamned big house cats in a box. And whistle! Why, they could puncture an eardrum if they wanted, or make music, or just give you a tweet, like a little bird.

And smoke ... a diesel didn't know how to smoke. Always the same color. Greasy blue-black. Why, that steam engine could blow blue smoke, or white smoke lighter than the clearest cloud, and make it disappear in a wink, if it wanted. It could spew out black smoke in clouds bigger'n the boxcars and blacker'n the inside of a windowless room with the doors shut. His old steam engine, 87, why, he could blow white rings that would get eight feet across and go fifty feet high. He could even put black punctuation marks in the air. And he could speak four languages and talk in a thousand voices. His deepest one could make a bullfrog sound like a soprano.

"Purr, you son-of-a-bitch," he said to the diesel, as it pulled back to the main line.

Poot looked in each open door of the five boxcars on the siding while he advanced toward the front. At the fourth car, he stopped.

"We got a stiff in here," he hollered to Squint Eye. When his partner reached him, the two railroaders climbed aboard. The stiff was propped up in the corner with a green duffel bag near his feet.

"Let's frisk him before we call the dicks," Poot said. Squint Eye grabbed Poot's arm.

"Better not," he said. "We could lose our job, retirement and everything. The railroad brotherhood wouldn't even help us if we got caught at this."

"We'll just take the cash, if he has any, then. They can't find our fingerprints on clothes."

"Bums don't have much cash, stupid. You'd take the risk for nothing."

"How about the duffel bag? We could take that. Nobody would know the difference."

"We would. Have a little respect for the dead, Poot. Come on, we'll call the dicks."

The railroad detectives and a deputy coroner arrived at the boxcar a half hour later. The coroner searched the dead man for valuables and identification. There was seven dollars in a worn cloth wallet, no pictures, no credit cards, and no driver's license, only a dilapidated identification card that must have come with the wallet. The Wisconsin telephone number on the front of the card had been penciled through.

Written in ink on the back was: *In case of emergency, contact Nancy Bartel, Holiday Forever, Norwood, Minn.*, and the telephone number. There were only a few old clothes and some rain gear in the duffel bag.

Nancy, Billy, Lilla Mae, and Dianne were on break in the kitchen at Holiday Forever. Les Morig had disappeared. Katey the cook had called, said she'd had it, and was quitting. Billy and one of the nurses had cooked the meals the first day after the raid, and Lilla Mae and Dianne had taken over since.

Lilla Mae added cream to her coffee. "Some of Katey's Jack Daniel's would be better, but, I can't find any. She must have finished off her stash before she went home" she said.

"Who made these cinnamon rolls?" Nancy asked.

"Ruth brought them up this morning, but said she had to get back to her shop," Dianne said.

"That nose of yours is one sore sight, Nancy," Billy said.

"It looks like she's been drinking Jack Daniel's for years—a real booze nose. Are you sure it's just from that cop throwing you on the floor?" Lilla Mae asked.

Billy walked with his cane to the stove, and added a quantity of ham to the bean soup in a large kettle.

"Don't stir that with your cane like you did the gravy the other day," Lilla Mae shouted to him.

Billy turned to the assembled group with a grin. "You guys quit teasing. You've been teasing me ever since you came to help," he said.

"But you're so easy," Dianne said.

"How will I ever make it up to you guys?" Nancy asked. "I never even called you—you just showed up and took over. Daddy, you've been just great."

Billy smiled. He never thought his life would be this good ever again. Lilla Mae and Dianne were treating him like family, and it felt so good to be doing something for Nancy—acting like a father.

Adele marched into the room. "Billy, you look like a preacher directing a Ladies Aide meeting," she said, appraising the group. "How come I wasn't invited?"

Nancy cowered in her chair and held up her hands. "We're afraid of you. We didn't know you knew judo until you cold-cocked that cop." Nancy said.

"Oh, I was just a little upset," Adele replied. "I hate to interrupt your little tea party Nancy, but there is a call for you in the office—a railroad detective in Seattle. Did somebody catch up to your past out west?"

Nancy went to the office and answered the call. "This is Nancy Bartel."

"This is Detective Robert Grimley with Burlington Northern. We found the body of a man in one of our boxcars this morning. His ID card has the name Les Morig on it, along with your name to contact in case of emergency. We need to know what to do with the body."

Nancy wished death weren't part of life. She'd experienced enough of death. Thoughts of her mother, Al Krankus, and Burton rushed through her mind. And now, Les. She held the phone at arm's length, wishing there would be no more. Faintly, she heard, "Hello, hello, are you there?"

"Yes," Nancy said. "But I can't help you right now. We'll have to make an inventory of his room. He was a guest here, and may have relatives in Wisconsin. I'll have to call you back."

"Okay," he said and gave her a number to return the call.

After Nancy hung up, she needed someone to talk to or she'd start brooding and getting angry again. Already, she was thinking—if it weren't for the police, Les would be alive. Police were supposed to help people, not make moral judgments and stupid raids that resulted in injury and death. "Damn them. Damn them. Damn them!" she said aloud.

Nancy searched the premises for Adele, and found Orson, pushing a dust mop along the hall floor. Nancy put her arm around his shoulder and told him about Les. She felt him shake, but he didn't look up. She asked him to let Burt and Naked George know about Les. Orson wiped the tears from his face with a big red handkerchief and nodded. Adele, Lilla Mae, Dianne, and Billy were still in the kitchen when Nancy returned. She told them about Les. Adele pounded her fists on the table. The others shook their heads in disbelief.

"Where did we go wrong?" Adele asked, exhaling through clenched teeth.

Nancy shrugged her shoulders. A faraway look came to her eyes. "Were we wrong?" Then she turned to Adele. "We'll have to call the Seattle people back."

"I think we still have the Madison number Les gave us," Adele said. "And we should check his room. I know he had a metal lockbox in his closet."

The padlock on the lock box was unlocked. "Be my witness, and I'll see if there's anything in the box," Nancy said.

There were two things: a white, unsealed envelope addressed to Nancy, and a magnificent pearl necklace. Nancy opened the envelope and read the letter from within.

If you've found this letter, I expect there is an emergency. If circumstances call for it, be advised I have left a will on file at the registrar's office in the courthouse. This letter should be sufficient authorization for you to obtain the will. Thank you so much for giving me the opportunity to contribute to mankind rather than just being a burden during these many months, even though I have made my contribution in an unusual manner.

The pearls are to be given to your wonderful aunt, Ruth Krankus. Don't be discouraged, Nancy. Hang in there "till the last dog is hung and the bitch to the gallows." (Shakespeare)

Les Morig

The will named Nancy the executor of his estate. It also named her the trustee of two trusts. The first trust consisted of bank certificates of deposit for nearly four hundred thousand dollars. The trust instructed the trustee to use the funds in efforts to pass federal legislation to legalize the use of marijuana for medical purposes. One hundred thousand dollars was to be given to NORML, the National Organization for the Reform of Marijuana Laws. The other trust listed stocks valued in excess of two hundred thousand dollars, to be used by the trustee as seed money to establish other facilities in the style of Holiday Forever. The remainder of the estate, forty-eight thousand, four hundred seventy-six dollars and forty-three cents, was bequeathed to Katey Long.

A codicil attached to the will asked that his body be cremated. *I'd appreciate it if perhaps Orson would put my ashes in an open cardboard box, weighted with a stone in the bottom, and set it in a freight car just as it pulls out of the yard. The ashes should be gone to the winds by the time the freight reaches its destination.*

The will was duly notarized and witnessed.

Chapter 44

AT MID-MORNING, COUNTY Attorney Ludweg fidgeted while the judge admonished him to come up with a miracle. "Do something to get us out of this dilemma," he said. Then he adjourned court for one week.

The next day, County attorney Ludweg, met with his assistant—Chief Douglass, and a cohort—the chairman of the county board of commissioners.

"This thing has the potential of turning into a political farce," he said. "I thought that raid would assure my re-election. The feds have backed off completely, what with Les Morig being dead. And I'm politically dead if it goes on like this. We'll have to plea bargain."

Chief Douglass didn't like how this was sounding.

"Plea bargain if you like," Chief Douglass said, slapping his palm on the desk. "But the police community will bury you in the election if somebody doesn't do some time for assaulting an officer. The sheriff doesn't seem to give a shit, but every other police officer in the county will be on your ass if somebody doesn't do some time."

Ludweg lit a fresh cigarette using the glowing embers of the cigarette he had just smoked.

"Commissioner, do I have your continued political support for plea bargaining, as long as someone serves time for assaulting an officer?"

"The bookie has to plead guilty to something too," the chief said.

"Oh, for Christ's sake," Ludweg said, "I'll see what I can do. I'll meet with the defendants and their attorney."

Andy Curtis represented all of the defendants, pro bono. He, Nancy, Adele, and Orson met with the district attorney. He proposed dropping all charges, except those against Adele for assaulting a police officer and against Minnow Grubs for bookmaking. Adele would serve sixty days in the county jail and have six months probation. Minnow would plead guilty to bookmaking and be fined $500.00.

Adele said she was worried about Holiday Forever and was ready to accept the offer if it meant the home could continue.

When Andy called Minnow, he said to tell them to stick it up their collective asses.

Andy made another suggestion, which Minnow said would be acceptable under the circumstances.

When the County Attorney came back to the room, Andy countered.

"Here's the deal. Adele will plead guilty to resisting arrest and get a sixty-day sentence to make you look good with your cops. Forty-five will be suspended after she serves fifteen days on work release. Minnow will plead guilty to a misdemeanor—creating a nuisance, and be fined one hundred dollars. The fine will be suspended on conditions of thirty days' good behavior.

Ludweg reluctantly agreed. Judge Plumb accepted and approved Andy's counterproposal.

County attorney Ludweg wasn't through yet. He had a score to settle with Nancy and that smug cunt and her tree hugging lawyer. He had political friends in high places. The governor's office, for one. So a week after the charges were dropped and the plea-bargain accepted, the State Department of Human Services made an unannounced inspection of Holiday Forever. And the next day, the State Health Department, the Fire Marshal, and the Public Safety Department arrived. Collectively, they sent a report to the governor recommending that, for the safety of the public, Holiday Forever be shut down and Nancy Bartel's state license to run a care facility be withdrawn. They cited, among other things, instances of prostitution, bookmaking, and contamination of the kitchen from preparation of food with illegal controlled substances, and they referred to the danger presented by a well-hidden, half-empty bottle of Jack Daniel's found in the kitchen.

Even if she didn't lose her license, enough work orders for compliance were issued to make it impractical for Nancy to continue.

Then, a representative of Continued Peace, a national chain of rest homes based in Minneapolis, gave a low-ball offer to buy Holiday Forever. Nancy knew the days were over for Holiday Forever in Norwood. After consulting with Adele and Andy, Nancy accepted the offer. For now, the bureaucracy had won.

But Nancy Bartel and cohorts did not give up. They merely moved.

Along with all his material goods, Les had saved for Nancy his list of contacts in the medicinal-marijuana movement. Many of these contacts were influential members of the Dutch and Belgian governments who became interested in adapting versions of Holiday Forever in their countries. Others on the list were persons whose lives had been made hellish by cancer and other painful diseases, and who had found in cannabis a respite from their pain and suffering.

And, at the invitation of the governments of Holland and Belgium, a successful chain of Holiday Forever guest homes were established and flourished in Europe.

Epilogue

A MONTH AFTER the sale of Holiday Forever, Minnow Grubs died from complications of diabetes.

Orson Bacon retired but continued raising purebred golden retrievers.

Katey Long bakes a few cookies and brownies for former contacts of Les Morig and saves a few for herself. She's known as "Grandma Marijuana" by an inner circle of approving health care workers in area hospitals.

Susan Pelt continues on at the home—living a more structured life, distributing Valium, rather than dildos, for ladies with an itch.

George Rudnik remained at Continued Peace in Norwood; he wore clothes, but only outside of his room, and showered up to sixteen times a day.

Burt Grench was allowed by the Continued Peace people to keep with the garden until fall. No provisions were in the Continued Peace master manual of rest home operations for a garden, so it was discontinued after the fall harvest.

The secret garden was another matter. On two consecutive moonlit nights in late October, Burt, with Orson's help, harvested Les's river plot. Later, in an out-of-the-way abandoned barn, they dried the product and put it in baggies, taking care to separate out the seeds so they could be planted in the spring. They placed the baggies of weed and seeds in the seed box of an old, rusted-out grain drill back of the barn, and informed Katey of the location.

Burt died of pneumonia the following February. He was ninety-three.

Adele did her time in the hoosegow. She teamed up with Nancy and attempted to establish a Holiday Forever in another state. By the time they were turned down in seven states, they realized they were nationally blackballed.

So now Adele Yorkland/Smith lives in Brussels, where she and her husband Roy Smith are managers of the Belgium branch of Holiday Forever. With the full support of the Belgian and Dutch governments, two more Holiday Forever guest homes are on the drawing board. Officials from Sweden and Finland have made inquiry about the establishment of Holiday Forever homes in their countries.

The Les Morig memorial trust has grant money available for approved franchise applicants. Donations to the trust have come in from throughout the world. At last count, the trust had in excess of ten million dollars.

Ruth Krankus has her own apartment in Amsterdam. She's regularly seen in Amsterdam's finest eateries, in the company of distinguished-looking gentlemen. She wears fashionable, long flowing gowns, complemented by an exquisite, lengthy pearl necklace. Dutchmen like Ruth Krankus. She has that warm feeling.

Nancy Bartel owns and manages Holiday Forever Amsterdam, where her father Billy is a guest and counselor.

Andy Curtis, the attorney for Holiday Forever, Inc., lives in sin with Nancy Bartel.

Twice each year, since moving to Amsterdam, Ruth and Nancy dress in their finest clothes for dinner at The Rembrandt.

They are a stunning pair as they lift their glasses in a toast. They color their lips with a glossy maple-leaf red lipstick they've named "Burton's Memories".

About The Author

Neil Haugerud is a former member of the Minnesota legislator and a county sheriff. In 1977 he was appointed chairman of the Upper Mississippi River Basin Commission by President Carter; where his major task was to provide congress and the President with plans and techniques for resolving conflicting issues between competing transportation, environmental and recreational uses of the Mississippi, Illinois, Chicago, St. Croix, Souris, Red and Rainy Rivers.

He has completed studies in public administration at Harvard and a mini Masters of Business Administration program at the University of St. Thomas. His law enforcement experience includes seven years as assistant commissioner with the Minnesota Department of Public Safety, eight years as county sheriff and a term as a member of the Minnesota Police Officers Standards and Training Board.

Neil is the author of *Jailhouse Stories*, a memoir published by the University of Minnesota Press, now in its fifth printing. In addition, Neil has written numerous short stories both fiction and non-fiction along with essays and commentaries for the *Minneapolis Star Tribune*. *Holiday Forever* is his first fiction novel and has received great reviews.